Totally Bound Publishing books by Barbara Sheridan:

Sweet Romance
House of Delilah

I0658853

FALLING THROUGH GLASS

BARBARA SHERIDAN

Falling Through Glass
ISBN # 978-1-78651-946-7
©Copyright Barbara Sheridan 2016
Cover Art by Posh Gosh ©Copyright April 2016
Interior text design by Claire Siemaszkiewicz
Totally Bound Publishing

FALLING THROUGH GLASS

Chapter One

Emmi Maeda couldn't help but smile as she stuffed the registration paperwork into her bag. Six months ago she'd barely wanted to live, let alone think of attending college, but now she had a chance at a new life. How freeing it was to finally be moving forward again. Nothing could bring her down today...

She paused in the middle of the wide corridor, sadness stirring to life at the sight of the memorial plaque honoring her father. Inhaling slowly, Emmi concentrated on the photo near the plaque. Her father's bright smile assured her that everything would be okay. At least it would be better. Stepping across the hall, Emmi touched her fingers to the photo frame and continued on her way. She clung to the hope filling her and bounded down the stairs into the sunshine bathing UCLA's campus.

She was standing outside looking over the list of books she'd need when her godfather, Jake, rang her cell.

"I'm done with translations, kiddo. I'm about to head out to that meeting. Do you want to come along and get a free lunch on the studio?"

"Sure. I'm over by the student center. There's a charity rummage sale happening. I'll be wandering."

"And buying."

Emmi laughed. "And probably buying some pretty, shiny thing I don't really need."

"Catch you in a minute, Em-chan."

Emmi tucked her phone into her pocket and stared at the long table before her. More specifically, she stared at the not terribly pretty and definitely not shiny thing that caught her attention. It was an old mirror, a vaguely familiar mirror.

The mirror was about eighteen inches tall and set in a badly tarnished brass frame. One of the side supports was loose. The rectangular, boxlike base had a dent on one side, and the silvered coating on the mirror's glass was flaking terribly around the edges.

An old Japanese superstition she'd learned as a young child echoed in her mind—like Alice's looking glass, there was another place behind mirrors where an oni, a demon, lurked. If you were careless and stared too long, or let the mirror look out into the room, you were leaving a door open. She'd thought it was silly, but could still hear her grandmother's words. '*The oni in the mirror will get you if you're careless, Emiko-chan. Keep the mirror covered if you're not in absolute need of it.*'

If any mirror had an ancient Japanese demon waiting to take her soul, this one did. Still, she wanted—she needed—to own it, weird vibes be damned.

She touched her fingertips to the mirror's frame, only to jerk her hand back. Surely she hadn't imagined it. The metal had vibrated. She touched it again, picked it up. The vibration became steadier. She should put it down and run the other way, yet she had to have it. Curiosity overrode her fear. She needed to have this—

"What? Did someone beat you to all of the pretty and the shiny?" Jake asked, interrupting her thought.

Emmi opened the trash bag the girl at the table had just passed to her. "I can make this kind of pretty and shiny, once I find something to polish it with," she said, a little defensively. "Do you think it's brass?"

"Could be. The overall styling makes it look Japanese."

"I know. It sort of reminds me of the wooden one my grandmother got from her grandmother."

Jake nodded. "After lunch, we'll find a hardware store and pick up some polish."

* * * *

The lunch meeting with the movie execs began with sympathetic looks and empty comments about how much Emmi's late father would be missed in the industry. Emmi smiled cordially when one said he hoped she, her mother and brother were getting on all right. Things were far from all right, they could never be right again, but Emmi decided to just nod and let them get on to their business with Jake—coordinating stunts for a historical action film to be shot partially in Kyoto and Tokyo.

With the topic of discussion turned away from her life, Emmi thought about staying with her grandparents in Hawaii for a while. They'd been asking her to come for months, and since she'd arranged to make up some of her classes via a new online program, nothing was holding her back. The thought of staying with her grandparents was starting to sound good, despite their ultra-conservative belief that unmarried girls under twenty shouldn't date unless an arranged marriage was part of the bargain.

Emmi was picking apart a breadstick and deciding between taking a tankini or a one-piece to Hawaii when Jake tapped her on the arm. That's when she noticed the casting director was staring at her. A lot.

"I'm sorry. Did you say something?"

The man nodded. "How would you like to be in the opening scene? There's no dialogue per se. All you have to do is look pretty and scream. You can scream loudly, right?"

"I suppose so."

"Let me hear."

"Now? Here?"

The casting director nodded. Jake smiled.

Emmi looked around. The place was crowded, and this was a nice restaurant, not a fast food joint. People just didn't go around "auditioning a scream" in a place like this.

Then Jake had to go and say, "Go for it, Em-chan. Kenny would want you to."

Emmi smiled. Her father'd had a twisted sense of humor, and he would have liked to have seen this.

Still, her heart pounded, and she felt like such an idiot. How could she scream for no reason? She was no actress. She wanted to work behind the cameras someday, not in front of them.

Jake grinned his encouragement, making her feel even more pressured. Emmi tried to remember everything she'd ever heard about actors calling up personal things to help bring life to scenes.

Then, it came to her—the accident. She saw the kamikaze gull heading straight for the car. She heard its screech and the squeal of the car's brakes as she instinctively slammed the pedal with both feet. She felt the impact of metal against metal...

Emmi screamed the way she'd screamed that day.

"Emiko!" Jake finally yelled, shaking her.

Everyone in the place was staring, and Emmi wanted to crawl under the table and die. She pulled away and ran for the Ladies room. Her body shook. Her stomach ached and tightened. She went to the sink and doubled over, certain she was going to throw up. It seemed like forever before the queasy feeling passed, but once it did Emmi splashed some water on her face and forced herself to go back out to the restaurant.

Luckily, Jake and his movie friends were finishing their lunch. Some people stared, but she kept her head held high. The casting director smiled at her.

"Miss Maeda, you've got the part in the opening scene if you want it."

Emmi looked at Jake. He gave her that same proud look her father used to give her. Tears stung her eyes— her dad would have been all over this moment. She was not going to cry. She'd embarrassed them all enough for one day.

"Thank you. I'd be honored."

* * * *

When they returned to Malibu, Emmi took the mirror up to her room. She wanted to clean it with the stuff Jake had picked up on the way home but an inexplicable unease prompted her to leave the mirror in the white plastic bag. Her grandmother once told her that kimono carried the feelings and, in rare cases, the spirits of their previous owners. Emmi wondered if the old superstition about kimono went the same for all personal possessions. Perhaps that was how the demon in the mirror legend began. Maybe this thing was haunted. Emmi put the bagged mirror into the closet then went downstairs.

Jake was out on the deck talking on his cell.

"Tinseltown's new starlet breaks onto the horizon," he said with a chuckle. He offered the phone to her. "It's Jonny."

Emmi's heart sank. She was certain her older brother had no desire to talk to her. She'd gotten the point months ago that he held her responsible for the accident. She shook her head then stretched out on the sofa and began flipping through the multitude of satellite channels, none of which had anything good on. She cycled through again and stopped on a documentary about samurai films.

She couldn't help but smile when they mentioned several movies devoted to the Shinsengumi. Her father had been quite a 'fanboy' of that shogunate police troop. At night he'd read her history books instead of the usual bedtime stories. She'd heard so much about the civil war that had brought down the last shogun that it felt more real to her than the boring renditions of American history she'd gotten in school.

* * * *

Unable to sleep that night, and with nothing to watch on TV, she decided to sit out on the balcony of the condo and finally polish her new mirror. It wasn't creeping her out quite as much. Emmi decided her silent chanting of, "There are no onis, there are no onis, there are no onis…" must have helped.

Despite being beaten up, the mirror really was a pretty thing. Emmi didn't understand why no one had seen past the grime and the dent. She put a bit of the smelly liquid polish on the rag and began gently rubbing over the raised petals of the sakura cherry blossoms.

The full moon had shifted position by the time she had removed the worst of the tarnish. Emmi set the mirror down on the small, glass-topped patio table before going to the kitchen to wash her hands. Making her way back through the darkened living room, she noticed that the room was slowly growing brighter, and she turned to see if the light reflected from the upper floor was caused by Jake coming down.

It was still dark by the stairs.

The weird glow was coming in from outside. "Ja—" Emmi clamped her hands over her mouth. She didn't want to wake Jake.

Emmi hurried to the sliding glass balcony door to look at the mirror, but once she stepped onto the patio, she realized the glow that she'd thought she'd seen was gone. She must have imagined it. A trick of the moonlight?

She slid the mirror to the center of the table and rested her head on her hands, her gaze gliding from one raised metal flower to the next. The craftsmanship was beautiful. It was like a sculpture in a way, so mesmerizing, and even more familiar now than it had seemed at the rummage sale.

The moonlight glinted off the glass. Emmi cocked her head to the side, certain she'd caught a glimpse of a bare-chested man with long black hair reflected in the mirror. She glanced over her shoulder. She was alone— it couldn't have been Jake.

She was reminded again of that weird, old legend about the oni in the mirror, and she wondered again if a ghost had started the legend rather than a demon.

"Daddy?" she whispered.

Emmi held the mirror in her hands and drew it closer to her face. Again, she felt that weird vibration when her skin touched the metal. Soon the humming began to flow through her. She wasn't afraid, even though part of her knew she should be.

She continued to stare at the old, mottled glass. There was a man in there, deep, deep within — as if he was at the end of a long, dark tunnel. He was Japanese, definitely Japanese.

"Daddy?" she whispered again.

Chapter Two

Shimabara Pleasure District
Kyoto, Japan
Spring 1864

"Aneko, I need you," Nakagawa Kaemon said.

"You mean that you want me. There is a difference," the woman across the room said as she slowly removed her elaborate wig.

Kae lay naked on the futon, touching himself as she teased, taking her time to carefully place the wig upon the wooden form on the small, red-lacquered cabinet. "I want you because I need you."

Aneko laughed. "You need me because you are young and always want sex, like every other man in Shimabara."

He frowned. "I am not like every other man in Shimabara."

Aneko knelt on the floor and bowed low. "No, Nakagawanomiya-sama," she corrected herself, using his honorific as well as his royal title. "You are not like them at all. You are far above them in every way. Please forgive this unworthy one."

"Since you asked so nicely."

Clearly relieved by the playfulness of both his tone and his words, Aneko crawled toward him, loosening her front-tied obi sash as she went. She knelt beside him and reached out to caress his cheek.

"What do you see in a woman of my profession, when you could have as your bride the most beautiful young girl in Japan?"

Kae sat up, taking her hand in his. "I don't want a wife. I want a friend I can trust completely. I've known you for ages. I can be myself around you without having to observe court protocol with every breath."

"Just like your father." Aneko smiled wistfully. "Is he happy these days?"

"As happy as anyone can be with the current state of things." Kaemon paused. "He fears for his brother's life."

Aneko gasped. "He doesn't really think someone would harm the emperor—no one would dare!"

"Wouldn't they?" Kaemon asked with a smirk before lying back down and folding his arms behind his head. "That rebel Katsura and the rest of the Choshu dogs will stop at nothing to gain control of this country, and what better way to do that than to gain control of the emperor?"

"But your father—"

"He stays as close to the emperor's side as possible, but, to be a proper advisor, he can't stay with him every moment. Should the emperor meet an untimely death, a twelve-year-old boy will ascend to the throne. And with his maternal grandfather being sympathetic to the radical faction..." The rebels would find a way to eliminate everyone who could keep them from manipulating the inexperienced boy.

Aneko sighed and poured them each a cup of sake. "If only I could do something."

Kaemon grinned, drained his cup and let it fall to the woven mat that covered the floor. "There is something you can do, that only you can do," he drawled before reaching for her.

"At least let me cover the mirror first."

"Leave it."

Aneko grinned and lay beside him. "Fine. When the demon woman comes from within to steal your soul, don't expect me to save you."

* * * *

Kae stared up at the ceiling, listening to the soft, even breathing of Aneko, who dozed peacefully beside him. Moving slowly, so as not to wake the prostitute, he untangled himself from her limbs and sat up. As he reached for the sake bottle, light from the floor lantern glinted off the prostitute's newest prized possession, a gift from a Western diplomat, and he smiled to himself at her earlier words.

'When the demon woman comes from within to steal your soul, don't expect me to save you.'

If pretty demons in mirrors were all he had to worry about, he'd be a happy man indeed —

Wait.

There *was* a woman in the mirror, and she was staring straight at him. He set down the sake bottle and reached for the razor-sharp katana that he always kept within arm's reach, even in the Pleasure Quarters. He climbed over Aneko, who stirred when he jarred her.

The mirror was turned slightly away from him, giving him the advantage over his ghostly enemy as he made his way toward the lacquered cabinet where it stood. He used the tip of his sword to turn the brass-framed mirror so he could look at the unnatural woman again. Strange. She didn't resemble any oni he'd ever imagined. She had long black hair and pale skin. Her dark eyes shone with blue flashes as a distant, silvery light reflected off her.

She seemed worlds away, and yet he could almost put his hand into the fathomless glass and pluck her out. She said something in a strange, lilting tongue and Kae pulled back, lest she suck him into her clutches and steal his soul as Aneko had warned. He prodded the mirror with the tip of his sword so that the glass faced the wall then covered it with the black silk cloth that Aneko used to keep the mirror's demons at bay.

Kae returned to the futon and finished off the bottle of sake, content that he was safe once again.

Yet, she had been a pretty little demon.

Over the course of the ensuing weeks, in those fleeting moments before Aneko covered her prized mirror, the demon entranced him. A few times in the dead of night, curiosity propelled him to lift the silken cover and peek at the reflective surface. Often the glass reflected only the room's objects, and he was certain the demon girl was nothing more than a trick of his mind, an odd play of light and shadow. Other times he'd see her deep inside, looking at him as if her captivating eyes called out to his very soul through the blue-tinted mist.

Chapter Three

Los Angeles
Present day

"You can't take that to Japan, Em-chan."

"But you don't understand. I have to keep this with me. If I put it in the checked bag, it will break."

Jake rubbed his temple and looked at his watch. "We have to get moving or risk missing the flight. If anything happens to it while we're gone, I'll find you another one."

"No!" Emmi shouted, hugging the mirror to her chest. "You don't understand! I saw Daddy in it—" She broke off, tears stinging her eyes. She turned away.

Gently placing his hands upon her shoulders, Jake turned Emmi to face him. "Tell me what happened, Emiko. All of it. I need to hear it."

"You'll think I'm crazy."

"I won't. I promise. Trust me."

Emmi accepted that Jake may have experienced something supernatural without question. Her dad, too, had never been one to hide his open-mindedness about things that pushed the boundaries of 'normal'. She explained to Jake what had happened that night when she'd first cleaned the mirror, and how she'd been getting up every night since, trying to see the image of her father again.

"I thought I caught a glimpse of him a couple times, but it was all blurry, like the glass was clouded or steamy — the way mirrors get when you shower." She sighed. "It couldn't have been Daddy. It probably was just a weird reflection."

"You don't have to brush the experience off because you think it's what I want to hear," Jake said softly.

"I'm not," Emmi said defensively. "At first I was positive it was Daddy, but this man is younger, a lot younger, around my age, and he looked so serious. Daddy never let anything get to him. He was always happy and smiling."

Jake nodded. "That he was." He looked at his watch again. "Tell you what. Let me call the prop master. I know there are a couple of pieces that he has permission to carry on. Maybe he can slip the mirror in with them."

* * * *

Halfway through the flight, Emmi had the uncontrollable urge to check on the mirror but forced herself to contain the impulse. Jake had been right back at the condo — airport security would probably consider the mirror a dangerous weapon if broken into shards. She should have left it at home. Even as she assured herself that the mirror was perfectly safe with the prop master's more fragile things, Emmi's stomach knotted with worry.

Emmi closed her eyes and tried to sleep, since there wasn't much else to do to pass the hours. A weird, dreamy vision came to her just as she began dozing off. It was like the dream she'd had before the accident—the flash of insight that had told her there was going to be a wreck, and that she would be behind the wheel. However, this was clearer and more than a quick flash. Yet it still didn't make much sense.

As if in a samurai movie, she saw herself on a street, being pulled against her will by a man in traditional Japanese clothing.

Emmi jumped in her seat and looked over to Jake, sitting quietly with his eyes closed. Was there going to be an accident on the set? *Please, don't let it be another omen*, she prayed. She couldn't lose Uncle Jake on top of everything else.

* * * *

"Finally moved up in the world, eh, Jake?" Dan Cruze, the film's director, joked when they joined the crew assembling near the front desk of the luxury hotel not far from the Imperial Palace.

Jake grinned. "Only the best for the stunt coordinator slash martial arts choreographer hyphen consultant."

The director flipped Jake off, which made everyone laugh, then he handed out the room assignments and hotel keys to Jake and the rest of the advance crew, who'd arrived ahead of the film's actors and other crewmembers.

Emmi was getting her mirror from the property master when the director approached with the keys.

"Giving away our stuff, Eric?"

"No, Dan, I was carrying it for Miss Maeda. It wouldn't fit in her carry-on, and I didn't want to chance it in the checked bags."

Jake gave the prop master a playful hug. "Eric is so sweet that way."

Everyone but Eric laughed, and the director asked if he could look at the mirror. Emmi didn't want to let him touch it, but Jake had that 'do it for me' look that coerced her to hand it over.

Cruze set the mirror on top of the hotel's check-in desk and did that framing the shot with his hands thing, which she'd never seen done except in movies featuring stereotypical movie folk.

"This would be fabulous in my opening shot. We'll pan across the room in the teahouse and show the ninja sneaking in to murder the sleeping samurai." He looked at Emmi. "You'll let us borrow it, right? I'll pay you a rental fee."

A sick feeling hit Emmi in the stomach, and she wanted to throw up. Having heard enough about Cruze always getting his way, she sensed she couldn't refuse. And yet... "I-I can't." She looked to Jake for support when Cruze's expression hardened.

"It's an heirloom, Danny," he lied. "Kenny gave it to her before...you know."

Cruze sort of winced and turned on Eric, the prop master. "You'll make me an exact replica by five a.m. tomorrow."

Eric sighed and guilt stabbed Emmi.

"Sure, Dan. I'll get right on it."

Cruze smiled. "Great. Later, people. I have an interview with a reporter from NHK in the bar."

Eric took a digital camera from one of his bags. "I need to get measurements and some pics, okay? Then I'll bring it to your room. You're in seven-one-eight, right? That's down the hall from me. I'll be careful with it. You'll have it back within the hour."

Emmi nodded. "Is there anything I can do to help? I didn't mean to make more work for you."

Eric laughed. "It's okay. I'll get a bonus out of the fearless leader for the aggravation."

Emmi smiled in return, but the sick feeling in her stomach stayed and got worse as she followed Jake through the garden-like atrium toward the elevators. Nothing could happen to the mirror. It just couldn't.

"You okay, Em-chan? You look like you got hold of a bad piece of sushi."

"I'm okay," she muttered. She craned her neck to see the mirror one last time before the elevator doors closed.

Except she knew everything wasn't okay.

* * * *

"There wasn't a thing to worry about," Emmi whispered to herself when Eric returned the mirror within the hour as promised.

She placed it on the desk and stretched out on the bed across from it. After a second, she impulsively got up to adjust the mirror so she could look into the glass when lying down, just the way she'd had it back home. It wasn't positioned quite right, so she repeated the ritual until it was. Finally Emmi lay on her stomach and stared into the mirror, so many thoughts going through

23

her head. Could it have been her dad's spirit she'd seen, after all? Was he unhappy wherever he was?

Jake came out of the bathroom, toweling dry his long hair. He sat beside her. "You okay?"

"Why didn't he listen to me?" Emmi blurted, voicing the question that had been nagging her for months. "If he'd believed me, he would still be alive."

Tears stung her eyes, and the torment she'd been struggling to control felt like it would explode inside her. She got up and paced across the room.

"I told him I couldn't drive him home from the eye doctor. I told him something bad would happen if I did. Why wouldn't he listen? Why?"

The tears flooded out, and Emmi's whole body shook from the force. She had to lean against the desk to keep from collapsing.

The mirror rattled, and she gripped the edge to keep it from tottering.

* * * *

Kyoto
1864

Certain he heard a woman crying, Kaemon paused while tightening the ties of his hakama pants as he prepared to depart the Pleasure Quarters.

"Aneko?" he called, walking toward the partially opened shoji to peer into the connecting room. It was empty, yet the faint sound of crying could still be heard. He realized that it came from behind him. He whipped around, surveying the room, his hand reflexively reaching for the hilt of his katana.

The crying came from…the mirror?

His dark eyes scanned the room once more for signs of an intruder. Finding none, Kaemon crept nearer the small cabinet where Aneko had set the mirror the previous night. Using the tip of his sword, he lifted the cloth from the glass. The cry sounded faint, almost like a bird's distant cry echoing on the summer wind. But it was unmistakable nonetheless. The sound of a woman crying came from within the depths of the mirror itself.

He leaned forward but abruptly jerked back, afraid that the crying was just a ploy by the pretty oni who lived inside.

Words tumbled from her unseen lips along with her sobs, and Kae understood a few of the odd words. They sounded like the English that his father insisted he learn to help those who translated imported books to ensure that no references to Christianity remained in the books that were allowed into the country.

Slowly he began to understand the oni's lament. Surely an oni would not lament the death of her father? Curiosity overpowered his better judgment, and Kae leaned in. He saw the shadowy shape of the pretty oni at the end of a long, murky corridor. She sat hunched over with her head buried in her folded arms. Her slim shoulders shook from her sobs. Impulsively, he reached toward the glass, wanting to ease the pain that carried across untold distances to touch him.

"Kae-sama!"

Kae jumped back, his sword drawn and at the ready. He relaxed. "It's only you, Aneko."

* * * *

Kyoto
Present day

"Oh, wow," Emmi said as the rental van entered the Uzumasa Movie Village, the Japanese version of Universal's famed Backlot. She could hear her father's words from years earlier echo in her mind.

'It was like being home, Em-chan, like walking into all those old stories great-grandfather Maeda used to tell. It was all smoke and mirrors, but it felt so real, just like I had stepped back a hundred years into the samurai clan that our people came from. And being there made me wish that the movie we were working on was true, that I could slip back in time to see it all for real just once...'

Though her father hadn't had a chance during that film shoot, or after, to make a trip to the Kanazawa area where their family originated, Emmi hoped this trip would afford her the chance to do just that both for herself and for him.

Jake nudged her. "Time for that big break into stardom."

Emmi smirked. "You mean time to be filmed and end up on the cutting room floor."

"Your scene will stay. Trust me."

Emmi smiled, feeling foolish for her behavior the night before. "I'm sorry I acted like such a baby last night," she said, finally finding the words she'd wanted to say all morning.

Jake hugged her. "Don't you apologize." He pulled back and tilted her chin up. "And don't you ever think that you're responsible for the accident."

Emmi nodded even though she knew the guilt would haunt her for a long time to come.

Jake led her to the dressing area and introduced her to a few makeup artists and costume fitters before taking his leave, assuring her she was in good hands.

The ladies immediately got down to business, working their magic with powders, hair ornaments and silk.

An hour later, as Emmi checked herself in the mirror, she didn't care if her 'big scene' did end up the director's afterthought. This was the coolest, most exciting thing she'd ever done — apart from the time her father 'directed' her brother and her in a homemade samurai epic they'd sent to their grandparents for Christmas.

Makeup and Costume had poked and prodded Emmi into a traditional Japanese prostitute. Last came the wig that was poufed and embellished with tortoiseshell combs and silver hair pins decorated with coral beads and fringed fans. She was dressed in layers topped by an elaborately embroidered silk kimono.

At the sound of Jake's wolf whistle, Emmi turned away from the large mirror in the extras' dressing room.

"Every single one of your ancestors may very well reach beyond the veil and strangle me for saying this, but if I was a nineteenth-century samurai on the make, I'd pay some big money for the pleasure of your company."

Emmi was certain that the burning blush she felt in her cheeks could be seen through the layer of white rice powder on her face. "Uncle Jake!"

"I mean that in a good way, really. If you twisted that obi around to the back like a 'respectable lady', you'd almost look like you'd just stepped out of the Imperial Palace." He laughed when Emmi rolled her eyes. He held out his hand. "Come on, I'll escort you to the set so you don't trip in those geta and break your neck."

"You make me sound like I'm helpless," Emmi said sharply, moving forward slowly on the high wooden sandals.

She'd just about reached Jake at the door when the bottom-most kimono slid from her grip and caused her to trip. Luckily, she fell right into Jake's arms.

"Don't even think it," she said, glowering up at him.

"What? That the death glare on your face looks exactly like your mother's?" he quipped.

Emmi was primped and prodded more as she waited for her big moment before the camera. Watching for the director's signal, she repeated to herself exactly what she was to do— Slip off shoes— Hurry down hall— Slide open shoji— Look in horror at dead bodies— Scream like banshee.

She repeated it so many times she was certain that, when she next spoke, those words would come out of her mouth. The crew seemed to take an awfully long time to get to the panning shot of the opening murder. During rehearsal, the cast had taken only a couple of minutes to run through the entire scene. Emmi peeked around the cameras, scattered equipment and people to figure out the cause of the hold-up. When she finally caught a glimpse of Jake in deep conversation with Director Cruze, she hoped he wasn't thinking of cutting her scene entirely.

At the wardrober's insistence, Emmi moved to wait near one of the sound stage's exits where she could get a bit of air, so as not to '*sweat up the merchandise*' during the filming delay. The wind was beginning to whip up outside, and the breeze had a cooling effect on her nerves and skin.

A Japanese television film was in production at the studio as well, and Emmi watched a large, formal procession being rehearsed. The whole scene reminded her of being near her great-grandfather's bedside during his last months. She had been a little girl but had listened raptly as he recounted the stories he'd heard as a young man about similar processions traveling from the main Maeda estate to conduct official business in Kyoto or Edo, which would later become Tokyo.

The Maeda clan ruled some of the most fertile land during the feudal era. Their resulting wealth from the abundant rice crops elevated nearly every Maeda male to the social rank of daimyo, which she'd always equated with dukes and princes. She remembered the passion in Great-grandfather's failing voice as he spoke of their ancestral domain, the Kaga han.

A wry smile curved her lips as Emmi thought of how vexed the ancient man had become when his thoughts turned to the Meiji Restoration, which had abolished the old, feudal class system. In protest of the military governor Tokugawa's overthrow, Maeda Takehito, her great-great-great-grandfather, had renounced his citizenship, sold everything and relocated to America. He'd considered it the perfect slap in the face to the new government, which professed support for the emperor but had no intention of letting him truly rule the land that was his by divine right.

"They need you on the set, Miss Maeda," one of the director's assistants called, jarring Emmi away from her memories.

She reverted to her earlier internal chant as she wove her way past the cameras, cables, technicians and actors to take her place on the set. Slip off shoes— Hurry down hall— Slide open shoji— Look in horror at dead bodies— Scream like banshee.

"And cut!" Dan Cruze shouted after Emmi did her short scene. "Nice job, kid. Looks like we have another 'One-take Maeda' in our midst."

Emmi blushed as Jake led the crew members who'd known her dad in a wild round of applause. Fortunately for Emmi's pride, Cruze called for everyone's immediate attention a moment later.

"Listen up, people. We're shutting down for the day." He paused as a murmur arose. He waited until his assistants had regained everyone's attention before continuing. "All I know is what the Toei Studio rep just told me. Some freak storm with hurricane force winds has come out of nowhere within the past hour, and it's headed right for us. Get to the hotel ASAP. That means go in costume and take the props in your hands with you. We'll collect them once we get there."

Emmi shivered as a deathlike chill blew over her. "Uncle Jake. I have a bad feeling."

He gave her a hug and urged her toward the exit. "It'll be fine, Em. It'll probably blow over before lunch."

* * * *

Emmi hadn't seen such a commotion in the streets since wildfires had spread through Southern California a few miles from her parents' house. She was very glad to reach the safety of the hotel—until she entered the room she shared with Jake and found her mirror missing.

"We were robbed! Uncle Jake, someone stole my mirror!"

"Emmi, Emmi, calm down. It wasn't stolen."

"But it's gone!"

"I had to borrow it."

"What?"

"The prop one was dropped, and it broke. Cruze insisted that he needed it for his shot. It will be all right. I'm sure Eric will grab it."

"Eric came back on the shuttle with us. He didn't have it. I have to get it!" Emmi darted for the door.

Jake grabbed the back of her kimono. "No!"

She pulled away. "It will get ruined! I need it with me!"

Jake grabbed her shoulders and gave her a quick shake. "Emiko! It's a mirror. It's just a mirror. I'm not letting you risk your life to get it."

"You said the storm was nothing!" she shouted back.

"Look, the Toei people wouldn't have ordered us out if it was nothing."

Emmi jerked herself free from his grasp. "Then I have to get it, or it will be destroyed!"

"No!" Jake took a deep breath. "Look, I'll call the studio. I'll make sure one of the security guys puts it in a safe place, okay?"

Biting back a snarky reply, she nodded and simply said, "Okay."

Emmi bit her thumbnail and tried to think of the quickest foot route back to the Uzumasa Movie Village as Jake went to use the phone on the desk.

"It's out." He reached for his cell phone, but it wasn't there. "Damn loose clip. I must have dropped it. Look, I'm going to the lobby to see if the phones work down there. You stay put."

Emmi said nothing. As soon as he left, she waited by the door. When she peered out, he'd already disappeared around the bend in the hall toward the elevators. The stairs were in the opposite direction, not far from their room. She yanked up the layered kimono

31

as best she could and tore off down the hall toward the stairs. She was thankful the wardrobe lady had given her a pair of thicker soled outdoor tabi sandals since the geta from the scene had been too loose.

The sky grew darker the closer she got to the movie lot. The winds picked up, pelting her face with debris and shoving against her like a football linebacker. She was running headlong into the approaching storm, but she didn't care about that or the looks that the few people scurrying by gave her. The mirror was all that mattered.

The decorative combs and hair sticks fell from her elaborate wig until it blew off. Soon her own long black hair came loose from its pins to whip about her face. She kept her mind focused on the mirror and kept her fingers clutched tightly to the layers of kimono that weighed her down.

The guard at the gate refused to let her in despite her pleas, but another guard, frantically trying to prepare for the coming storm, called him away. Emmi slyly slid the edge of her kimono in the gate opening, and it was just thick enough to keep the lock from catching all the way. Once the guard was gone, Emmi slipped inside and ran toward the set where they'd been filming.

A torrent of rain exploded from the sky just as she got inside. The building's metal roof vibrated, and the wind whistled through whatever tiny cracks it could find. The lights flickered and went out just before she reached the set. It was so dark she had to feel her way along the walls.

The soundstage shook from the wind and rain hitting the building, and Emmi felt like Dorothy about to be sucked up into Oz. The storm ripped the functional shutters off the window across the room a moment before Emmi stepped inside the set. The outer soundstage window broke, and Emmi screamed as the driving wind propelled tiny shards of glass against the back of her neck.

There it was, on a red lacquer cabinet. She lunged for her mirror and hugged it to her chest seconds before part of the set wall blew in, shoving her against the furniture and burying her in debris. Her foot was wedged beneath the small cabinet where the mirror had rested, and she screamed in pain as something else fell on top of the pile. She could feel the wind gusting outside her cave-like prison. She heard a crackling noise and soon smelled smoke.

A fire!

"Please help me!"

You're in Japan, Em!

"*Tasukete kudasai!*"

"Help me! Help me! Please!"

The smoke grew thicker. Her lungs protested at the noxious fumes. She kept calling for help between coughs.

"*Onegai! Onegai...tasukete...*" she pleaded. Her grip tightened on the mirror as her lungs constricted. "Help me!"

Chapter Four

Kyoto
1864

Kae's eyes flew open the instant his senses recognized the smell of burning wood. He was on his feet, katana in hand, before his consciousness registered that this was not the fire-prone Imperial Palace and that the smell was distant, somehow not quite real.

Please help me!

Kae looked down at the empty futon. Aneko was gone. She'd had an appointment with an outside customer that she couldn't cancel. He went to the door leading to the corridor and peered out. Only the usual sounds of merriment and sexual encounters drifted back. There was no smoke smell.

Help me! Help me! Please!

His eyes finally adjusted to the faint light of the small lantern Aneko had left lit, and he was certain that a wisp of smoke came from beneath the cloth covering

Aneko's mirror. Again, the mournful cry for help followed.

Help me! Please!

For a number of years his father had sent Kae to serve as a retainer to the Matsudairas, the leaders of the Aizu clan. There he'd learned the wariness of a battle-ready warrior, and now that training sprang to the forefront.

It was another trick of the oni in the mirror to steal his soul. Yet...

Please, help me.

The terrified wail was too much to bear, too similar to the pain-filled cries of his father's mistress that night when he was ten years old and the palace had caught fire, trapping them both and killing her after she'd shoved him out of a window to safety.

The wisps of smoke coming from beneath the cloth grew thicker while the cries for help grew weaker.

The fire that long ago night had caught the hem of Yumi's kimono even as she'd lifted him to the window, to safety. As Kae had tumbled out backward, he'd seen her engulfed in fire, seen her writhe in utter agony, seen her hands reach out, seen her skin bubble and melt...

No. It would not happen again.

Help...

Kaemon plunged himself forward, tore the cloth away, and, with a *kiai*, a loud battle cry, he thrust his hand through the glass. The mirror did not shatter, and he felt his fingertips at last connect with smoldering silk.

He stretched his arm until his shoulder collided with the mirror's frame then let out another *kiai* while he used all his strength to pull backward on the handful of silk in his grasp.

The tatami mat scratched Kae's back when they hit it and slid. It took a moment for him to catch his breath. The smell of singed fabric prickled his nose. Instinctively he rolled out from under the stunned woman and threw a blanket from the futon over her, patting it to smother any hint of fire.

Within seconds, Emmi began coughing. She flailed her arms and legs, swatting a blanket from her face.

Her brain took its own sweet time processing the Japanese words someone called out. "Calm down. You're safe now. You're safe."

Coughing, she sat up and scrambled to her knees as much as the cumbersome layers of clothing and the blanket covering her would allow. She bent forward, taking in large, gasping breaths, hacking to expel the smoky air from her lungs.

"Daijoubu desu ka? Daijoubu desu ka, oni?"

Was she a demon? What the hell kind of question was that?

Still kneeling, Emmi straightened and swiped her tousled hair from her eyes. She then turned to look over her shoulder. Had her mother sent some distant relative to watch over her and taunt her with the demon epithet in her stead?

"Are you a demon?" the man kneeling before her asked again.

Emmi blinked and wiped her eyes, which still stung from the smoke. She glared at her supposed rescuer. "Yes, I'm all right, and I'm not a demon, you idiot."

She looked around. This did not look like the soundstage. Where was the storm? Where on earth was she?

"What?"

Emmi looked back at the confused man. He was around her age and seemed rather familiar somehow.

"What?" she asked in answer to the very same question from him.

"*Nani? Nan desu ka, oni?*" he repeated.

"Look, I know I should be grateful to you and all, but..."

She broke off as his look of bewilderment grew. She closed her eyes a moment. She hadn't carried on any long conversations in Japanese since she'd last seen her grandparents at the funeral. In fact, that hadn't been quite normal, since a lot of the time they chose to use the old, classical Japanese...

Which was exactly what this guy was speaking.

She spoke to him slowly in Japanese, hoping he'd get it straight that she was not a demon and that she was indeed all right.

"What is i-di-ot?"

Emmi coughed and wondered if coughing more might distract him from wanting to know what idiot meant. However, when he repeated the question, she knew that wasn't much of an option. She looked at him and translated 'idiot' as best she could.

She gave a start when the look of bewilderment, which she thought might be his natural expression, turned to one of fury. He jumped to his feet and grabbed the katana lying on the floor a few feet away, and Emmi knew without a doubt that he was not holding any movie prop.

It didn't look like any unsharpened practice or prop sword she'd ever seen, but it did look exactly like the antique sword her father had owned. She knew without a doubt that this katana was very much the same — very real and very deadly.

She looked around the room again. Why wasn't she in the same room? Why wasn't it a shambles? Where were the security people or the paramedics, the police and the firefighters? Where the hell was she?

Before she could figure it out, the man ordered her to stand. She knew that to refuse would not be wise — even if he insisted on calling her a demon.

He pointed the katana at her. "Go back to where you came from, demon. Now!" he ordered in Japanese, pointing the blade to the mirror lying face down on the floor near a small lacquered cabinet.

The mirror!

Emmi ran forward, fell to her knees and picked it up, making sure it was unharmed.

It was her mirror, but it was different. It looked newer, shinier, and while it had a dent on the right side, the other nicks and dents were missing from the base. Where had the cloth tacked onto the back come from?

"Go back inside, demon! You will not have my soul! Not now or ever!"

"Wha — ?" Emmi's voice died the instant she turned. The guy had the tip of his katana a fraction away from the base of her throat.

"Go back inside to where you came from."

What was happening?

Was she dead and in some kind of hell for causing the accident that killed her father?

Was she unconscious and having some freakish dream?

"Go back now, demon!"

Shaking in fear, Emmi blinked back the tears that formed in her eyes and prayed she wasn't screwing up any old Japanese pronunciations. The last thing she wanted was to say something wrong, something that would push this guy over the edge.

"I'm not a demon. I swear I'm not. I don't know how I got here. I was caught in a storm at a place I was working. The wall fell on me. There was a fire. That's all I remember. I'm not a demon. I swear I'm not. My name is Emiko. Maeda Emiko."

"Maeda?" he asked.

"Yes. My family comes from Kanaz—the Kaga han," she added.

His eyes narrowed suspiciously. "Then how did you come to be in the mirror? He pointed the tip of the sword to her throat. "Prove to me that you are human."

Chapter Five

Kyoto
Present day

Even as the hunt for Emmi was going on within the hotel, Jake knew where she'd gone. He tried to follow but didn't make it past the hotel lobby as the weird storm hit the hotel dead on. Then, as quickly as it had engulfed them it was gone, much like the devastating tornadoes near his hometown in Oklahoma. The wind died to nothing. The rain stopped and brilliant sunrays poked through gobs of fluffy white clouds.

At the Uzumasa Movie Village, the nightmare hit him full force. The soundstage they'd been using was a smoldering shambles, and though the authorities tried to hold him back, Jake used his size and strength to shove his way past the rescue workers and into the thick of the devastation.

He prayed to any deity who would listen to see that Emmi had survived this.

Calling out her name, he began pawing at the fallen sheetrock, twisted metal and broken glass. After hours of searching and repeated pleas for updates from a sympathetic cop, no trace of Emmi was found.

Oh, shit. He had to call her mother and brother.

He was picking his way back through the rubble that had been their set when excited voices of nearby rescue workers caught his attention.

A miracle!

No miracle. Dark magic. Drop it. Get away.

Jake spun around. The sunlight pouring through the mangled roof glinted off unbroken glass. It was the mirror, Emmi's mirror.

Where the hell was she?

* * * *

Kyoto
1864

Emmi licked her dry lips and tried not to flinch. "How do I prove I'm human? Maybe by dying if you stab me?"

"Perhaps," he said flatly.

She did her best to bite back a scream and clutched her hands into fists on her lap. "P-please don't kill me. I'm a real person. I swear."

The man—the samurai, she realized—lowered his sword a bit. "Then perhaps I'll smash your mirror and make you my slave."

"No!" she shouted, rearing back. "Please don't break it. How will I get home if you break it?"

"You mean how will you capture my soul if I break it?"

"No—"

A pounding on the other side of the shoji door leading out of the room interrupted her.

The samurai went to the door, but his gaze never left Emmi. He slid the shoji open a few inches and glanced out. "What's the problem?"

"Fujiwara-san! You must leave at once! Downstairs is crawling with rebels. I recognized one of them from the other night."

The samurai muttered an obscenity, then sheathed his katana and stalked back across the room. He grabbed Emmi's arm and jerked her to her feet.

"What are you doing?" she shrieked.

"Quiet! I'm not leaving you until I find out what you are."

He pulled her forward.

She pulled back. "The mirror. I need the mirror."

"No."

"Fujiwara-san. Please hurry," the samurai's friend pleaded in the doorway.

The sound of men's raucous voices echoed from the direction of the stairs.

The samurai grabbed the mirror with his free hand while the other still grasped Emmi's arm.

"Matsuyama, this way," Fujiwara instructed as he led the way to a secret door and passage hidden within the wall in the adjoining room. He pulled Emmi in after him.

Her body shook with fear, but she let the samurai drag her along the narrow, dusty corridor. She stumbled on the long hem of her kimono and fell forward. Her hand collided with the small bones of some long-dead creature whose skeletal teeth cut into her flesh. The man behind them, Matsuyama, tripped over her, and his foot connected with her ankle.

"Oww!" she cried out.

"Quiet!" Fujiwara ordered, pulling Emmi to her feet and continuing.

She limped along as best she could, ignoring the grumbling of Matsuyama behind her. At last the dusty corridor gave way to fresh air. They were outside in a darkened courtyard of some type, where the samurai had the decency to pause... At least until he barked more orders. He set the mirror on the ground.

"Straighten yourself! Stand up straight!" He yanked Emmi's hands from her middle and grabbed for her wide silk obi. "Slide this around."

He froze when he saw a blood smear on the obi. He took hold of Emmi's hands. There, on her left palm, were two gashes from the teeth of the dead whatever.

He surprised Emmi by taking a handkerchief-like cloth from the sleeve of his haori jacket and wrapping it around her hand. He finished adjusting the obi to his satisfaction and pulled the edges of her kimono closer together.

"What are you doing?" she asked when the samurai began combing his thick fingers through her hair.

"Making you presentable," he said. He set to braiding her hair. He turned to the man who'd accompanied them. "Your chopsticks."

Matsuyama grimaced then pulled two gold-trimmed, black-lacquered chopsticks from the sleeve of his own jacket.

Emmi was at a loss. These guys carried more junk in their sleeves than she did in her backpack.

"Oww," she said when the demon-hating samurai twisted her braid and jammed the chopsticks into the hair to hold it atop her head.

He reached down to retrieve the mirror then propelled her toward a gate in the courtyard fence.

"Where are you taking me?"

"You'll find out when we get there."

"But—"

"Quiet," he said roughly as they exited into a narrow side street.

Patches of wetness lingered on the ground, suggesting it had rained earlier. Was this part of the movie backlot? It didn't look familiar, and there should have been lights and clean-up people at the very least.

The farther they traveled, the more afraid Emmi became. This wasn't a movie set. This was a real street. These were real, solid, complete buildings. What had happened? Where was she?

The old Kyoto from the movie they'd been filming stretched before her, but that was impossible. Wasn't it?

Matsuyama brushed past Emmi to walk alongside the other samurai. He whispered something she couldn't quite make out, but it sounded suspiciously like "You're giving her to the wolves?"

"For tonight at least."

"If you are human, and truly a Maeda, what did you do to disgrace yourself? Why would your family send you here to Shimabara to be a whore?"

Emmi stopped dead. She tried to pull her sleeve from the grasp of the samurai. Though fear shook her inside and out, she did not back down at the look of anger the samurai gave her.

"What do you think you're doing?" he asked.

"That's my question. What gives you the right to give me to someone for the night? I'm no prostitute, and I don't plan to be one."

"And yet you dress like one and appear in a brothel. You merit no explanation."

He tugged her sleeve. She still would not budge.

"I want to know where you're taking me. Who are you taking me to?"

The young samurai glowered, and common sense tried to tell Emmi that he wouldn't tell her a thing. Yet he surprised her, and from the fleeting look in his dark eyes, he surprised himself as well.

"I'm taking you to a secure place until I can figure out what to do with you. To friends who will not fall for your tricks and who fear no demons."

"Because they are the demons," Matsuyama murmured.

Emmi gave them both a hard look, though she wanted very much to cry and run away as fast as she could. "No."

The samurai smirked and lifted the mirror into her line of vision. "Fine. I'll smash this and put an end to you now."

"No!" Emmi lunged for the mirror, but the samurai handed it to the other man, who stepped away. "Please don't break it. I'll go."

She had no choice but to follow meekly.

Her free hand reached into the collar of her kimono so that she could touch the gold dragonfly pendant around her neck. She was glad the wardrober had found a way to conceal it within the kimono collar when she insisted that she couldn't take it off. She'd had the pendant as far back as she could remember. It was a Maeda family heirloom, and her father once told her that as long as she wore it, she had nothing to fear. The pendant would protect her with the strength of every generation of the samurai family it had passed through.

Emmi sensed there was a lot to fear if she was being taken "to the wolves" as that Matsuyama guy had said. That phrase "to the wolves" nagged at her as they continued onward. However it all fell into place once Emmi saw men dressed in matching blue haori jackets with bands of large white triangles along the sleeves' edges. Fujiwara was handing her over to the Wolves of Mibu, the Shinsengumi, one of the Tokugawa Shogunate's most feared police troops.

"Oh shit," she muttered. She couldn't end up in Alice's Wonderland. No, she had to end up in nineteenth-century Japan during one of the bloodiest civil wars in history.

"Quiet," Fujiwara ordered as he continued toward the patrol troop, which had now noticed them.

The men carrying lanterns came forward to illuminate the three strangers, and the looks they gave Emmi reminded her very much of a pack of ravenous wolves. Her stomach churned and she prayed she would not be their midnight snack in any way, shape or form.

Nearing the "wolf pack," she noticed the stains on some of the men's clothing. Bloodstains. She stumbled, and Fujiwara shot her a fierce look before grabbing her arm a moment to steady her.

"Harada-sensei," he called.

A man carrying a spear stepped forward. His gaze immediately swept over Emmi and lingered before he turned his attention to her captor. He broke into a toothy grin. "Another night, another pretty girl, eh?"

The Demon Hater and his friend laughed.

"Very pretty," one of the patrol troops called. "Between the two of you and Kato-kun, you maybe wore the ladies out so they had to hire new ones?" another said, eliciting more laughter.

Of course Mr. Demon Hater Fujiwara laughed. "I think she is not that kind of girl, Harada-san."

"Then why is she with you?"

There was more laughter, and Emmi's cheeks burned in embarrassment. She looked around for a way to escape but decided against it. She certainly wasn't guilty of any wrongdoing, but if she took off, these guys would slash first and not question at all.

"Is Yamanami-san in?" Fujiwara asked.

"He is," Harada said. "You need to see him?"

"Yes. It's important."

The man nodded. "Follow us."

"Follow" wasn't exactly how it went. The patrol group surrounded Emmi, her captor and his friend as if they were all prisoners. More than once men purposely brushed up against Emmi, but she didn't dare take notice even though she wanted to punch them.

Surprisingly, her demon-hating samurai captor did notice, and he instructed his companion to move behind her while he took a position to her right. He glared over at the Shinsengumi member to her left as if warning him to keep an appropriate distance.

"Thank you," she said softly.

Not surprisingly, the samurai didn't bother to respond or acknowledge her gratitude.

Finally they came to a halt in front of a wide wooden gate guarded by two uniformed men.

The patrol captain, Harada, asked one of the guards for the whereabouts of Vice-Commander Yamanami. Once inside the gates of the Shinsengumi compound, the men drifted away, leaving Emmi with Harada, her demon-hating samurai and Matsuyama, who still carried her mirror.

The group veered left and stepped up on the engawa, the porch that ran the length of the building. Three-quarters of the way down Harada stopped and tapped lightly on the frame of the shoji. It slid open to reveal a rather sad-looking man dressed in a simple dark gray yukata, a thinner, less formal kimono.

"Is there a problem, Sano?" he asked before noticing Emmi and her male companions. He smiled a smile that didn't quite reach up to brighten his eyes. "Ah, Kaemon-dono. What a pleasant surprise. Come in."

Harada bade them a quick farewell and jogged off around the dark corner.

So, Mr. Demon Hater Fujiwara's given name was Kaemon.

When the two samurai slipped off their sandals, Emmi removed her dirty tabi socks so as not to get any mud on the clean tatami mats within the older man's room. Surprisingly, her captor, Kaemon, she reminded herself, turned to his companion and asked him to head back home. Then he took the mirror and followed Yamanami inside, gesturing for her to do likewise.

Yamanami cleared a sheaf of papers, a calligraphy brush and an ink stone from the low table in the center of the room and motioned for them to sit.

"Would you like some tea?"

"Yes," Emmi said.

"No," Kaemon said at the same time.

Yamanami suppressed a small smile. "I was about to have a cup myself, Fujiwara-san. I'll be back in moment."

Fujiwara Kaemon—Demon Hater. That sounded like a cheap direct-to-video movie. Only her brain would think of something so lame at a time like this.

With Yamanami gone, Emmi turned to Kaemon. "Why did you bring me here? What are you going to do to me?"

His dark eyes impaled her. "I brought you here for safekeeping until I can find out exactly what you are and where you came from."

"I told you I'm Em—Maeda Emiko. I don't know how I got here, but I know the mirror has something to do with it, and I need it to get back to my time."

"Your time?"

Before Emmi could even try to think of a way to explain, Yamanami returned with a steaming pot of green tea and three cups.

Also on the tray were a cloth bandage and a small jar. He gave the bandage and jar to Emmi, saying that the jar contained a healing ointment. While she tended to her cut hand, he sat and poured the tea. He took a long sip from his handleless cup and studied Kaemon and Emmi.

"What can I do for you, Fujiwara-dono?"

Yamanami's reversion to formality struck Emmi as odd after he'd initially addressed him by his given name. Apparently it struck Kaemon the same way, though his expression betrayed nothing. Emmi detected quite a bit more rigidity to his posture than had been there a moment ago.

Kaemon put down his cup. "I have something of a favor to ask, Yamanami-san." He paused then turned to Emmi. "Wait outside."

"No!"

Kaemon placed his hand on the mirror that rested on the tatami between them. "Wait outside."

Exhaling a defeated sigh, Emmi took a quick sip of her tea then rose. "Fine."

She gave them a quick bow, then went out to the engawa and sat on the step a few feet away from Yamanami's room. Since she doubted she'd like anything she might overhear, she saw no point in eavesdropping.

She was conscious of the curious and suggestive looks she received from the men who passed through the compound or stood talking on the porch of the building across the way. They reminded her of the jocks back in high school who checked out the cheerleaders and rated them on their potential "bed-ability."

By the way her luck was going, she might as well have "fresh virgin" tattooed on her forehead. She propped her chin on her palm and stared down at the ground. Maybe if she ignored them, they'd go away. Maybe if she prayed hard enough, she'd go —

A gruff voice broke into her thoughts.

"Who are you?"

Emmi jerked her head up and found herself face to face with yet another one of the Mibu wolves. She recognized him from the history books her father had collected. He was Hijikata Toshizou, and, though he wasn't an especially tall man, the sheer force of his presence loomed over her.

Emmi stood, stepped up to the engawa, then bowed deeply and backed away as he stepped up as well. She straightened to find the man's dark eyes fixed sharply upon her. His hand hovered over the hilt of the katana at his side.

"Who are you, woman?"

"Em-Emiko... I-I..."

The shoji slid open and Yamanami stepped out. "Ah, Hijikata-san. I'm glad you're here. Please, come in. And don't worry, the—er—young lady is accompanying a friend of ours."

Emmi shrank back when Hijikata shot her a most unsympathetic look before striding past. She struggled to swallow her heart, which seemed to have stuck in her throat. Talk about looks being able to kill.

As a preteen, she'd developed something of a fangirl crush on the drop-dead gorgeous man in the photos that had survived the years. Now, after seeing him in the flesh and getting that look that said he'd be quite fine killing her for no reason other than that she seemed "suspicious," Emmi knew that crush was never to return. No wonder historians had referred to Hijikata as the Demon of the Shinsengumi.

"What?" Hijikata bellowed from inside, breaking into Emmi's thoughts.

She sank back against the building's wall and groaned. No doubt Kaemon had just hit the vice-commander with the "She's an oni from the mirror" bit. No, he wouldn't do that. No one would believe him, and Kaemon would not take the chance of alienating these men, if what she knew about them was correct.

But then again, this was the nineteenth century, and Japan wasn't the major world power that it was in 2009. In fact, it was just coming out of three hundred years of isolation from the rest of the world.

Not caring that a 'proper young Japanese woman' wouldn't intrude, Emmi got up and wandered toward the room containing the men. They had exited Yamanami's quarters and stood, still conferring, near the door.

"We have two cells empty as far as I know," Yamanami said.

"Then it's agreed," Kaemon answered.

"I don't like the idea at all," Hijikata said, casting a menacing look Emmi's way.

She stayed where she'd stopped, a few feet or so behind Kaemon.

"Hijikata-san, I wouldn't ask if it wasn't important," Kaemon said. "I could have gone to the Mimawarigumi, but we both know that sometimes the integrity of that group leaves something to be desired."

"I must agree with that," Yamanami said. "I wouldn't put any woman's safety in their hands."

Hijikata cast Emmi another hard look. "Fine," he said flatly before stalking away to a room farther down the hall.

"There's Captain Harada," Yamanami said. "I will ask him to have men ready a cell and have a food tray prepared."

"Thank you. I'm sure Maeda-dono is hungry and tired."

Yamanami stepped away, and the reality of the situation hit Emmi. Impulsively, she grabbed Kaemon by the arm. "Are you insan—" she began in English, quickly shifting to Japanese. "What are you doing? Are you having me arrested? I'm no criminal! I haven't done anything!"

"I told you earlier that I'd like you to speak with the governor of Kyoto. Until then, I need to keep you secure in Kyoto. You can consent to the questioning and be a guest for the night, or continue to be difficult and become a certified prisoner for an indefinite period. The choice is yours."

Wonderful. So this was the story he was passing around, that she must be some informant or something and needed to speak with the "Feds," as it were. Emmi exhaled a long, defeated sigh as Yamanami came back onto the porch and went into his room for something.

"Fine. I'll cooperate."

Chapter Six

"But I'm afraid," Emmi said as the harsh truth sank in. She was a prisoner.

"It's only for tonight," Kaemon said. "I'll come back for you tomorrow."

Emmi swallowed back her unease and nodded. He almost seemed to care.

"What about my mirror?"

"Yamanami-san will see that it is secure."

She nodded again and lowered her gaze, determined not to cry in front of this guy. She looked up when he spoke again, his tone much softer than it had been all night.

"Yamanami-san, could you assign a guard to her for the night?"

"Of course."

"Could you choose someone totally trustworthy? Someone who would never think to take advantage of the situation?"

Yamanami placed his hand on Kaemon's shoulder. "I've been having difficulty sleeping lately. Let me lock her mirror away, and then I'll go stay with her."

Kaemon bowed deeply. "I am in your debt, Yamanami-san."

When the older man left, Kaemon looked at Emmi a long time, and she tried to figure out what was going on behind those piercing dark eyes of his. For the first time, she took a long look at her "rescuer." He was young. She doubted he was much older than she was.

In fact, he was awfully good-looking.

Yamanami returned from his room and Kaemon left without saying another word or even looking back.

"I won't lie to you, Maeda-dono," Yamanami said as they walked toward a small L-shaped building at the far end of the compound. "The men we have detained are typical dogs, and, even though we rearranged them to place empty cells adjacent to yours, they'll still be able to glimpse you coming in, so don't be surprised if they say things you might not be used to hearing said to a lady."

Unnerved at the thought of being stuck in an actual jail with violent criminals, Emmi stumbled.

Yamanami placed a steadying hand on her arm. "It will be all right. I'll see to it that you're not alone in there."

"Thank you."

As predicted, the prisoners began calling out when she stepped inside the jail. Emmi was glad they spoke so quickly. She couldn't process it all, but even the gist of their words made her want to throw up.

"Silence!" Yamanami yelled in a voice infinitely more commanding than his measured speaking tone.

Emmi kept her eyes focused on her feet. She followed the vice-commander to the middle of the three small cells that formed the shorter portion of the L. Blankets had been hung on the sides as makeshift walls. Yamanami picked up the clean chamber pot from the floor outside and placed it in the right corner behind a small bamboo screen.

"It isn't the privacy you're used to, but I think you'll be comfortable enough."

"Thank you," Emmi said, stepping inside. Though she wanted to scream when Yamanami shut the door and placed a large iron lock through the wooden bars, she kept silent.

"I'm going to check on that food tray, and then I'll be back."

"All right."

When he left, Emmi unrolled the thin futon mat and curled up in the center. She prayed that this was all a nightmare, that she'd wake up and find it had all been a bad dream. That wish fell apart quickly once the male prisoners began calling out to her a few minutes later.

"They bring you to entertain us?"

"You smell sweet."

"I get the first taste."

Emmi covered her ears and hoped Yamanami would return soon. When the outer door to the jail slid open, she crawled to the front bars and looked out.

She could make out Yamanami in the dim lantern light. He was carrying a dinner tray. Behind him was another man, who veered off toward the prisoners' cells.

Emmi gasped when she heard scuffling and what could only be the sound of men being beaten. A man's voice issued threats and orders of silence.

"Pay it no mind, child," Yamanami said as he set the tray down then unlocked the door.

"But—"

"They savaged and murdered a woman who was gathering information for the shogunate. They don't deserve your mercy."

He slipped the open lock through one of the door crossbars, then picked up the tray and set it on the floor beside the futon. Emmi's empty stomach rumbled at the smell of the soup, steaming tea and flat bread. She noticed that there was enough for two.

"If you don't mind, I thought I'd sit here with you."

"Well..."

Yamanami smiled a rather sad smile. "It's quite safe, I promise you."

"Yamanami-san," a man said.

Emmi looked up at the man who had accompanied the vice-commander inside. He was dressed in a dark kimono, his black hair pulled back into a high ponytail.

"Forgive the interruption. I don't think you'll have any further trouble tonight from that scum."

Yamanami sighed, and Emmi had the distinct impression that he didn't have much of a stomach for this part of the job.

"Thank you, Saitou-san." He turned back to her. "Maeda-dono, this is Saitou Hajime, captain of the third unit."

Emmi managed to stop herself from saying "I know." Saitou was portrayed quite often in anime and manga. The drawn versions didn't come close to grabbing the intensity of the real man.

Saitou bowed to her then addressed his commander once more. "I will be making rounds through the compound tonight if you need anything."

"Thank you."

The fierce samurai headed to the door, pausing long enough to order the prisoners to cease their groaning and sniveling else he'd "make them stop."

"I think he's more frightening than Hijikata."

"You might be right." Yamanami removed the cover from the food dishes. "We'd better eat this before it gets cold."

* * * *

At the sound of the quiet knock, Hijikata Toshizou turned toward the inner door. "Enter."

His chief investigator slipped inside and knelt, bowing deeply.

"As of now, my sources within the Shoshidai have no information on any girl scheduled to be questioned in connection with rebel activities. It's possible the girl may have information on another matter, or it might be that the confusion surrounding the current changeover between governors has let something slip through the cracks."

Hijikata stroked his chin. His eyes narrowed with suspicion. "This bureaucratic confusion is all unbelievably convenient for our friend, Nakagawa no miya—oh that's right, he calls himself Fujiwara in public." Hijikata snorted. The emperor's nephew shouldn't go about putting on the pretense of a commoner. Men of the court had no stomach for war— particularly a prince with a weakness for pretty faces.

"Sir?"

Hijikata dismissed his speculation with a wave. "And the girl?"

"I didn't find any information specifically on her, although it seems that she and Fujiwara were coming from the direction of the Inamoto-ro. However, they have no women fitting her description. I checked with people at the other first-class houses, but they had nothing either." The spy paused. "Shall I check with the lesser houses?"

Hijikata shook his head. "Fujiwara wouldn't dirty himself at a lesser brothel." He drank a small saucer of sake, offering some to his spy. "Something about the girl didn't come across as a prostitute, though she was dressed like one. She had no shoes, and her hair was a mess. Such slovenliness is not good for business." He poured himself another drink. "What exactly could our 'friend' be up to?"

"You don't think he has begun to side with the rebels, do you?"

Hijikata shrugged. "Katsura and his people want to be the power behind the throne, and what better way to get close to that throne than through the son of the emperor's closest advisor?"

"But if the girl is a Choshu spy, then perhaps that's why he wants to hand her over to the Shoshidai."

"That's entirely possible," Hijikata agreed. "However, I don't trust our current governor, Inaba. When Matsudaira takes over in the next few days, we may know more."

The spy, Yamazaki, bowed and stood. "I'll keep trying to find out who the girl is and see what I can dig up on Fujiwara's recent activities."

"Fine."

* * * *

In his bedroom in one of the residence buildings of the Imperial Palace, Kae stared up at the moonlight glinting off the gilded ceiling trim. He reached beneath his thick futon and pulled out the stained cloth he'd wrapped around the pretty oni's hand earlier. The stains certainly appeared to be human blood. She could feel pain and fear. She had cried. These things certainly seemed to prove her claim that she was no demon. Yet the undeniable fact was that he had pulled her from Aneko's mirror with his own hands. How could she have come from within a mirror and not be some otherworldly being?

'I told you, I'm Em – Maeda Emiko. I don't know how I got here, but I know the mirror has something to do with it, and I need it to get back to my time...'

Her time.

What did that mean? For that matter, why did she have such an odd accent and where had she learned foreign words?

Kae got up and tossed the bloodstained cloth into the small brazier that did little to warm the room. He went back to his futon and pulled the cover over his head. He closed his eyes, doubting that sleep would come any time soon.

It wasn't just this business with the pretty oni — Emiko, he corrected himself — that troubled him. The very condition of Japan itself preyed upon his mind.

His father did not like the political trouble the Choshu clan and their followers stirred within their various domains. While they insisted that they revered the emperor and wanted to expel all foreign barbarians, the truth of the matter was that this Sonno Joi philosophy of theirs was merely a means to overthrow the Tokugawa. With the shogunate gone, they would be in the position of power to make the rules that benefited themselves and not necessarily all of Japan.

Kaemon bolted upright as a preposterous thought hit him.

Of course! His pretty oni was a human girl—her odd appearance was all part of the rebels' plan.

Before Aneko had left the brothel, she'd had one of the serving girls bring him sake. While he doubted that Aneko could be any kind of accomplice, it remained entirely possible that the Choshu had found out exactly who he was and had found the perfect opportunity to drug him.

Kae stood and paced the room. It all made perfect sense. The episode with the mirror was nothing more than a drugged dream and the acting of a devious girl playing tricks with his mind.

But if that's true, then why didn't they poison me outright?

Chapter Seven

Emmi woke a bit before dawn and sat up to see Yamanami had fallen asleep sitting against the side of the cell. Emmi took one of her blankets and gently draped it over him.

He was such a nice man that she found it hard to believe he was actually one of the leaders of this fierce group of samurai. She'd detected sadness in him when he spoke of their recent run-ins with the Choshu samurai who were seeking to overthrow the shogun. It was clear that he fought when he had to, but each time he raised his sword against another man, he did so at a great personal sacrifice.

Emmi wished now that her father hadn't read her those history books as bedtime stories when she was younger. It broke her heart to know what Yamanami Keisuke couldn't. His conscience would not allow him to violate the Shinsengumi's cardinal rule—once you joined, you could never leave. Yamanami would die because of it.

Her mouth was bone dry. Emmi reached through the open cell door and poured herself a bit of the now cold tea that was left in the pot from the night before. It wasn't her usual morning latte, but it wasn't so bad. Unfortunately, it was just enough to fill her bladder to the overflowing point. She stifled a groan as she thought of the chamber pot waiting behind the screen in the corner.

She tried thinking of something, anything, to take her mind off her need, but all her imagination would conjure was a remembrance of sitting on the beach near Jake's condo. The beach. The ocean. All that water, pounding against the rocks. Wave after wave...

Emmi nearly dove toward the screen to use the dreaded ceramic pot. She struggled to get situated, but once she did, she shut her eyes and hoped that Yamanami would sleep through the sound, which seemed as loud as the gushing of Niagara Falls. Though her bladder felt so much better once the deluge ran its course, there was still one small problem.

Or not.

Finally, Emmi appreciated Grandma Maeda's weird fixation that a lady should always carry a tissue or two tucked in the center of her bra. It wasn't quite the abundant quilted softness she was used to, but it was close enough.

Carefully, Emmi finished up and stood, making certain not to tip over the pot or let the hem of the kimono fall in it. She peeked around the screen then stepped out. Luckily, Yamanami was still sleeping, and if he wasn't, at least he had the decency to pretend to be.

Emmi lay down on the futon again but knew she'd never fall back to sleep. Her brain buzzed with a million and three questions, the first being—how was she ever going to get back home when she wasn't even quite sure how she'd gotten here?

She sat up and crinkled her nose. A breeze blew through the tiny window set high in the wall outside the cell, and the smell it carried reminded her of the chamber pot's existence. Bad enough that the place stank from the male prisoners' waste, but she really didn't want anything of the sort to be closer to her than necessary.

Yamanami had gone out last night to relieve his own bladder. Emmi didn't recall him unlocking the outer door before exiting, so it might remain unlocked now. She could go out, leave the pot, then come back and wait to be formally sprung. After all, it wasn't as if she was a criminal prisoner or anything.

Emmi retrieved the chamber pot carefully, moving slowly so as not to spill it. She tiptoed between the futon and the sleeping samurai leader, hoping he didn't decide to stretch out his legs. She stepped over him without any disaster and breathed a quick sigh of relief. Emmi inched to the door, not wanting to draw the attention of those criminals down the way.

Almost home free! Emmi thought, testing the door by nudging it with her foot. It gave way a bit, and she shifted sideways to push it open with her shoulder.

The door flew open just as Emmi shifted her weight. Emmi pitched outward, and the pot flew out of her hands, right into the center of Hijikata Toshizou's chest. He roared an obscenity so loudly Emmi was sure it woke half of Kyoto.

She fell to her knees partly as a sign of apology, partly to pray he wouldn't slice her head off. Gaining an ounce of courage, she glanced up and winced. The tissue she'd used as toilet paper had deposited itself right in the center of his low obi.

Emmi bent her head to the ground and apologized profusely in Japanese as best she could. She begged his forgiveness, adding that she was a complete fool who didn't deserve his mercy.

"Can't you do anything right?" he shouted.

Emmi bit back the tears and shook her head, thinking he was addressing her until she heard the other vice-commander speak.

"It was an accident, Toshi. An accident."

"Was it an accident her cell wasn't locked?"

"She's a harmless girl—"

"And that could very well be what the rebels want us to think! She wouldn't be the first spy sent to try to murder us in our sleep."

With that he spun around and stalked off, flinging the wet tissue from his obi to the ground.

Yamanami touched Emmi's shoulder. "You can get up now, Maeda-dono."

"I'm so sorry. I didn't mean to get you in trouble."

"It is nothing you did. It's me. He finds fault with everything I do these days." He paused and rubbed the bridge of his nose with his thumb and forefinger. "Come with me. I'll show you where you can wash, and I'll try to find you some clean clothing."

* * * *

Alone in the bathhouse, Emmi stood and stared at the supplies she had been given. One of the items reminded her of the long table runner her mother brought out on Thanksgiving. The other was a small sewn cloth bag filled with something almost rice-like.

Evidently these were the bath towel and soap, since there was nothing even remotely resembling a real towel or soap in sight.

Emmi undressed, then filled the nearby wooden bucket with some of the tub water. She dipped in the scratchy little soap substitute and scrubbed it over her skin before climbing into the large wooden tub to soak. She submerged herself to her chin, wincing at first as the hot water slid over her skin. Once settled, she closed her eyes and tried to relax, though it was next to impossible to keep her mind from spinning with an endless stream of unanswerable questions.

Finally the warmth of the water and the pleasant scent of cedar from the tub worked its magic, and all the hows and whys of her situation drifted to the far reaches of her mind. On the brink of dozing off, Emmi jerked her head up. Reluctantly, she climbed out of the soothing warmth. She dried herself as best as she could with the pitifully thin towel and donned her bra and panties before pulling on the blue men's kimono Yamanami had given her. She used the narrow obi like a bathrobe belt. She was just reaching for the skirt-like hakama to place over it when the outer door opened.

"What is taking you so long?" Kaemon demanded.

"None of your business!"

Emmi watched his gaze fasten on to her chest, and she wanted very much to slap him—until his expression changed to a mixture of confusion and fear.

"What are you doing?"

"Trying to put this on," Emmi said, shaking the hakama pants. "Wait outside."

"What are you doing with your kimono that way?"

"What way?"

He pointed again, appearing quite agitated that Emmi wasn't getting the clue. She looked at herself again, and it finally hit her. She'd thrown the kimono on like she would a bathrobe. She had the right side overlapping the left, the traditional Japanese way to dress a corpse prior to a funeral.

"I'm sorry. I wasn't paying attention," she said, turning away to open and adjust the kimono. She stayed with her back to him and stepped into the hakama, trying to pull up both the front and back sections at once.

How in the hell did her father and Uncle Jake slip these things on and get the long ends tied like it was a piece of cake? This was ridiculous. When she grasped the front ties the back fell, and vice versa. What she wouldn't give for a nice pair of jeans about now!

"Let me," Kae grumbled, coming up behind her.

Emmi sucked in her breath when his large, rough hands swept across hers as he took hold of the ties from the front section. He fastened them around her waist, then reached down and took hold of the hakama back. He slid it up and tucked the kimono inside, brushing against her rear as he did so.

"Hey!"

"Sorry," Kae said quickly, although he stepped closer still as he began to wrap the long back ties of the hakama around her waist and fit them into a precise square bow at the front.

Emmi tried not to notice the way he allowed his arms to linger around her waist after he finished tying the hakama. She thanked him in a whisper and wondered if she was imagining the attraction between them.

Nope, not imaging a thing, she thought when he drew her back against him.

He kissed her neck. His lips were a warm and inviting prelude to the way he slid his tongue up the side of her neck and nibbled on her ear.

Had that odd whimper just come from her? Did it even matter?

Kaemon coaxed her around and drew her nearer, into a slow kiss. Emmi wrapped her arms around his waist and pressed closer. Giving in to his expertise, she let the play of his lips and tongue unleash a flood of sensation that she'd never fully experienced.

She'd been on dates. She'd been kissed, but not like this. Never like this.

Daylight flooded the bathhouse, and Kaemon and Emmi jumped apart. The scary man from last night—Saitou—stood in the doorway, struggling to conceal his amusement. He cleared his throat.

"Hijikata-san wants to see you both in his quarters."

"Thank you, Saitou-san," Kaemon said, bowing.

Emmi did likewise and took a long deep breath in an effort to slow the thudding of her heart. When she straightened, Kaemon was staring at her. His deep, dark eyes burned with an intensity that both frightened and attracted her.

Without a word, he tore a thin strip from the towel-like cloth and tucked the end into the waist of his hakama. Using his fingers as a comb as he had the night before, he smoothed through her damp hair and drew it up into a high ponytail similar to his own. He wrapped the cloth strip around her hair to secure it in place.

"Now you'll appear to be my servant."

"Hey!"

"Would you rather look like my courtesan?"

A servant or a hooker? That was a no-brainer. Emmi shook her head and followed him outside, slipping into the sandals left for her, also courtesy of Yamanami-san. At least people were generally smaller in this time, and she wasn't stuck trying to wear huge men's shoes that would fit someone like her father or Jake.

Emmi kept looking toward the ground. She tried to ignore the pointed glances and suppressed snickers of the men milling around the compound. Emmi's cheeks flushed with embarrassment when Captain Harada approached and clapped Kaemon on the back, leaning in to whisper something about the bathhouse.

For all their fame in the history books as dedicated warriors, the Shinsengumi bunch wasn't that far removed from the jocks back home who liked to tell tall tales in the gym locker room.

"Shouldn't your unit be on patrol, Captain Harada?" Hijikata Toshizou called loudly from the porch of the building across the way.

"Understood, Hijikata-san!"

Emmi glanced at the vice-commander and followed Kaemon toward him slowly, not anxious to be in the ever-irritated man's presence.

Chapter Eight

When they stepped inside the vice-commander's quarters, Emmi bowed far lower than Kaemon. After all, when confronted with angry men who brandished sharp, dangerous objects, it seemed wise to push aside one's modern pride and grovel.

Especially after one had dumped a pot of pee on them.

However, Emmi didn't expect the oppressive silence that sprang up between Kaemon and the older man. This reminded her very much of some Wild West showdown at high noon on the main street of Dodge City.

The tension grew oppressively thicker until finally Hijikata said, "Who do you serve, Fujiwara-san? For whom would you give your life in battle?"

"I serve the emperor as you do, through Governor Matsudaira-sama."

Emmi glanced at the two men still staring each other down. She hoped this would end soon, mainly because her modern, American-born legs and ankles were beginning to go numb from sitting in the traditional kneeling seiza position. She really should have paid more attention to her father's and Jake's mind-over-matter meditation lessons.

At last the standoff ended when Kaemon took a small, silk-wrapped bundle and slid it across the tatami mat. "Accept my apologies for the inconvenience caused you. I would be honored to have this accepted in return."

He bowed, and Emmi did likewise because it seemed the best thing to do.

Hijikata's reply was a curt "Hn" sound, but Emmi was quick to note that he wasted no time in scooping up the bundle, which made a distinctive metallic clink.

"I trust this will be your last such imposition, Fujiwara-san?"

"Hopefully," Kaemon said, offering a quick bow of his head. "Thank you again for your help."

The forced politeness of the words hit Emmi hard, and she was not at all pleased to see the gleam of superiority in Hijikata's hard gaze.

The older man merely nodded, and, thankfully, Kaemon took his leave and Emmi trailed behind. A young man who'd been waiting outside handed Kaemon a cloth sack with something wrapped in paper. It might be her mirror. She hoped it was. Kaemon slung the strap of the sack over his chest and positioned it so the weight hung across his back.

Biting back a 'Take it easy with my ticket home, bud,' Emmi hobbled along behind him until the pins and needles subsided in her feet and ankles. She stopped when she saw the kindhearted vice-commander,

Yamanami Keisuke, a short distance away and veered off in his direction.

Kaemon was halfway to the front gates before he noticed that Emiko had gone to speak with Yamanami-san. Kae could see the immediate effect her presence had on the older man. He always seemed preoccupied and morose, but when Emiko spoke to him he stood straighter, and a rare smile curved his mouth. When she placed a swift kiss on Yamanami's cheek, the man fairly shone with a fleeting moment of happiness.

Kae knew exactly how he must feel.

He forced his memory to stop replaying their kiss when his body responded. Perhaps he had been wrong in his conclusion the previous night. Perhaps she wasn't simply a temptress sent to leech secrets and information from him. Maybe she was some type of demon with the power to enchant and capture the souls of men.

Emmi rushed back toward Kae and said, "I'm sorry, but I had to say goodbye and thank him for being so kind to me."

"It's all right," Kae said, heading toward the gates once more.

Something odd or almost sad lingered in the depths of the samurai's eyes, and Emmi rushed to keep up with his quick pace. He seemed quite surprised when Emmi gripped his haori to stop him.

"Are you sure something isn't wrong? Back there you looked...I don't know, like a lost little boy."

Kaemon said nothing but turned away quickly. He kept walking, taking long strides so that Emmi had to hurry to keep up with him. Lovely. Just what she needed—she'd left the lair of one big, bad wolf only to be stuck with another.

"Where are we going?" she asked when they had to stop and step aside as two large wagons loaded with bulging rice sacks blocked the street.

"To the military governor."

"But I don't know anything about anything military."

"What you know or don't know is not the issue. We have to go because Hijikata has his spy watching to see that we arrive at the offices of the governor."

Emmi whipped her head around. "Spy? Who? Where?"

"It doesn't matter, but there is one nearby," Kaemon said, beginning to walk again. "I know Hijikata, and I know I'd send someone to check my story if I were him."

Emmi sighed to herself and kept trotting along with her attention focused on keeping up with the cranky samurai as he led her through every side street and grungy back alley in Kyoto. Just her luck—she was in the company of a man who was tall for the era, a man who had a long, fast stride and took full advantage of it.

And he's a good kisser. Don't forget the kissing part, her brain added on its own.

Emmi wished he'd slow down for a minute, or change his route so she could at least see some of nineteenth-century Kyoto. She'd gotten more of a tour out of Uncle Jake's quick spin around the movie backlot before they started filming yesterday.

Unfortunately, Kaemon didn't slow until they were confronted with another knot of people. Emmi caught her breath and massaged her side to ease the stitch she'd gotten from the unaccustomed hike. Looking around, she realized they were on the edge of a bridge that spanned a wide moat.

Emmi shifted and stood tiptoe to see clearly over the heads of the people in front of her. Finally, she saw something familiar. Up ahead was a massive front gate set in the high stone walls surrounding the Nijo castle compound. They'd passed Nijo on the way from the airport to the hotel, and although she'd only gotten a quick glimpse, Emmi was certain that this was the same place.

It seemed to take forever to reach the main gate then pass through to another. Kaemon explained why he was there to the guards and produced some type of identification paper for the men to inspect. Emmi took the time to look around and admire the workmanship of the entrance to the rambling palace complex containing the shogun's official Kyoto residence and various offices and official meeting rooms.

Incredible barely described it. The dark wood of the gateway's massive support beams was a sea of majestic decoration. Lifelike carved cranes flew amid intricately carved flowers, all of it surrounded by a myriad of golden chrysanthemums and set into golden scrollwork cartouches. Why the shogun would have ordered so much of the emperor's chrysanthemum crest to be incorporated, as if it was his own, was beyond Emmi, but she couldn't deny the beauty or commanding impression it gave.

The bottleneck at the gates eased considerably once they were inside the courtyard. Emmi didn't have much of a chance to examine her surroundings as Kaemon grabbed her sleeve and propelled her forward.

It seemed as though he led her around and through each of the palace's interconnected buildings twice. The place was bustling with men rushing here and there, most carrying handfuls of scrolls, stacks of ledger books or wooden boxes. She noticed that the majority of men knew Kaemon. The guards stationed throughout the place waved him through with curt bows, as though his face was the only ID he needed inside.

At last he slowed his quick pace, and her aching feet gave thanks. Emmi noticed the squeaking of the floorboards as they, and the few people that passed them, moved along the corridor.

"What, Tokugawa can't afford a decent carpenter?" Emmi murmured.

Kaemon stopped short. Emmi almost ran into him and had to grip his waist to steady herself. Her hand seemed to burn from the feel of muscle beneath his silk clothing, and Emmi snatched it away but gave him what had to look like a guilty smile.

"You truly don't know anything at all, do you?"

"What?"

He glanced down. "You claim to be a Maeda, and yet you don't know about the floors. Are you so far removed from the main branch of the clan that none of your people have ever been here?"

"It's been a long time for them, if that's all right with you." Stupid nervousness making her spit out the stupid carpenter comment. Of course she knew the floors were supposed to squeak like an old school burglar alarm. She prayed Kaemon wouldn't press the issue.

He shook his head and surveyed his surroundings. He then stretched as if he too had finally tired of this wild goose chase. He returned the greeting of two men who came out of a side room. Once they disappeared around a corner, Kaemon gave her a hard look.

"Time for your questioning," he said, grabbing her hand.

A cold chill ran through Emmi when he dragged her to a silk tapestry set into an alcove on the left.

Before she could finish saying "What the hell are you doing?" Emmi found herself pulled behind the tapestry, through a sliding panel, and into another corridor, which was lit only by thin bands of sun coming through slits in the ceiling.

"Do you know every secret passage ever created in Kyoto?"

"No. Only the ones in Shimabara, here and those in the Imperial Palace," Kaemon said matter-of-factly.

"The Imperial Palace, as in where the emperor lives."

"It's also where my father, I and a host of other people live as well."

"Bu—"

Her words were cut off when Kaemon shoved her against the wall and held her in place with his muscular body.

"You know all that, though, don't you, Maeda-dono?" he sneered, saying the name and honorific as though it were the biggest exaggeration in the world.

Emmi shivered. Her pulse raced, and a thin sheen of sweat formed on her face following the unmistakable scrape of a weapon being drawn from its sheath. She sucked in her breath when he placed the blade of a long dagger almost against her throat.

"Those men we just saw will be gone for hours, and they're the only ones in this part of the residence during the day. I could torture you, and no one would hear your screams well enough to know where they came from. And, even if they did investigate, I assure you I can convince them that you tried to kill me first."

Emmi trembled and prayed that she wouldn't shake enough to bring her throat closer to the blade in his hand.

"W-what is wrong with you? Why are you doing this?"

He snorted his contempt. "What did you drug me with? What did you put into the sake that I couldn't detect?"

"I don't know what you're talking about. I swear I don't."

Kaemon smirked and tilted the blade so that what light there was glinted off its edge and hit her in the eye.

"I will get the information out of you," he said in a menacing whisper. "I'm sure such a drug would be useful to my father."

Emmi clutched her hands into fists so tightly her nails dug into her palms. "I don't know what you're talking about. I didn't give you any drug. Maybe it was Yamanami. He gave you tea, I gave you nothing."

Kaemon pressed the flat edge of the blade against her throat. "Do not play the fool with me," he ordered. "At the brothel. The sake was drugged. You led me to believe that you were trapped within the mirror and made me think I pulled you free."

"No, I didn't—"

"Do. Not. Lie."

Emmi winced when the very tip of the blade pressed on her neck, and, though she clamped her eyes shut, she could feel the tears slide from beneath her lashes as drops of blood trickled down her neck.

"I didn't. Kill me if you want, but I swear on my life that I didn't drug you or trick you."

Kaemon was again reminded of the courtesan, Koyuki, who had so loved his father and had been like a mother to him. He'd been playing with his cousin and hiding in a chest in his father's room. Father and Koyuki had come in arguing—she protesting her innocence in betraying him with another man and he insisting that his informant was beyond the reproach of a whore no matter how noble of birth she was. His father had been as close to severing Yuki's head as he himself was at this moment with this woman.

"Look at me."

Emmi opened her eyes. More tears slid down her cheeks, but she shakingly met his gaze.

He tilted the blade of the tanto away from her throat and stared into her eyes. He'd killed traitors before, and he'd seen the deceit lingering in the backs of their eyes even as they professed their innocence. The woman who'd lied to his father about Koyuki had had that look of betrayal in her own eyes before his father had killed her.

Even through the sheen of watery tears, Kae knew the look in the depths of Emiko's eyes was nothing like those of the true betrayers. He put the tanto away then gently wiped away her tears with the pads of his thumbs.

Maybe I am Alice stuck in a topsy-turvy world, Emmi thought when Kaemon kissed the spot where he'd nicked her throat. First he wanted to kill her, now he wanted to comfort her. It made no sense, but, for the life of her, Emmi couldn't push him away.

When he leaned in to kiss her, she didn't even try to make sense of it anymore. All that mattered was the fire that seeped into her blood when his lips met hers. She'd never been kissed like this. This was a man's kiss, not the kiss of the boys back home who were too intimidated by her father to ever dare take possession of her mouth the way Kae was doing.

He broke the kiss long enough to gaze into her eyes before he captured her lips with his again. He slid his mouth from hers to kiss a trail to her chin then down her neck. He licked the small cut he'd given her.

"Forgive me," he whispered before teasing her with featherlight kisses up and down her neck.

Emmi breathed a long soft sigh and arched into his touch when he slid his hands along her midriff. He drew back to look at her again, and Emmi melted inside from the intensity of his gaze. She shifted, and the boards beneath her feet creaked softly. They creaked again when Kae changed his own stance and removed the sack holding the mirror.

He set it on the floor beside her and gripped her waist, his hands snaking inside the side slits of the hakama she wore.

Emmi whimpered when he cupped her rear through the soft fabric of the yukata and again when he pulled her hips toward his. She could feel his erection but was too lightheaded from the pleasure to consider the consequences.

"You must be some type of oni," he said before kissing her neck again. "What magic do you use to make me behave this way?"

"I-I'm not—"

He chuckled, and Emmi felt embarrassment flame her cheeks. The instant he peered intently into her eyes, the heat coursing through her body settled itself deep within her center, and she shivered.

He grinned, and Emmi was certain she heard a muffled growl rumble in his chest. He claimed her mouth with his once more. His tongue sought out hers, teasing her, coaxing her, while he slipped his hands inside the hakama again to part the thin yukata.

Emmi shivered again when Kaemon's rough fingers glided over her belly and hips. She barely noticed the squeaking of the floorboards as he strummed a gentle rhythm over her burning flesh. He hesitated when his fingers brushed the stretch lace of her panties, but then he slipped his fingers beneath the thin fabric. With slow precision he stroked and caressed, pressed and prodded her sex until she was quaking beneath his experienced touch.

Common sense screamed that this was a bad idea, but she was powerless to resist. Maybe he was the demon who had her under a spell. She barely heard the creaking boards any longer, never paid attention to the sound of the hidden panel sliding open until Kaemon stiffened and stopped dead.

"Why am I not surprised to find my son here?" an annoyed male voice asked from behind Kaemon. "So your taste is running to young pages these days, is it? This is exactly why I told you not to befriend Takeda Kanryuusai and the rest of that Mibu-ro trash."

Kaemon sucked in his breath and Emmi tried to shrink back into the wall. Her father and brother had had a couple of standoffs like this, and they hadn't been pleasant.

"My tastes are as they have always been," Kaemon said curtly before turning. "I don't understand why you dislike the Shinsengumi. They've quelled more disturbances than any other force in Kyoto."

"They're nothing but farmers with swords. That will never change, no matter how many rebels they slay or favors they're granted."

The low growl that rumbled in Kae's chest chilled Emmi, and she instinctively grabbed the back of his haori, hoping to stop him from saying or doing something he'd regret. He relaxed, and she rubbed his back a moment before removing her hand.

Kaemon's father cleared his throat. "Send your playmate back to wherever you found her then meet me in my quarters within the hour." He left, shutting the sliding panel with a sharp bang.

Kae grumbled and turned back to face Emmi. She looked up at him with a combination of worry and curiosity.

"Why did you do that?" he asked. "Why did you rub your hand over my back?"

Emmi shrugged. "I don't know. I guess because my parents did that to each other. They didn't get angry very often, but that was their signal for the other to stop and think before they said or did anything they'd regret later."

Emmi paused as the awkwardness of the situation engulfed her, making the brief silence uncomfortable.

"So that was your father?"

Kaemon smirked. "Yes. His Imperial Highness Prince Nakagawa."

Emmi shivered. No wonder he seemed so dictatorial—

"Prince? Your father is a prince?"

Kaemon nodded. "He is an adopted brother to the emperor."

"The emperor?"

Kaemon smirked. "He's the emperor as long as the rebel swine never get their way."

Emmi's mind spun. For as long as she could remember, there had been a large portrait of the Emperor of Japan above the living room mantel in her grandparents' house. Even in old family photos it was there.

Kaemon's father was a prince, the adopted brother of the current emperor and that meant...

Shouldn't she fall to her knees and bow? *He practically had his hands in your pants,* a sarcastic inner voice said. *Don't you think you're a wee bit past the formality stage?*

"You're an imperial prince?" Emmi asked in a shaking voice, hoping she'd gotten it all wrong.

"Yes. And I'm going to be a prince awaiting his funeral if I don't get to my father's quarters in time. Come on."

He dragged her out of the secret passage and rushed through various rooms and corridors, causing the squeaky Nightingale Floor to sing.

"I can't go to the Imperial Palace looking like this."

"No, you can't," Kaemon said. "That's why I'm leaving you here."

"No!"

Kaemon stopped and glared at her. "I will not leave you to run loose here or through Kyoto. I'm taking you to the wife of the castle warden. I'll return for you later."

Knowing that she didn't have much choice in the matter, Emmi let him lead her to the spacious kitchens of Ninomaru Palace. There a bevy of maids dressed in matching salmon-colored kimonos with dark green obis bustled about preparing food to place on the dozens of *ozen* — meal trays — that sat waiting with small bowls and plates atop a series of long plank tables set against the far wall.

While Kaemon didn't acknowledge the attention that their entrance into the room attracted, Emmi noticed the many covert looks the young samurai got from the maids as they passed. The one he sought out, however, was an older lady dressed in a somewhat drab, dark gray kimono with a black and white obi.

"Shinjuku-san," Kaemon said in a singsong tone as he approached the woman from behind. "May I speak with you a moment?"

She spun around, and Emmi felt like an impetuous child bothering an impatient mother.

"I don't have a moment!" She gestured around the kitchen. "Look at this! With Inaba going out, and Matsudaira coming in, and all of their retainers wanting to be fed, there isn't enough time in eternity to get it all done, and you want to ask me favors."

"I didn't say anything about favors," Kaemon said, before that lost little boy look colored his expression almost as it had back at the Shinsengumi compound.

Shinjuku-san clearly wasn't buying it, and Emmi lowered her head to suppress a smile at the familiarity he allowed the older woman.

"Well, there is a favor, but it's a small, important favor," Kaemon said, reaching around to grab the front of Emmi's kimono and pull her forward.

Shinjuku-san gave her a cursory look. "Do your problems ever not concern a girl?"

Emmi shot the samurai a look, but he ignored it and addressed the older woman again.

"Maeda-dono is a nice girl, but she hasn't eaten today, and I must meet with my father. Or else."

"So you give me yet another mouth to feed. As if the two hundred I have now aren't enough?"

Emmi shook her head "I don't want—"

Kaemon interrupted. "But look at her—she's small. She hardly needs to eat. You can give her the table scraps. Just let her stay here until I return."

Shinjuku-san's laugh was clearly derisive. "Until you return from your father's tonight or from Shimabara in a few days?"

Anger stirred within Emmi, and she wanted to smack Kaemon not only for saying she deserved only scraps, but also for having the nerve to try to make her yet another one of his conquests.

"Only until tonight. I promise."

Shinjuku-san dismissed it with a wave. "The sooner you leave, the sooner you return. Go."

Kaemon flashed a smile that reminded Emmi of what her father used to call Jake's 'ladykiller' smile. She had no doubt Kaemon took full advantage of that smile's effect whenever he could.

"Stay out of the way. I'll return for you soon," he said to Emmi before rushing out the door.

He left behind a bevy of sighing kitchen maids, an irritated matron and one very cheesed-off descendant of the legendary Toshiie Maeda.

"Leave it to that boy not to even introduce you," Shinjuku-san said pleasantly.

Emmi looked at her, surprised by the friendly tone and the sudden warmth appearing in her brown eyes.

"Having you wait here is no trouble, but I try not to encourage his bad habits."

"I take it that he has many bad habits?"

Shinjuku-san grinned. "You haven't known our Kaemon long, have you?"

"No."

"His faults are many, but nothing more than those of any young man of wealth and power let loose in the world for the first time."

"I see," Emmi replied flatly. She remembered the tales of arrogant stars and 'suits' that her father and Jake had had to deal with in Hollywood.

Shinjuku-san laughed softly, and Emmi looked at her but didn't reply. Instead, she simply followed the older woman.

Chapter Nine

"You see, Toshi? Yamanami told you there was nothing to be suspicious of, and Yamazaki confirmed it," Shinsengumi Chief Kondo Isami told his vice-commander.

Their senior investigator had just left, after giving his report on Kaemon and the girl. Kondo lay sideways on the tatami, propping his head on his hand.

"Fujiwara-san took the girl to the Shoshidai, left her, and then went to the Imperial Palace to report it all to his father."

"And his father is exactly what has me bothered," Hijikata grumbled as he cleaned the blade of his katana. He rested his sword across his lap and looked at his lifelong friend. "The elder prince has never made a secret of his political leanings, not even when the shogun exiled him and confined him to that dilapidated outbuilding at the Shokoku-ji Temple."

"But he was released and allowed to return to life outside the Buddhist order."

Hijikata huffed and returned his katana to its sheath. "Have you forgotten that he was released only a year ago? And how many of his friends and supporters were exiled or killed during the Ansei Purge? If I were him, I'd want my revenge on the house of Tokugawa."

Kondo sat up. His expression turned as serious as Hijikata's. "You have a point, but many think highly of him, even those loyal to the shogunate."

Hijikata shrugged then turned to place his sword back on the lacquered sword rack beneath his smaller wakizashi.

"All I'm saying is that the young one bears further watching, especially since he insists on keeping his true identity a secret outside the palace walls."

Kondo folded his arms into his sleeves. "I suppose I can't argue with that point." He summoned his page and had tea brought in. "Will you be accompanying me to Edo to recruit new men?"

"And leave Yamanami in charge?"

"He's a capable officer, Toshi, and you need to get away and relax."

"I'll think about it." He sipped his tea. "You said last night that you have some promising prospects to interview?"

"I do. Including one Kawashima Daishiro."

"Kawashima? He's willing to leave his position in Edo to come here?"

"It's possible."

Hijikata's reply was a scowl.

* * * *

Prince Asahiko paced the length of his reception room in the Imperial Palace. "Mori Takachika sent one of his retainers to approach me today. I was too busy to receive him and will remain too busy to receive him until I know exactly what Choshu's plans are."

He stopped and faced his son. "You have important business to attend to, Kaemon. And, while I realize the best place for you to get the information we need is in Shimabara, your mind needs to stay on the business of the Court. You cannot waste precious time by fornicating with servants in the halls."

"Honored Father, I do take what I do for you seriously. And I was trying to get information from the girl, but... I was mistaken about her..."

"So you decided to pass the time in more pleasant ways."

"No—"

Asahiko held up his hand for silence and began pacing again. "I heard you had trouble in the Licensed Quarters earlier this week."

"It couldn't be helped. A group of the Choshu attacked one of the courtesans-in-training at Narihisaro. The *kamuro* was a child of only ten. I had to get involved."

The elder prince stopped and stared at Kae. "What business did you have in a third-class house like that? The men with the information we want wouldn't be there." He paced again. "You do realize that the men of Choshu han guard this palace. They have acquaintances from their home domain arriving in Kyoto every day. All it takes to spell disaster for us is for one of them to recognize your description."

"Understood," Kae said, bowing deeply. He looked up to see his father sink down onto a low, painted chest that held maps. Throwing protocol to the winds, Kae rushed over. "Are you ill? Do you need a doctor?"

Asahiko shook his head. "I'm tired." He gestured for Kae to sit beside him. "Japan is on the brink of death, Kaemon, and I want to hold it off as long as possible."

He rubbed his eyes and exhaled a weary sigh before continuing. "You and I have a responsibility to be the voices of reason in Emperor Komei's ear. We need to find a way to voice that same reason to young Prince Mutsuhito, because one day he'll be emperor, and if the rebels have their way, it will be long before he's ready to assume the role."

Prince Asahiko placed his hand on Kae's shoulder. "This incident with the *kamuro* and the servant girl prove to me that you are too much like your mother, Kaemon. Men such as we can never indulge the whims of our hearts. Never. Remember that."

Kae nodded. "I will remember, Honored Father. You have my word."

Chapter Ten

The meal that the wife of the castle warden served was far from a plate of table scraps. In fact, if Emmi had been wearing her favorite jeans instead of the loose kimono and hakama, she'd have had to undo the top button. Emmi raised her hands when Shinjuku-san tried to coax her into another sweetened rice ball for dessert.

"Just one more. After all, Kae-san likes his women with some meat on their bones."

Emmi gasped. "We're not— I'm not one of his women. I'm far from home and lost, and he was kind enough to help me."

The older woman gave her an enigmatic smile in return then began collecting the used plates. Emmi hurried to help and followed Shinjuku-san to the trough in an adjacent room where the kitchenware was washed.

Twin girls, who couldn't have been more than twelve, were working like mad, scrubbing pots and woks, bowls and cups.

"I'll stay and help them if that's all right with you, Shinjuku-san."

"You are a guest. This is their job."

"Please?" Emmi asked. "I'd like to repay you for helping me."

"All right," Shinjuku-san said after some consideration. "If you're not done when Kae-san returns, I'll send for you."

One of the girls helped Emmi tie her kimono sleeves back and then whispered something to her twin. They both giggled.

"What's so funny? Come on, you can tell me."

"We think you make a very pretty boy dressed that way."

Emmi laughed. "Thank you. Why don't you two sit for a while and let me wash this mess?"

The girls shook their heads. "No," the taller of the two said. "Shinjuku-dono will be angry if we don't work."

"We must work," the shorter girl said. "She bought us."

"She bought you?"

"From Shimabara," the girl said.

"Bought from Shimabara," Emmi repeated softly, unable to believe that these little girls had been bought from the sex district. She gripped the edge of the sink trough, afraid that she might throw up. What kind of person was Mrs. Shinjuku really? For that matter, what type of person was Kaemon? What other sorts of "favor" did he ask of the older woman?

"Shinjuku-san heard that we were going to be sold to customers, so she had her husband buy us from the master. We live here and can help with the work after we come from the Temple school."

"Oh," Emmi said. She was relieved she'd been mistaken about the motivation but still hated the thought that these kids had to work in a kitchen to repay the favor.

It made her realize just how far from home she truly was and how she might never again have the everyday comforts or security of the life she'd taken for granted back in the twenty-first century.

As she helped wash the dishes, Emmi did her best to translate into Japanese some of the lame jokes her brother used to bug her with when they were younger. The jokes didn't translate all that well, but the twins, Chidori and Namiji, found them amusing enough to be entertained.

However, they stopped laughing and bowed low the instant Shinjuku-san came into the washroom.

"Get up. Get up," she said. "You two can go out and enjoy the sunshine before dinner."

The twins thanked her, bowed from the waist, and bowed again to Emmi. "Thank you, Emiko-dono."

"Thank you for being so nice to me."

They ran off giggling. Emmi set the last dish aside, dried her hands and offered the older woman a deep bow. "I owe you an apology, Shinjuku-san."

"Apology? Why?"

"I told the girls to let me do their work mainly because I thought you were being cruel to them. When they told me you had bought them from Shimabara, well… I'm sorry for what I was thinking."

Shinjuku-san studied her for a long time, and Emmi felt like a total fool. The older woman would probably get one of those scary guards to take her away to a dungeon until Kaemon came back.

If Kaemon came back.

"You have a caring heart," Shinjuku-san finally said. "Kae-san needs someone like you in his life."

An invisible punch hit Emmi dead in the stomach, and she could barely make her lips form words. She shook her head.

"No. It isn't going to happen. He's a prince, and I'm not...from around here. I don't think I'll be here long."

Shinjuku-san smiled another one of those enigmatic smiles.

"For however long you are here, it will be a good thing for him." She gave Emmi a gentle prod toward the door. "Come. I'll show you where things are. Then we will sit in the garden and watch the children play."

Chapter Eleven

Kae was on his way back to Nijo Castle when a familiar young servant girl ran up to him.

"Aneko-han...wishes to...see...you at once," she said between gasping breaths, as if she'd been running all over Kyoto to find him. She handed him a note.

My mirror is missing. You have been enchanted with it of late. If you have it, please return it at once. I will make the inconvenience up to you any way you like. I also have some news from a distance for you.

News from a distance usually meant news pertaining to the rebel ronin infiltrating the city. Kae folded the crisp rice paper and tucked it into his kimono sleeve.

"Tell her I will stop by later tonight if I have time."

On the verge of tears, the girl fell to her knees in the center of the street. "Please, honored sir. She told me that if I didn't find you and bring you back at once, she would have me beaten again."

She looked up, and Kae fell prey to her frightened eyes. He reached down, took hold of her arm and coaxed her to her feet. He took some money from the pouch inside his sleeve and gave it to the girl.

"Aneko-san asked me to return something of hers that I borrowed. You get yourself something to eat while I retrieve it, and I will meet you by the Sanjo Bridge very soon."

* * * *

Emmi stared across the wide pond at the twins skimming tiny stones across the water and ran her fingers through the thick grass beneath her. She wondered what had happened between Kaemon and his father. It was probably something unpleasant, judging from the older Nakagawa's tone and demeanor.

"Think of the demon and he appears," Shinjuku-san teased before tapping Emmi on the shoulder.

Emmi looked up and followed the older woman's gaze to see Kae approaching. He looked so impressive striding toward them with his back straight, his gait sure and balanced like one long-schooled in the martial arts. His katana and wakizashi bobbed at his hip. The ends of his open haori blew slightly in the breeze while the kimono he wore beneath gaped slightly with his movements, revealing a flash of his well-toned chest. As he drew nearer, Emmi noticed his dark eyes instinctively scanning the surrounding area for any signs of trouble, even though there was unlikely to be any this far inside the compound.

Shinjuku-san stood and brushed off the back of her kimono. "I need to round up those girls. They have a bit more work to do before dinner." She grinned at Kaemon. "I trust it is safe to leave Emiko-chan alone with you?"

"Absolutely safe," he said, casting a look to Emmi that made her warm all over.

It didn't seem too terribly safe from where Emmi was sitting, but she wasn't about to complain.

The older woman left, and Kae extended his hand. Emmi took it and allowed him to help her up. He held on to her hand after she was on her feet, and Emmi stepped closer, wanting very much to kiss him again.

"How did the meeting with your father go?"

Kaemon shrugged. "As our meetings always do. He lectured me on my responsibilities, and I told him I would follow his wishes."

He let go of her hand.

"I have a small errand to run. It won't take long. I know Shinjuku-san will let you stay until I return."

"I can come with you."

"No," he said quickly. "It won't be safe for you. I need to see someone back in Shimabara."

"Oh," Emmi answered flatly.

Kaemon began to walk back toward the compound's main building, and Emmi followed a few paces behind. She could imagine his business was of the sex variety with that hooker friend of his. Of course, that was none of her business. It wasn't as if she owned him or was even involved with him. It certainly didn't matter to her that he planned to go picking up sleazy women.

"What are you going to do with me? Later, I mean," she wondered aloud, suddenly feeling more lost and alone than she had since her bizarre arrival.

Kaemon stopped short, and Emmi ran straight into him. The metal-tipped sheath of his sword caught her just above the knee, and she cried out.

He turned. His dark and dangerous expression emphasized his scalding tone. "If you continue to walk beside me and on the left you'll stick out more than you already do. And doing that will get you killed in Kyoto these days."

Emmi rubbed her knee and moved to his right. "It's not like I'm doing it on purpose. I can't help it if I stand out. I'm not from around here, remember?"

"Walk behind me and to the right. Even women from Kaga aren't as stupid as you appear."

"Well, I happen to be from Am—" Emmi stopped herself short. She knew enough about the period to understand that proclaiming herself one of the 'barbarians' everyone wanted to exterminate and expel from Japan was not a wise move.

Kaemon's eyes narrowed suspiciously. "You are from where?"

"A long, long way from here."

His harsh gaze drilled into her, reminding her far too much of the way he'd looked when he pulled the tanto on her earlier.

"You need to get going to your appointment, don't you?" she prodded.

He said nothing before turning and walking away at a pace she hurried to match.

* * * *

"Really, Kae-sama," Aneko said, placing her mirror back on the low chest in her quarters. "Are you so fascinated with the thought of a female oni that you wanted to try to conjure her?"

"Of course not. I wanted to have that dent removed and have it polished as a gift to you, but I didn't have the chance."

The prostitute slid her hand along Kae's arm. "You are too good to me. You know, if you were to buy out my contract, I could secure a small house near the palace and be good to you and you alone."

Kae pulled away when she licked his neck.

"I wouldn't want to deprive your long-time customers of their favorite entertainment."

He went to the table across the room and poured himself some sake. He removed his swords and sat with his back against the wall.

"What is the latest news you have heard from a distance?"

"They're just idle rumors so far. It can wait," Aneko said.

She came to him and undid the obi securing her embroidered red kimono. She dropped it to the tatami, then knelt before Kaemon and ran her hands up into the wide leg openings of his hakama.

Kae grabbed her wrists. "Not tonight. I need to know what you found out."

"Fine." Aneko closed the front of her kimono and sat back on her heels. "As I said, it is a rumor overheard by one of the *kamuro*, and those little wretches can't really be trusted."

"What is it?"

"A plan to burn Kyoto to the ground to prove how ineffectual the shogunate is in keeping the peace. The girl said she overheard a man while she was in the garden. He said, '*If Japan can't protect her people from the bad element from within, however will they succeed in protecting us from the barbarians waiting to devour us from without?'"*

Chapter Twelve

The sun was fading when Emmi sat down to eat dinner with the twins and Shinjuku-san. Shinjuku-san's husband looked at her even more suspiciously than Kae had. She didn't want to lie to the man when he questioned her about her origins, since she sensed he had what Jake's twin sister called 'an inbred B.S. detector'.

"My family is from Kaga. My father died in an accident almost a year ago. My mother and I don't get along, so I was staying with my adopted uncle. I came here with him on business, but we were separated." Emmi paused to sip tea. "Kae—Nakagawa-san found me and said he would help me."

Mr. Shinjuku simply nodded then finished his second bowl of rice.

With her insides a jumble of nerves, Emmi could barely touch what was on her tray. She sensed that he still wasn't quite buying her story, but what could she do? It was as close to the truth as she could get without them believing she was some freakish demon or, worse, some kind of spy.

Mr. Shinjuku set down his bowl and caught her eye with his fierce gaze once again. "Your manner of speaking, your accent, does not sound as though you're from Kaga."

Emmi shrugged. "I can't explain it. I've always been 'different.' I suppose that's why my mother hates me so…"

Emmi wiped her eyes and bowed to the Shinjukus.

"May I be excused? Please?" she asked.

Shinjuku nodded, and Emmi went out to the side porch of the castle warden's residential quarters. Emmi had thought she'd cried all the tears in the world when her father died, but apparently there were more. She gave in to the lingering grief while darkness settled over Nijo Castle.

She sat in darkness for several minutes before her pity party was interrupted.

"Emiko-dono?" the twins Chidori and Namiji said softly in unison just after Emmi dried the last of her tears.

"Oh. Hello." Emmi wiped her eyes once more. "You must think I'm silly."

"Oh, no," Namiji said. "Our father died too."

"His new wife sold us to the brothel," Chidori added.

Sadness washed over Emmi again, this time for the girls. She had to blink the forming teardrops away when Kaemon appeared behind the twins. He smiled at her, and the sisters giggled. They hurried back inside the Shinjukus' quarters, closing the sliding door firmly behind them.

Emmi turned to look out toward the gardens. At least she hadn't been wearing mascara and didn't look like a raccoon. But jeez... Of all times to have puffy red eyes.

The samurai settled down beside her on the porch. Kae placed his hand on the small of her back and rubbed it in a circle. Lightning shot through her.

"Why were you crying?"

Emmi faced him, offering a sheepish smile. "It's nothing. Shinjuku-san asked about my family. My father died a few months back. I was missing him."

"One never gets over the death of a parent." He jumped off the porch. "Walk with me."

Placing her hand in his, Emmi jumped down and told herself it was stupid, stupid, stupid to get so jittery inside. Especially when he came into close contact with her.

"I know. Walk behind you and to the right," Emmi said, scooting over to his other side.

He laughed, tucked his arms into the sleeves of his haori, then led the way.

Large paper lanterns had been lit and placed at various spots on the castle grounds. The lanterns reminded Emmi of a big anniversary party at her grandparents' home in Hawaii. After the guests had gone and the caterers had cleaned up the mess, Emmi had joined her parents and grandparents out in the spacious back yard where the paper lanterns still hung.

Her father had put away the party CDs and brought out what he deemed 'make-out tunes'. Emmi had sat on the wide veranda and watched her parents and grandparents dance. How in love they all were! Emmi had wondered if she would ever find someone to look at her the way her father and grandfather looked at their wives.

Fat chance of that now, her inner voice announced.

Emmi knew that the worst-case scenario had her stuck here and signing herself into some house in Shimabara to keep a roof over her head and food in her stomach. Of course, some kindhearted family might adopt her, which would lend her some social status. Or, if they were merchants, perhaps they would offer her a job. Even then, her status wouldn't be much.

With the way things were headed for the samurai class, even if she could find patrons in one of their families, she ran the risk of a future of destitution anyway. If she happened to fall for a guy who was still affiliated with the shogunate when the current political climate turned to depose the Tokugawa regime, he would lose everything and they'd both be relocated to a desolate detention camp out of pure spite by the leaders of the winning side.

That could be any day, in fact, unless her freaky time warp did something to screw up history. If it didn't and events stayed the same, then this year was somewhere between 1863 and 1865, since Shinsengumi Vice-Commander Yamanami hadn't been killed yet.

Wrapped up in her thoughts, Emmi never noticed that Kaemon had stopped a few paces ahead. She ran into him yet again—her nose collided with his broad shoulder. Emmi rubbed her aching face.

"Why do you do that?" she asked.

"I did nothing. You are the one never paying attention to where you walk."

"Asshole," Emmi said under her breath.

He grabbed her shoulders and pulled her closer. "You spoke the barbarian words. Admit it. You spoke like the 'Merican sailors do."

Emmi swallowed and wracked her brain, grasping for Great-grandpa Maeda's deathbed reminiscences.

"Uhh…" *Come on, think!* "Um, to be honest some of my family traded with the Americans for guns — to stand with the shogun. Only because you can't defeat the enemy unless you can match his might."

Kae stared down at her. With his left hand, he cupped her chin none too gently.

"So you say."

He increased the pressure of his grip on her chin and shoulder as he riveted his gaze upon her even harder.

"Tell me again."

"What? That some of my family traded with the Americans for weapons to fight when the shogun told them to?" A sick knot formed in her stomach. "You aren't going to have my family charged with anything, are you? Oh, please don't. Please."

Emmi placed her hands on Kae's wrist. "You have to believe me. I don't know about the rest of the clan, but I know that Maeda Takehito would sooner give up everything he owns and leave Japan forever than stand with anyone who would try to unseat the shogun or dare to try to control the emperor."

Kae released his hold on her then stepped back. "You realize that I have the means to have this looked into."

"I know that, but I don't know if Grandfather Takehito will be willing to admit publicly that he's breaking the law by trading illegally — even if it is in the best interest of his retainers, should they be called to war by the shogun."

Kae's expression grew harsh, and he stepped closer. Emmi shrank back. "I know enough about Maeda Takehito to know that he isn't old enough to have legions of grandchildren."

"No, but he has a son named Sadanori who will have a son in 1897 also named Takehito and that Takehito is—was—my great-grandfather, and when he was dying, he told me about this point in time."

Emmi held her breath, knowing that to voice this insane truth might very well make things far worse than they were. When she heard the sound of Kae's katana sliding from its sheath, she closed her eyes and awaited her fate.

Chapter Thirteen

At the sound of other blades being drawn, Emmi opened her eyes to see four men surrounding them, circling like a pack of wolves eyeing their prey.

And Emmi was very, very glad that both her father and Jake were fourth dan black belts. She just wished that she'd listened to them and stuck with it long enough to get past the lowly white belt. Of course, from the looks of this bunch, she and Kae were toast. These guys were mean and probably very skilled, judging from the way they held their swords as they closed in one by one.

Kae broke the mounting tension. "The soba stall isn't near here. Clearly, you scum are lost."

"We have no taste for noodles, boy, only tainted Imperial blood."

"They want me. Run," Kae said over his shoulder.

Suddenly all four men rushed at Kae and Emmi, and the world turned into a Kurosawa movie in fast forward. Battle cries and the clang of steel against steel filled the air. Emmi ducked out of the way of one assassin who jumped over her to get to Kae.

Emmi picked herself up and sprinted back toward the castle, screaming for help, only to be seized around the neck by a burly arm that reached out from the cover of bushes.

Coughing and choking, Emmi was dragged backward by the smelly assailant. Then he spun her to face the way she'd come.

Splattered in blood and breathing hard, Kaemon stood amid the corpses of the dead assassins.

The unknown man's arm fell to her shoulders, and Emmi gasped for breath.

Kae rushed forward. An instant later, a wakizashi was against her throat.

"Drop it," the man ordered.

Kae let his sword fall and took a few steps closer.

"And the other," the man said.

Kae dropped his own short sword.

Emmi didn't see the tanto tucked into Kae's belt, but she was sure he had the dagger concealed somewhere.

"Let the girl go," he said, advancing slowly, his hands held out at his sides.

The man laughed. "I'll do that just long enough to kill you."

Emmi waited until the man lowered the sword from her throat. He pushed her aside, but she kept her balance and kicked his knee with all the force she could muster.

Kae was on the man the instant he fell and plunged his tanto into the man's heart.

Emmi watched with grim fascination as he wiped the blood from his blade onto the dead man's clothes — that was, until a bobbing light in the distance caught her eye.

"There are more…" Emmi said.

He turned to look over his shoulder. "It's all right. They're Tokugawa guards," he assured her. He picked up his katana, shook off the blood, then sheathed the weapon. "Come with me."

Emmi followed. A chill skimmed down her spine as she stepped around the blood-soaked patches of ground surrounding the bodies of the first assassins. Nakagawa Kaemon, who couldn't be that much older than she, was taking this all in stride, as though he'd done it before.

A weird silence engulfed Emmi and she looked around, realizing that she could smell the scent of the dead men's blood. Her stomach lurched and she ran for the cover of bushes, making it to their edge just before she heaved.

She was on her knees after the spasms passed, and jumped when Kaemon knelt beside her. He gently rubbed her back, relaxing her.

"Let's get you back inside."

He helped her up, placed his hand around her shoulder, then tilted her chin up. His fingers brushed lightly across her neck. "The bastard cut you."

"No worse than you did when you thought I drugged you," Emmi said, pulling away.

Kae stepped into her path. "I'm sorry."

"So you said."

Emmi brushed past him and started back toward the Shinjukus' quarters.

Kae wanted to be angry with her but couldn't. In fact, he was more impressed than anything. She'd handled herself well tonight, better than most women would have. The way she'd brought the last man to his knees had been extraordinary. While he knew many women who could wield the spear-like *naginata*, he'd never known one who could use any type of kenpoist moves.

Still, he doubted that the Maeda taught their women to fight like men.

The Shinjukus were waiting outside for their arrival. Shinjuku-san's wife took Emmi inside immediately, while Kae conferred with her husband.

The older man dropped to his knees and bowed low. "Forgive me, Nakagawa-sama. The guards will be censured for not catching them the moment they breached the walls. If any of them is found to have been an accomplice, he'll be dealt with severely. I will inform the Shoshidai of my failure myself. I will commit seppuku if so ordered."

"Matsudaira-sama will not order that. I will speak to him. The men were after me specifically. They must have followed me, and probably were following me a long time to have found a way to sneak in between patrols."

Shinjuku-san looked up. "But who would be after you?"

"Anyone wanting to distract my father long enough to harm the emperor."

Shinjuku gasped and stood, stepping in close enough to whisper, "You don't think someone would try to harm him, do you?"

"I think the rebels will do anything to overthrow the shogun and attempt to assume control. Anything." He paused and glanced down at his bloodied clothing. "Could I trouble you for a bath and something to wear? I can't go home looking like this."

Shinjuku-san bowed. "Of course."

* * * *

"I think he left, child," Mrs. Shinjuku told Emmi. "My husband went to report to the Shoshidai, and I have no idea where Nakagawa-san is. I didn't see him in the kitchens where he usually sits."

Emmi sighed and sipped her tea. She swirled the last of it in the small, handleless cup then looked up.

"I wonder what I should do, then. About a place to stay. I have no money and nowhere to go…"

Emmi remembered her pendant. Her father had given it to her when she was tiny. She'd worn it every day since, and it was like a part of her. The thought of selling it made her ill all over again, but what choice did she have? *Forgive me, Daddy.*

Emmi removed the pendant and showed it to Shinjuku-san.

"Do you know of any place I might sell this? It's been in my family a very long time, but it's all I have of value."

The older woman took the necklace and studied it. "It is beautiful, possibly the most beautiful thing I've ever seen."

Emmi tried to smile through the pain flooding her soul. "That's our family crest on the front, and the dragonfly on top of it is just like the one Toshiie had on his golden battle helmet. On the back, you can see the names of the eldest sons and the eldest daughters that they gave the pendant to. I'm the last one. The last one…"

Shinjuku-san handed the pendant back to her. "You cannot sell this. You will stay here tonight. Tomorrow,

I may be able to have you kept on as part of the staff. If not, I'll help you find work."

"I hate to impose on you."

The older woman shook her head then brushed the stray strands of hair back from Emmi's face as a concerned aunt might. "It's no hardship."

Emmi placed the pendant back in Shinjuku-san's hand and closed her own over it. "I want you to hold on to this until I can repay your kindness."

"That isn't necess—"

"It is to me."

Shinjuku-san nodded. "I will lock this away. Why don't you go to the bathhouse and relax in the tub for a while? I'll send one of the twins with something clean for you to wear."

Although she knew it wasn't quite proper for this era, Emmi got up and hugged the older woman. "Thank you."

As she walked the short distance from the kitchen to the bathhouse, Emmi let down her hair and began untying the knots Kaemon had used to fasten the hakama. Emmi stepped inside, set the door latch and allowed the hakama to fall to the floor. Kicking the garment aside, she undid the knot in the obi fastening the yukata, and froze when someone—a man—cleared his throat from behind her.

Emmi spun around, clutching the yukata closed.

"Who's there?" she demanded, scanning the dimly lit room until she saw the wooden screen in the right corner.

Kaemon stepped out wearing only a fundoshi, the Japanese equivalent of underwear that resembled a Native American breechclout. It was a red fundoshi, no less.

"What are you doing here? Shinjuku-san said you'd left."

"Obviously, she was mistaken."

Emmi pointed to the door. "Go. Now."

"I was here first."

"Well, I'm here now."

A grin played upon his lips. "What will you do if I choose not to leave?"

"I'll pull off your fundoshi."

He laughed and came to stand before her. "Do it."

Damn. He would be the type to call her bluff.

A knock sounded on the door, followed by the voice of one of the twins. "Emiko-dono. We have your things, but the door is locked."

Emmi motioned for Kaemon to get behind the screen. He shook his head no. Emmi grumbled, then went to the door and opened it just far enough to grab the fresh sleeping yukata.

"We can help you wash your hair."

"N-no. I'm fine, but thank you." Emmi closed the door and placed the clothing on the stool.

She turned and promptly bumped into Kae, who'd snuck up behind her.

"I can help you wash your hair," he said, toying with the loose strands. "Or your back," he added, allowing his hand to slip down and caress her spine. He leaned in to whisper in her ear. "Or I can wash your front..." His voice trailed off as he ran the tip of his tongue along the side of her neck.

A flash of heat shot through her and made her squirm, but Emmi had the presence of mind to place her hands on his chest and push him back.

"Oh no you don't."

"What is that?" he asked, prying her yukata farther apart with his fingers.

Emmi groaned and pulled the edges of the yukata together again. "It's my underwear. You have your fundoshi and I have my...bra and panties."

"Brrra... Pan-tees," he said.

Her face flushed. Emmi nodded. He made it sound so...obscene, yet exciting.

"That's what we call 'em."

Kae stepped close again and gently tugged the edges of the yukata again. Try as Emmi might, she found she could not control her traitorous fingers, which simply let him.

I told you guys this was a bad idea, Emmi silently reminded her fingers as Kaemon slid his large palms across her lace-encased breasts. She bit back the moan that tried to escape when he teased her further by running his index finger all along the top edge of the bra cups.

"You shouldn't do that."

"You don't like it?"

"I do. I like it too much."

He chuckled and bent down, allowing his tongue to retrace the trail his finger had made moments before. She groaned.

"You have to stop. Please."

He pulled back and looked at her. His dark eyes glowed with desire as his hands settled upon her hips. Emmi shivered when his fingers drifted down to tease her skin just beneath the edges of the panties.

"You don't want me to stop, do you?"

"No, and that's why I need you to stop."

His grip on her tightened, and he brushed against her. The thin layers of fabric separating them did even less to conceal the hardness of his erection than the multiple layers of clothing had earlier.

"Do not take me for a fool, woman. You are no virgin. Not with the way you kissed me today, not with the way you let me touch you now."

Emmi's mouth grew dry as morality and primal need began to war within her. She slid her hands to Kaemon's strong shoulders in a vain attempt to keep him at bay.

"I'm not playing you for a fool. I've touched guys before, let them touch me, but I am still a virgin. Things are different where I'm from, but... I wanted it to be right...to be special..."

Kaemon stared down at her. Even in the dim light from the floor lantern, he could see undeniable truth shining bright in the depths of her warm brown eyes. She hadn't been bedded. She was eager for more yet afraid of the consequences.

Nevertheless, he was a man, a prince of the blood. He could have any woman in the land in any way he wished. Even if she was a daughter of the Maeda, no daimyo had the power to deny him.

He wanted this woman with every fiber of his being.

And he would have her.

He pulled her fiercely against him. He slid his fingers up her back, her neck, tangled them in her hair and tugged her head back to kiss and nip the flesh of her throat. She whimpered as he worked his way down, kissing and licking the delicate skin just above her strange undergarments.

He lifted his head, turned his attention to her mouth. She parted her lips without any coaxing. Her tongue sought his first, and she wound her arms tightly around his neck, kissing him back so fervently that his body ached and strained against the confinement of the fundoshi.

He kissed her throat again. She sighed his name. The words drifted in a soft, mewling sound. He kissed his way back up her neck and pulled her into a crushing embrace. She grew bold, flicked her tongue across his shoulder.

She whispered close to his ear, "I'm afraid. Promise you won't hurt me."

Kaemon's inborn sense of duty and obligation reined in his lust. He couldn't do it. He couldn't bring himself to take what should be his. For the life of him, he didn't know why.

Chapter Fourteen

Emmi gaped in surprise when Kae pulled away and began throwing on his clothes. "What's wrong? What did I do?"

"I don't want a woman who thinks I take my pleasure from her pain."

"I didn't mean—"

It was too late. He left the bathhouse in a rush, banging the door behind him.

Her body was still warm and tingly from his kiss. Emmi breathed a sigh, then locked the door and undressed. She slipped into the large wooden tub, not caring that the fire beneath the bathhouse had died down, allowing the water to cool. It was just the kind of wake-up call she needed, and she'd be damned if she made the same mistake again.

* * * *

Kae didn't take his usual route into the Imperial Palace. He went via the direct route and straight to the main entrance gate. He put up with the Choshu guards' critical inspection of his identity papers, though it galled him to do so. If it were the last thing he did, he would see to it that the dogs of that domain were removed from Kyoto once and for all.

Far too often they tried to allow their leaders to sneak in and beg an audience with the emperor or someone close to him. They succeeded enough to bend the ear of Nakayama Tadayasu, the maternal grandfather to the emperor's twelve-year-old heir, Mutsuhito.

Unfortunately, there was no empirical proof, only speculation on the part of his father. But Kae completely trusted his father's judgment in the matter. As long as Mutsuhito was a child, he would need a guardian — a regent to advise and counsel him — should he happen to ascend the throne. And to whom would that illustrious honor go? Nakayama-sama, of course. Kae suspected Nakayama might be quite generous with those who'd made a positive impression upon him — such as those rebel swine.

Kae welcomed the anger that heated his blood as he walked along the covered walkway at the rear of the palace. At least it was beginning to extinguish the painful desire that had plagued him earlier.

Catching the rustle of silk from the shadows, Kae slowed his gait and placed his hand on the hilt of his katana. He sensed the follower closing in and spun, unsheathing his weapon as he did so. Instinctively he began his swing high, aiming for a beheading, and just barely stopped short of slicing off the top of Crown Prince Mutsuhito's head.

Kaemon dropped his arm to his side then fell to his knees, bowing forward. "Forgive me!" He looked up when he felt the prince's slender hand touch his shoulder.

"I could demand that you commit seppuku, cousin."

"And I will, my Lord." He reached for the tanto tucked into his belt. The prince stopped him.

"If you slice your belly, then who will be my friend and talk with me when I can't sleep?"

Kaemon relaxed and settled back on his heels, tucking away the tanto and replacing his katana in the saya.

He made a show of thinking. "Hmmm, perhaps your grandfather, Nakayama-sama? Or perhaps his friend Katsura-san?"

The prince made a most unpleasant face, and Kae couldn't hold in his smile. Mutsuhito laughed and sat facing his cousin.

"You are my only true friend, Kaemon. Everyone else is always telling me how I must behave, and how I may talk, and what to eat and what to wear, and they make me practice my writing over and over and over until my fingers hurt." He reached out to touch Kaemon's hand. "You're the only one who treats me as a friend. You're the only one who lets me run and laugh."

"You're a good friend to me as well."

"Will we always be friends, Kaemon?"

"Always," Kae said sincerely. He grinned. "I heard a joke in Shimabara the other day..."

* * * *

The mirror could still be in that secret passage.

That was the thought that haunted Emmi's mind the entire next day. She hoped that one of the duties she eagerly accepted from Shinjuku-san would take her back to that hall where the entrance to that secret passage lay, but none did. As the day wore on, she grew more agitated about it.

She needed that mirror. But how to get it? She couldn't go sneaking around the squeaky-floored private residence halls without a reason, and she doubted that her princely 'friend' was going to make an appearance any time today.

What could she do?

She was helping sort the guards' laundry when she remembered the maid who she was on sorting duty with had been one of the ones who kept stealing glances at Kaemon.

"Akiko, does Nakagawa-sama come to visit every day?"

The girl sighed wistfully. "No, sometimes we don't see him for weeks."

Lovely. She so did not have weeks. Her attention was drawn again when Akiko sighed a very long sigh.

Akiko picked up a familiar brown haori. "This is his," she said, tracing the outline of the crest on the back of the garment.

Realizing that Akiko was staring at her, Emmi dismissed her remark with a wave of her hand, picked up another haori and began to examine the inside of the sleeves as she'd seen Akiko do. There was a folded piece of paper in the sleeve of the next garment.

"What do we do with this?"

Akiko shook her head. "Those men. I don't know how they get around Kyoto with the way they forget their papers." She gestured to a small box on a shelf to the left. "Put it there with anything else you find. Shinjuku-san will go through them later and return them to their owners." She giggled softly. "It's too bad that Nakagawa-sama didn't leave anything in his jacket."

Akiko held Kaemon's haori up to her cheek one more time then tossed it onto the pile of things to be washed.

Emmi wasn't sure if she should be bothered or amused.

* * * *

Later that evening, Emmi walked alone in the garden adjacent to the Shinjukus' quarters. Emmi wondered if she might be able to go in search of the mirror when who should appear behind her but the devil himself.

His velvety voice reached out and caressed her from behind. "I could have been another assassin. You shouldn't be out here alone."

Emmi stopped walking and turned. Why did he have to look so damn good in the moonlight? Or any light...

"I heard that the patrols have been increased."

"Then you don't need a chaperone?" he asked with that oddly appealing lost little boy look in his eyes.

"I do if he can chaperone me back to my mirror."

"I can't."

Emmi folded her arms across her middle and gave him a hard look. "Why not? I need that mirror to get home. You know I do."

"How can that get you home? You are a demon from the other world, aren't you?"

Emmi lifted her hands in frustration and walked away. "Will you stop with the oni business already? I am the same as you, except I'm from the future!"

Emmi gave Kae a dirty look when he grabbed her shoulder and spun her around to face him.

"Future?"

"I told you that yesterday, remember?"

Kaemon placed his free hand on her shoulder as well. "When in the future?"

"Two thousand and sixteen," Emmi said softly. "Around a hundred and fifty years in the future."

"One hundred fifty," he muttered. "Will everyone in Japan speak the gaijin tongue then?"

"A lot will be able to as a second language. I'm not from Japan. My parents are—were—third generation Japanese Americans. My ancestors left Kaga after—" Emmi stopped short and lowered her head. *Way to go, Em-chan.*

Kaemon tilted her head up with a tender prod of his fingers. "They left Kaga after what?"

"After Takehito had a falling out with his brother," Emmi said, omitting the fact that the brothers' disagreement was a result of the fourteenth Lord Maeda publicly aligning himself with the rebels' side after the battle of Toba-Fushimi in 1868. Her ancestors' defection was yet another death knell for the Tokugawa.

Kaemon considered what Emmi said for a long time, but thankfully he didn't question her for more details. He dropped his hands to his sides and began walking. Emmi went with him.

"So, will you go get my mirror from that passageway?"

"It isn't there."

Emmi stopped and grabbed his sleeve. "What do you mean it isn't there? Where is it?"

"I gave it back to Aneko. It is rightfully hers, and she wanted it."

"Who the hell is Aneko?"

"She's a *tayuu* in Shimabara."

"You'd better go get it."

"I will not."

"Then I will," Emmi said, whipping around and hurrying back toward the castle.

Emmi yelped when Kae grabbed her by the obi and spun her around. "You will not go to Shimabara."

Watch me, Emmi fumed silently before pulling away and going back inside.

* * * *

Emmi tossed and turned for what seemed like hours on the futon in the small room she shared with the twins. She had to get that mirror. "But how?" Emmi whispered to the darkness a moment before realizing that the shorter of the twins, Chidori, was looking at her. Emmi motioned for her to go back to sleep then turned on her side facing away. Within seconds, her conscience started fighting with her desire to get home.

She can help. She has to know a way out!

I don't want to get her in trouble! Sure, the Shinjukus are nice, but if this girl breaks some major house rule because of me, she'll be the one to suffer!

The mirror is your ticket home.

Home.

With a lump in her throat, Emmi turned back over. Chidori was still watching her. Biting the inside of her cheek to distract herself from her nagging conscience, Emmi motioned for the girl to come closer.

"I have a favor to ask," Emmi whispered. "I need to get something of mine that was lost. It's in Shimabara, but I don't know how to get out of Nijo without anyone seeing me. Do you know a way?"

The girl nodded.

Emmi took hold of her hand. "I don't want you to get in trouble. You don't have to show me if Shinjuku-san will punish you."

"I can show you. I want to help my new friend."

Some friend you are, Em-chan, possibly getting her in trouble with the people who saved her from being a hooker for life.

Emmi did her best to silence her nagging conscience. She didn't belong here. She needed to get home before it was too late. Still, she couldn't do anything that might hurt this trusting little girl. Emmi sighed and turned on her back.

"Never mind. I can't ask you to do this."

Chidori tugged her yukata sleeve. "I will help. Hurry. I will not be punished."

Emmi caved. She put on the hakama she'd worn the other day and tied her hair up in a ponytail, hoping to be able to pass as someone's servant again. She dashed into the laundry sorting room, took two identity papers from the lost and found box, and tucked them into her sleeve.

Her mind was nearly numb with fear, but she followed Chidori through the maze of darkened corridors and through the moonlit gardens until they came to a small gate overgrown with weeds. Chidori opened it and gave Emmi a gentle shove out.

Though Emmi was sure her heart was pounding loud enough to be heard all the way to Osaka, Emmi took a deep breath and headed in the direction Chidori had indicated while an old school friend's words echoed through her mind.

'It's easy to get into a premiere, girlfriend. Anyone can get past the velvet rope. It's all in the attitude. All you gotta do is walk into the place like you belong there…'

Emmi took a deep breath and kept walking as though she knew exactly where she was going and what she was going to do once she got there. Emmi tried not to notice a guy using the space between two buildings as a bathroom and forced herself to look away from the kids robbing a drunk. Emmi stepped aside quickly and averted her eyes when a squad of Shinsengumi ran past chasing three bloodied men.

She walked like she belonged here, and when, off in the distance, the huge gates to Shimabara appeared, Emmi kept walking like a servant in search of an errant master. She even ignored the gruff command that came from somewhere to her left.

"You there! Stop!"

"Boy! Show us your papers!"

Emmi froze when she heard men drawing their swords.

Holding her hands out to her sides to show she was unarmed, she turned to face them. They wore matching headbands and breastplates with a kanji that Emmi couldn't make out in the center. This must be one of the other patrol groups who acted as police in Kyoto.

"Papers. Now," the meanest-looking one demanded.

Emmi dug in her yukata sleeve and produced one of the two she'd taken. She handed it over, hoping her look was one of an honest citizen being unjustly detained.

The man looked at the paper and his expression grew even meaner. He threw it at her. "Do not toy with me, boy! Show me your papers or die!"

Oh great. What had she grabbed? Emmi pulled the other papers from her sleeve and handed them over as calmly as she could. Unfortunately, this didn't seem any better.

"You do not look like a forty-five-year-old retainer from Edo in Kyoto for a meeting with the new Shoshidai."

"It's my master's paper. He took mine by mistake. I was trying to find him and give it to him."

"So you have no papers?"

"The Shinsengumi know who I am," she blurted. "You can ask Vice-Commander Yamanami-sama or Captain Harada. He knows me."

Emmi breathed a small sigh of relief when the men conferred, though she was not pleased when the leader had two of the others grab her by the arm and drag her off toward Mibu.

The guards at the Shinsengumi compound gate said that Vice-Commander Yamanami was away, but Vice-Commander Hijikata was in and would handle the matter.

Hijikata was in his quarters with Saitou Hajime, the captain who'd beaten up those rude prisoners, and another man that Emmi didn't know. Hijikata and Emmi exchanged looks of mutual loathing as the other police types explained the situation and handed over the papers she'd filched.

"I am acquainted with this lowly person," Hijikata told the men. "Leave the young fool and go on about your business. I will see to it that this matter is taken care of."

Hijikata fell silent and remained that way until the other cops were gone. He cleared his throat then handed one of the papers to Saitou.

"I believe this haiku refers to you, Hajime."

Emmi's heart skipped a beat when the intimidating captain growled under his breath and tossed the paper to the floor. She couldn't help but look at it.

A smell in the air
people walking past me gasp
Ah, my fundoshi.

Great. Just great. She'd gotten two of the fiercest swordsmen in Japan to hate her without even trying.

"As amusing as that bit of poetry may be, Maeda-dono, your possession of this identity paper, which is clearly not yours, is a serious matter. Explain. Now."

Screw formality, Emmi thought as she went from the kneeling seiza position to one a bit more comfortable with her aching legs to the side. "I borrowed it. I just borrowed it from the lost items box in the laundry room at Nijo Castle. I was going to put it back when I returned there, I swear."

"Why were you in the laundry room at Nijo?"

"Kae—Fujiwara-san left me there after I was questioned." Emmi paused. "I was questioned and released from any official investigation, I might add." She valiantly managed to hold on to her "velvet rope attitude," cleared her throat, and continued to meet Hijikata's cold gaze with one of her own. "All I wanted to do was get to Shimabara. I lost something there and I need it back."

"What? Your virginity?" Hijikata asked with a leering grin.

Saitou and the third man laughed.

Emmi scowled. "I lost my uncle. We were last together there, and I'm afraid something may have happened to him."

"His name is?"

Shit. Think, Emmi, think. "Yamauchi," Emmi said managing to translate Jake's last name into its components hill and house. "Yamauchi Mamoru," Emmi added, pulling the Mamoru out of some recess of her brain that equated the word "protector" with Jake.

Hijikata stared at her with such ferocity that Emmi wanted to confess to bad things that she'd never even considered doing, but she managed to keep chanting the velvet rope theory in her mind. *Act like you belong. Act like you belong. Act like you belong...*

"May I leave now?" she asked, throwing a bit of attitude into it.

"I should put you back in a cell without the benefit of the comforts Yamanami arranged for you the last time."

Hijikata glared again, as did his feral-looking companions, but her fear of these men, who'd taken many lives in the course of their duties, was being replaced by an inborn sense of nobility and the knowledge that her own background was far loftier than theirs were.

As Kaemon's father had so succinctly put it the other day, these men were just a bunch of farmers with swords, while the blood of highly ranked samurai ran through her veins. In fact, it was some of the same blood shared by the current shogun himself.

Emmi swept her gaze over the men and stood. "Fine. Put me in a cell. I'm sure that when Kaemon finds out where I am — and he will — he'll just ask his father to get me a pardon, signed by his uncle, the emperor."

Oh shit. The semi-concealed surprise in Hijikata's smug eyes told Emmi she'd screwed up and blabbed Kaemon's secret. Of course, it was too late to back down now. She took a deep breath and folded her arms in front of her. "Well?"

Hijikata smirked then pulled a fan from his obi and began to fan himself lazily. "I suppose detaining you would be more trouble than you're worth, Maeda-dono."

Emmi let the dig slide, though it pissed her off to do so. She'd taken one step toward the door when Hijikata stopped her. Emmi turned back to see him writing something with a thin brush and ink. He fanned it dry then folded it in thirds and handed it to her.

"This should get you where you need to go."

"Thank you," Emmi said sharply, taking the paper and leaving quickly.

Emmi waited until she was outside the gates of the compound before opening the paper. Her kanji skills weren't all they could be, especially when it came to this old style of writing, but she made out enough to get the gist, that this "obnoxious upstart from the Kaga Han" was awaiting the arrival in Kyoto of the relative they'd been separated from and who retained their official travel papers.

Gee, thanks, Emmi grumbled to herself as she headed back toward Shimabara, instead of being practical and returning to Nijo. She paused when she realized Hijikata hadn't made mention of being dressed like a guy. He'd even indicated she was male in the paper he'd just given her. A bad feeling hit her, but she pushed it away. Kae had dressed her like this before. That was the reason Hijikata was going along. She wasn't turning back now. She couldn't.

She had to find where this Aneko was and get the mirror back.

Chapter Fifteen

Emmi didn't know how late it was, but she was glad that the aggravation of being in Hijikata's presence had gotten her adrenaline going enough to make her wide awake. She walked quickly, forcing herself to ignore the potentially distracting sights and sounds surrounding her. At last the gates to Shimabara appeared in the distance once again.

Shimabara was brighter, noisier and more crowded than the streets leading there had been, and Emmi felt slightly relieved. Here she would be able to blend in with the milling crowd. Emmi doubted that anyone in these parts would be checking IDs, unless there was trouble, and she planned to stay as far from trouble as possible.

Weaving her way past two palanquins, Emmi looked at each of the buildings she passed. Restaurant, restaurant, teahouse, brothel — by the looks of the women seated near the windows flirting with male passersby...

Emmi ignored the painted women's calls of "Oh, boy, visit with us!" and kept on walking. Receiving quite a few looks from some creepy men, Emmi wished she'd had the sense to ask Hijikata for the loan of a short sword or at least a dagger. Of course, he probably would have blown off that idea.

Oh well, best to keep with the 'velvet rope' attitude and keep looking like she knew where she was going and what she was looking for.

Chidori had mentioned that Aneko was a premiere courtesan at the Inamoto-ro, one of the top brothels in the Licensed Quarters. Emmi slowed her pace just a bit and turned to look back the way she'd come. Inamoto-ro was supposed to be not far from the main gates.

There were signs posted, but they weren't the clearest. Emmi made a note to practice her kanji reading when she got back home — just in case she ever needed it again. At the first sign with a 'moto' in the name, Emmi entered.

Somehow the scruffy, glaring bouncer, or whatever he was, did not give the impression of the 'first-class' house Chidori had described. Emmi backed away from the half-curtained doorway as a couple of men exited and more entered.

She walked down the street but didn't see anything with 'moto' in the name, so she then returned to the first place. To enter, she snuck in alongside some rather fat old guys wearing garish green haoris.

Emmi followed them through the spacious main room. She tried not to sneeze or choke on the thick, heavy incense that filled the air. Why couldn't they use that nice, unobtrusive sandalwood blend that they had at Nijo? This stuff was bad...

Emmi was distracted by the sight of a large screen in a smaller room to the left. Not thinking, she stepped inside to gawk at it. It was unusual to say the least, and she wondered what Uncle Jake would make of it.

It depicted men. Lots of men doing lots of...things with each other. Emmi stepped closer and tilted her head to the left. Was that what she thought it was? Was the pretty guy in nothing but a gold haori really doing what it looked like he was doing to that other guy? Was it even possible to be in such a position and enjoy it the way they seemed to be doing? And those three in the right corner. Could two guys even do that to another guy at once? Damn, that looked painful.

"Interesting piece, isn't it?"

Emmi swallowed hard. "Yes. Interesting." She tensed when she felt the person step up very close behind her.

He chuckled. "Nervous? Surely, this isn't your first time?"

Emmi stayed facing the screen, though it did nothing but add to the awkwardness of this whole situation. "I'm actually looking for someone. I thought he might be here."

"Oh, so you've been referred by a satisfied client."

"Something like that."

The screen was really getting to her, so Emmi decided to take her chances by turning. Not the brightest idea, she realized when the finely dressed man behind her got this strange look of...awe upon seeing her.

Emmi hoped her male cover wasn't totally blown. He beamed a smile, which might have been quite nice if it hadn't freaked her out so much. She felt like that cartoon chicken being slobbered over by that bug-eyed weasel thing.

"Oh, I know who sent you."

"You…do?"

"I do." He took hold of her elbow and urged her forward. "Please follow me."

Emmi tried backing away. His grip tightened, and surprisingly so, considering his rather geeky appearance and slight build.

"I think you're mistaken about me."

The man's slimy smile fell. "I am not."

"You are," Emmi said roughly, trying to wrench away again. "I'm looking for a woman named Aneko who works out of Inamoto-ro. I'm in the wrong place. I'm sorry."

From seemingly out of nowhere, two big guys came and flanked her as the thin guy moved aside. Each of the gorillas grabbed Emmi by an arm. She tried kicking them, but it was to no avail.

The thin guy stepped in front of her and brandished a small knife.

"Enough."

"Listen to me," Emmi said, hoping he could hear over the pounding of her heart. "I have papers verifying who I am. I'm looking for my uncle from Kaga."

"I thought it was a woman you wanted."

"No. I mean yes. I thought she could help me find him."

The thin guy jerked his head, and the gorillas dragged Emmi behind the painted screen and through a door hidden behind it.

"I know the Shinsengumi," Emmi blurted.

The thin guy laughed. "As do I and the one who is buying you for the evening."

"Buying me?"

The thin guy chuckled but said nothing.

Emmi struggled with the men who pulled her through the shoji and into a dimly lit room with another obscene picture screen in the corner and a big futon unrolled in the center of the room.

"No, no, no!" Emmi craned her neck to look at the thin guy. "Look at my papers!"

The thin guy replied with a disgusted look then motioned for the others to let her go.

Emmi took the advantage. She darted past the thin guy and out through the shoji. She pushed over the big floor screen and ran to the other door and into the narrow corridor, pushing her way past those in her path. She made it to the front door and ran, shoving through the crowd, cutting off pedestrians and palanquins alike. Emmi didn't slow or stop, though she could hear shouts of "Stop that boy!"

Emmi sprinted through the streets. It was not supposed to go this way. She was supposed to find that Aneko woman, get the mirror, then sneak back into Nijo. Why couldn't things just go the way they were supposed to go?

Emmi almost ran into a couple coming from a side street but managed to veer right at the last second. Unfortunately she ran into a palanquin bearer, knocking him off balance. The heavy conveyance shifted, and the man fell with a sickening crunch of broken bone. The palanquin hit the ground. A passenger inside shrieked, and the bearer in back cried out as his foot was crushed under the weight of it all.

"Ohmygod!" Emmi cried out, not knowing what to do. She picked herself off the ground and tried to help the trapped man in the rear. Two men who'd come running to help shoved her aside.

"Aneko-han!" two young girls shrieked, running from a building up ahead. They fell to their knees and helped the palanquin's occupant out. The woman had a large, bleeding cut across her cheek. Two of her three decorative hair sticks were broken and sections of oiled hair came loose from the elaborate coiffure.

Emmi reached out. "Let me help—"

Her words died when Nakagawa Kaemon pulled himself out of the palanquin after the little girls had helped the woman to her feet.

"What are you doing here?" Kae and Emmi asked in unison.

"Do not move!" Kaemon ordered before he hurried to help the woman who'd been injured.

The woman screamed when she realized her face was bleeding, and she lunged at Emmi. Kaemon grabbed her around the waist and lifted her off the ground.

"Come inside, Aneko. It doesn't seem that bad. You'll be fine."

Aneko?

Emmi took a step forward but stopped when Kae whipped around and shot her a look that froze her in her tracks.

Damn. So close and yet so far.

Chapter Sixteen

A wave of guilt washed over Emmi as she watched someone tend to the injured palanquin bearers, until a shout of "There he is!" caught her attention.

Emmi turned to see those gorillas from before rushing through the crowd. She looked toward the front of the brothel that Kaemon had entered then ran inside calling his name. Emmi called out every Japanese variation of "I'm sorry" she knew as she plowed through the busy rooms, bumping into and stepping on customers and prostitutes alike.

Many shouting, angry people were hot on her trail by the time Kae showed his face in a room at the rear of the building. Emmi ducked behind him and crouched down in a vain attempt to hide herself in the folds of his haori. She cringed when she heard the sound of weapons being drawn. She scrunched her eyes shut seconds before she was shoved backward to land flat on her ass.

Emmi opened her eyes to see Kaemon standing in the center of the small room. He held his sword with both hands, but low — pointing downward in front of him, in the position her father and Jake jokingly called the "stupid wannabe" stance.

It was strictly a movie-type maneuver, they said. A *real* swordsman wouldn't use it since a *real* swordsman wouldn't be stupid enough to invite an open attack from a dozen guys and still think he could come out on top.

Of course, Nakagawa Kaemon hadn't ever seen a movie to know any better...

Two older women shrieked for the men to stop, but no one paid attention. The first one rushed Kae and had his attack easily deflected. Two more rushed, then a third circled behind Kae, followed by another. Emmi mashed herself into the corner and shut her eyes again. She didn't want to hear the clashing of steel blades, didn't want to hear the sound of breaking wood or the ripping of rice paper-paneled walls and silk screens.

And Emmi absolutely did not want to hear the grunts or cries of men being injured and killed or feel the hot, sticky spray of blood hit her face.

Emmi looked, hoping it wasn't Kaemon's blood.

It wasn't, and Emmi found herself watching the single-minded artistry in this life or death situation. He sidestepped an attacker and spun to gash another's forearm. He switched his katana to his left hand and crouched to avoid a rush. He kicked the man's legs out from under him, then seized his short sword and pierced the man's heart.

He was clearly on the defensive, and yet he switched gears better than a choreographed stuntman and attacked those who got in too close.

A man fell in front of her, his sword hand bleeding profusely. Even as Kae reached for his tanto, Emmi instinctively kicked the man in the head. She lunged for the fallen dagger herself, but the man grabbed her. She slashed backward with his tanto and scrambled away. A wave of nausea washed over her when reality hit and she saw the gaping wound she'd caused, but the queasiness vanished in the rush of adrenaline that followed.

Out of nowhere came a small throwing knife that hit Kae in the upper thigh. He staggered and lost his footing in a slick puddle of blood. Not thinking, Emmi dove at the knife thrower, who sought the advantage over Kae. She jammed the tanto into his groin.

Silence fell for a moment, and Emmi looked around the jumbled, blood-spattered room. Kae was a few feet away, down on one knee. He was supporting himself partially by leaning on the hilt of his katana, the blade of which was stuck into the tatami mat covering the floor. The throwing knife still protruded from his thigh, and Emmi scrambled to him.

"Don't touch me," he snapped and yanked the knife free.

A woman with a bandage covering her cheek rushed into the room. She knocked Emmi out of the way and began tending to Kae, who seemed quite content that she do so.

A formidable-looking man came in and began barking orders, and the onlookers who had come in to see the outcome of the battle scattered. Soon a bunch of men wearing an all too familiar uniform appeared, and Emmi found herself being escorted once more to the Shinsengumi headquarters.

* * * *

Emmi knelt with her head bowed as Hijikata Toshizou read — with more than a little glee it seemed — the list of crimes she'd committed in the short time since she'd last been there.

"Willful destruction of a valuable painted screen at the male teahouse Fujimoto-ro, causing a serious accident resulting in injuries to both the palanquin bearers and their passengers, willful destruction of multiple pieces of property and various physical assaults on patrons of the Inamoto-ro and finally, starting a violent confrontation that resulted in grievous physical injury to His Most Imperial Highness Nakagawa no miya Kaemon."

Emmi glanced up. Hijikata paused before delivering the fatal blow. "You do realize that last item alone is punishable by an immediate death sentence? Why Takeda-san failed to carry that sentence out on the spot is beyond me." He paused again and turned his dark, deadly gaze to the captain of his fifth squad. "Enlighten me, Kanryuusai," he said coldly.

Takeda bowed until his forehead touched the floor. "Hijikata-san, I would never fail in my duty, but Nakagawa-sama requested that I bring the girl here. He also requested that I ask you to wait for his arrival before meting out any punishment."

Hijikata smirked then looked at Emmi again. "So it appears Buddha smiles down upon your miserable hide once more."

Lucky, lucky me, Emmi thought miserably as two surly guards took her away. Apparently part of 'Buddha's smiling upon her' included all of the regular cells being filled, so they had to improvise by placing her in solitary confinement.

Chapter Seventeen

Emmi sat in the humid, dark storage room off the kitchens and wondered how much time had passed since Hijikata had her placed in here to await Kae's arrival. She glanced toward the tiny barred window at the far end of the shed but couldn't really see the sky. It seemed that it was just beginning to lighten, but a few large paper lanterns had been strung around the compound, so she wasn't quite sure about this light or its source.

She tried to erase the image of Kae's furious expression from her mind. Why did he blame her? It wasn't as if she'd planned to have all that stuff happen. Okay, so maybe she shouldn't have gone busting through the Inamoto-ro, but she'd been scared. Those gorilla guys were after her, and she didn't even want to think about what their slimy boss had planned for her back at his place. It had been obvious that he'd had her pegged for some new male prostitute or other, but once they found out she was a woman there was no telling what they would have done.

What did the arrogant prince expect her to have done? Let them take her or try to go politely in the brothel and asked sweetly for Kaemon to come to the door and reason with the gorillas?

As if that would have worked.

Emmi sighed and leaned back against a pile of rice sacks. She closed her eyes while sending silent farewells back to Jake, her mother, her brother and her grandparents as she imagined her tombstone—

Here Lies Emmi Maeda, Executed A Century Before She Was Born

* * * *

Though Kaemon pretended to rest in the palanquin that took him from the Imperial Palace to Mibu, he covertly peered across the carriage to his companion and personal retainer, Matsuyama, who had been conspicuously absent during the incident at Inamoto-ro.

Supposedly Matsuyama had been so occupied with one of the new whores he hadn't realized Kae had returned unexpectedly with Aneko and was involved in the commotion. That account did not agree with the one from off-duty Shinsengumi captain Takeda Kanryuusai.

The palanquin stopped.

"My Lord," Matsuyama said. "We've arrived."

Kae sat up and made a show of rubbing the sleep from his eyes before following his retainer out of the carriage. They entered the Shinsengumi compound, where the chief officers and a few of the captains waited.

Following an imperceptible nod of Kaemon's head, Hijikata Toshizou instructed two of his men to escort Matsuyama away.

"M-my Lord—"

Minutes later, the girl was led in and Chief Kondo read the list of charges. Kaemon stared at her with the same deadly expression that he'd used when condemning his friend to death only moments before.

Kae didn't know what to make of her. More importantly, he was at a loss to explain this warring within himself about her punishment. It was entirely likely that she had been in league with Matsuyama all along. In fact, it was the only sensible conclusion, and yet something about her—that look in her eyes— swayed him as it had before. As damning as the evidence before him was, he felt in his heart that she was innocent. He broke off from his musing when Isami Kondo addressed him.

"Nakagawa no miya-sama, by virtue of your station, it is your right to hand down sentence upon the accused."

Kae looked at her. She met his gaze boldly, so unlike he would expect of any woman, let alone one so close to a sentence of death.

"It is clear to me that Matsuyama had an accomplice in recent attempts upon my life."

He paused and studied her again. She was terrified and shaking, yet she held firmly to her control as only a true Maeda could. He continued.

"The punishments that are my right to inflict are many—imprisonment, beating, execution—"

"M-may I stand?" Emmi interrupted in a shaky voice. "My ankles are numb."

Kaemon nodded at her, and captains Saitou and Nagakura drew their short swords before taking positions closer to the exit doors lest she try to escape. She stepped back against the wall and placed her hand atop a red-lacquer box that rested on a wooden chest.

Kaemon continued with his dark gaze centered upon his pretty oni, "As I said, the choices of punishment are many, and I am certain I could even demand crucifixion and not be denied—"

Chapter Eighteen

Emmi's knees seemed to give way with that pronouncement and the lacquer box, perched so close to the chest's edge, could not support her. She stumbled. The box fell, hitting her and spilling its contents upon the tatami at her feet.

She stared in morbid fascination at the colorful woodblock prints that littered the floor. They were what she could only describe as old-fashioned porn — men with men, with women, women together. It was like the big screen at that brothel, and the reality hit that she might be facing something similar before they killed her.

Killed her.

Raped her, then killed her.

Maybe even crucified her.

Her stomach heaved at the thought and emptied all over the prints at her feet.

Vice-Commander Hijikata swore and shoved her out of the way so he could scoop up the unsoiled prints.

Kae reached for the katana on the floor beside him, but he stilled the impulse and glared at Hijikata, who picked up his box and jammed the unmarred pictures back inside while ordering Emiko's removal.

"No," Kae said in a tone that froze the two captains who'd advanced.

"Toshi, why don't you call for someone to clean this mess?" Kondo asked.

Once he stepped through the door, the other vice-commander, Yamanami, approached Emmi with two cloths. He handed one to her, helped her to her feet, then placed the other on the floor. He looked to Kondo and offered a faint smile, clearly trying to ease the tension.

"I told you your *shunga* collection would turn up sooner or later, Kondo-san."

Kaemon smirked. The ladies' man, Hijikata, had clearly "appropriated" another man's *shunga* collection for his own use. Kae turned his attention back to Emmi, who'd eased herself into a corner and was leaning back against the wall. He continued to stare at her, and she finally averted her gaze. Her knees gave way once more. She slid to the floor and lowered her head.

Kaemon stood, and Kondo did as well.

"Gentlemen, perhaps we should continue this discussion elsewhere."

On his way out, Kae asked the captains guarding the doors to allow Emmi a bit of privacy to compose herself.

Blinking furiously to clear her eyes of the tears blurring her vision, Emmi watched them go. They were going to discuss the details of her execution, and there wasn't a damn thing she could do about it. She bit her lip and lowered her head once more.

Uncle Jake, I wish you were here…

With her eyes closed, her thoughts went to the scene she had witnessed as she was led from her solitary cell.

'No one betrays me, Matsuyama, and lives. No one.' Those softly spoken words had chilled Emmi to the bone as guards led her past the man she recognized as Kae's friend — the friend who'd gotten them out of the brothel the night she'd arrived.

The man had struggled only to be knocked to the ground, bound with rope and dragged away to a darkened corner. Light had glinted off a katana blade as it sliced through the air seconds after Kaemon's former friend cried out for mercy…

And she was next.

Two strong hands clamped onto her arms and jerked Emmi to her feet, bringing her to face the livid Hijikata Toshizou confronting her. He was every bit the deadly, demon-like vice-commander her father once told her about. Her blood ran cold.

He could kill her this instant, and no one would do a thing to him. He had the position and the respect so that anything he said to cover a murder would be believed.

But Emmi would not let him see how scared she was. To keep from crying out, she clamped her jaws so tightly her teeth ached.

"You listen to me," he hissed. "There is something about you that's not right. If it's the last thing I do, I'll find out what you're up to with Nakagawa. Your woman's tricks will get you only so far."

He was so close that Emmi could feel his breath on her skin, the heat of his anger seeping through his clothing.

Kae stopped short the instant he set foot inside the door. His back stiffened at the sight of Hijikata holding Emmi. Though he couldn't make out the low conversation, he was certain he heard something about a woman's tricks. Was this how it was? Was she one of Hijikata's many women being used to get close to him and get information on what was going on within the Imperial Palace?

He stepped farther into the room. His hands rested lightly on the hilt of his katana with the right one poised, ready to draw in an instant.

"Is there a problem, Hijikata-san?"

Hijikata dropped his hands — and Emmi with them — and turned slowly.

"Not at all," he said with a curt bow. "I was simply advising Maeda-san to release any information, no matter how trivial she thinks it may be."

"Information on — ?"

"Any potential rebel plots, of course."

"Of course," Kae said flatly. "Emiko, come with me."

His silence was driving her crazy. Apart from the bossy, *'Emiko, come with me,'* he hadn't said a word to her. If he'd wanted her dead, he'd have it done here and now as he had to that Matsuyama guy. What was going on? He led her to a palanquin, one so large it took four men to carry it.

"What's going to happen to me?"

"Get in."

Swallowing hard, she did.

As soon as they were inside, the litter bearers took off at a quick, steady pace.

Within the confines of the shadowy conveyance, Kaemon studied her like a bug under a magnifying glass, and Emmi felt certain that the sun must be streaming through that imaginary magnifying glass, because she felt like she was about to burst into flames. She turned her head to escape his unblinking gaze and noticed something familiar through the gauzy cloth covering the palanquin windows.

Emmi turned back. He was still staring. "Why are we going through the Shimabara gates?"

"This is where you will stay."

Her jaw sagged open. She hugged her arms around herself and felt like throwing up again.

"You can't do that! You can't sell me to one of those places as punishment for whatever you imagine I did! I'm no prostitute, and I won't be one!"

"I could do that and more, and there isn't a thing you or your family could do to stop me—providing you even have a family who care."

Emmi launched herself at Kae, tried to punch him and scratch his face. He deflected her and grabbed her wrists. As the palanquin jostled, the bearers struggled to compensate for the weight shift and movement.

Emmi didn't want to cry like a frightened child, but she felt very much like one at that moment. She blinked the tears back as soon as they formed.

"Don't do this. Please don't do this to me."

"Why?" Kae asked, angling his face nearer hers. His dark gaze was all but paralyzing.

"I don't want to be a prostitute. I don't want strange men touching me…"

"You let me touch you."

"I… It wasn't the same. You…" Her voice died, and she lowered her head.

"No other man will touch you."

Emmi felt her breath catch in her throat. Slowly, she looked up. The power in Kae's eyes held her captive as firmly as his strong, rough hands held her wrists.

The last thing she expected was for him to kiss her, but he did. He stared at her. The desire in his eyes was alive and almost frightening in its intensity. He drew her closer still, flicked his tongue across her lips to tease them apart before covering her mouth with his and claiming her. Then, without warning, it was over.

He released her wrists, pulled away and stared at her a moment. The palanquin had stopped without her quite registering it, and he threw open the sliding door. He pulled Emmi out and led her to a side door of the brothel where the fight had occurred earlier.

An older man and woman immediately let them in and ushered them up a short flight of stairs and down a dim hallway. In a set of connecting rooms, a girl was removing dust covers from the few pieces of furniture while another carried in a thick, folded futon and placed it in the center of the smaller room. A third girl rushed in carrying a number of garments, which she placed atop one of the low cabinets in the bedroom.

"I want this tatami replaced as soon as possible," Kaemon said. "And I want better screens. One for each room — light, bright colors."

The older couple bowed deeply. "Yes, Fujiwara-sama," the man said.

Still using the Fujiwara alias? Emmi wondered.

"Have you secured a guard yet?"

The woman bowed deeply. "We couldn't find one worthy enough. Forgive us. We will find one tomorrow."

"Forget it," Kae said. "I will secure my own in the morning. Tonight I will stay here myself. You may go. Send in some sake, tea and a few sweets."

The couple and their servants bustled out. Large floor lanterns, one in each room, cast a warm yellow glow, and Emmi couldn't help but notice how handsome and noble Kae looked as he removed his longer sword and leaned it upright against the wall near the unrolled futon in the adjoining room. He said nothing but walked around the rooms until the serving girls brought what he had requested. When they left, he latched the shoji behind them then sat cross-legged in front of the food trays.

"Well?"

"Well what?" Emmi asked.

He gestured to the trays. "Sit. Serve."

Serve? His tone and expression made her want to serve the food and drinks right on his head, but Emmi didn't think that would be the wisest idea, especially tonight. Emmi eased down her bruised pride and sat on her heels facing him. Emmi poured him small cups of sake and tea and placed two of the sweet-looking cakes on a delicate plate. She placed the plates on the empty tray directly in front of him.

"Have something as well," he said when Emmi sat back, her hands resting lightly on her lap.

Emmi took one of the cakes and nibbled on it, not looking at him. She was both unnerved and excited by the possessive way he kept staring at her. He held out his small sake cup and Emmi looked at him, questioning. He indicated the bottle on the tray with a nod. Grumbling to herself, Emmi poured him another drink.

"How old are you?" she asked.

He seemed a bit surprised by the question, but he answered after eating one of the cakes. "Twenty-one." He paused. "And you?"

"Nineteen, a couple months ago," Emmi said, pouring herself some tea. She sipped it and winced. It certainly wasn't the gourmet tea her mother insisted on importing from Tokyo.

Kae downed what was in the tiny cup then poured his own sake this time. "Why aren't you married? Surely a Maeda woman would not lack for suitors."

"Things are different back home. I was busy studying, and besides, most of the guys seemed afraid of my father."

Kae smirked. "In Kyoto, most fathers fear me."

Emmi rolled her eyes and reached for the sake herself. She coughed after the first sip seared a path down her throat. This wasn't the stuff her grandparents bought at Christmas, either. Still, it was better than the bitter tea.

"So, what am I supposed to do here, Fujiwara-san?"

Kaemon's expression hardened. "Firstly, you will not say anything about who I truly am. One word to one person, and I will kill you."

Emmi swallowed hard and poured herself another sake. "Not a word."

Kae ate the last cake.

Emmi stood to stretch out her aching calves then sat back down cross-legged like Kae. "So what else am I supposed to do here?" she asked, too nervous to have him confirm the most obvious answer—be his personal, unpaid hooker.

Kae shrugged. "I would advise you to stay in these rooms once the customers begin arriving in the early afternoon, unless you have your guard with you."

"Guard? You were serious?"

"Do you value your reputed virginity?"

Emmi scowled. "I do, and it's not reputed."

"Then you will simply be here, provided for, until someone from your family appears in Kyoto looking for you, or until I figure out what to do with you permanently."

Of all the things he could inflict on her, she supposed this was the best. Still, he hadn't said he wouldn't use her for his personal bed toy. She hated herself for not being more upset at that prospect than she was.

She took another sip of sake, then got up and went to the bedroom. She lay on her side on the futon, half curled into a ball. She looked up when she heard movement. Kae had entered the room and slid the shoji shut. He removed his wakizashi and set it beside his katana. He began untying his long hakama straps.

Emmi sat up as he let the hakama fall. He then stepped out of it and folded it into a neat square. She tried not to let the sight of his well-muscled thighs beneath his gi top distract her. "What are you doing?"

"Getting ready for bed," he said, calmly untying his obi and removing his top so he wore nothing but a pale blue fundoshi.

Emmi looked around the room. There was no other futon anywhere. "This is my bed."

Kae unfolded the quilted blanket at the foot of the futon. "Correction," he said, settling himself on the mattress, taking up more than half. "I'm renting these rooms and everything in them. It's my bed."

Chapter Nineteen

Emmi stared at the waning lantern light flickering off the smooth glossy surface of a low table. The room was very quiet except for far-off voices and the faint chirp of crickets outside, most likely in that small garden area they'd gone through when he'd first taken her from the mirror.

If only the quiet sounds were enough to cover the voice that had been running through her mind, but the deep, sexy, oh so confident male voice insisted on replaying bits and pieces of their conversations.

'I'm renting these rooms and everything in them. It's my bed... You let me touch you... No other man will touch you... I could do that and more, and there isn't a thing you or your family could do to stop me...'

Emmi clung to the edge of the futon so as not to brush against Kae in any way. When her right arm started to tingle from lack of circulation, she turned onto her left side and regretted it instantly. The fundoshi that he wore was not the kind her father and Uncle Jake wore in the movies. At least those covered them fully. This one was more like a thong that did nothing whatsoever to conceal his tight, rounded cheeks.

Damn, but Kaemon had a nice butt.

Emmi breathed a soft sigh and closed her eyes. Of course sleep would not come because of that voice in her head. His voice. So deep, so sexy... She opened her eyes and gasped.

He was facing her, staring at her with those big, dark eyes that made her want to die of pleasure. Or throw herself at him. Both very bad ideas but very strong compulsions.

"Why are you not sleeping?" he asked.

"I don't know. I just can't."

He seemed to hide a grin. The rat was grinning at her because he knew why she couldn't sleep—the nice butt... Broad chest... Strong shoulders...

Emmi flopped over to her other side.

Kaemon reached out and turned her onto her back then lifted himself on his elbow and hovered over her.

"You cling to the edge of the bed. Are you afraid of me?"

Oh, he was enjoying this way too much. She could tell by the gleam in his eyes.

"No," Emmi snapped.

She turned her head to the side. Kae turned her face back toward his. He stared at her again for a long time without saying a word.

Emmi became extremely conscious of how close he was. She could feel his bare chest brushing against her upper arm. And he was next to naked. Thank goodness she had the yukata on under her hakama.

Damn, but he turned her on.

She was doomed.

"You don't have to be afraid," he said at last.

"I'm not."

He chuckled. Damn him.

"I could have taken you any number of times these past few days."

"Why didn't you?"

'Why didn't you?' Her practical side informed her obviously insane side exactly how dangerous that question was.

Kae seemed as surprised by the question as she was. "Did you want me to?"

Say it and die, slut girl. "Um, no, not really." *Oh yeah, that's convincing…*

"Then you would never want me to do this," Kae said before gently stroking his fingertips across her cheek. "Or this," he added, allowing his fingers to trail down into the vee of the yukata top.

"Um…no. You, uh, shouldn't do that."

He grinned.

She felt a quiver between her legs. Oh yeah, she was doomed.

"Ah, I see. Then this is most certainly an unwelcome thing," he said an instant before covering her mouth with his.

His kiss was slow, his lips whisper-soft against hers. He teased her upper lip with the tip of his hot tongue and did the same to her bottom lip. He eased over to kiss her jaw, the side of her neck, the lobe of her ear.

Emmi tried her best not to squirm or sigh. She valiantly pretended she did not make that dirty little moaning sound when he licked his way back down the side of her neck then to the base of her throat. She felt hot and cold and tingly and very, very uncomfortable in certain parts of her anatomy that she was trying not to acknowledge.

Kae stopped suddenly, raised himself up, settled back on his heels and gazed down at her again. Emmi was all too conscious of the fact that, although he wasn't much older than she was, he was a very experienced man. He was looking at her the way such a man looks at a woman he plans to have.

And she knew she wasn't going to protest.

He reached out, pulled her into a sitting position, then unbound her hair from the ponytail. He combed through her hair with his fingers, all the while peering deeply into her eyes. He caressed the sides of her neck. His touch was skilled, and the roughness of his fingertips scratchy but exciting. He slid his hands to her shoulders. Oh so slowly, he eased the front of her yukata apart and tugged it loose enough to pull it down past her shoulders and free her arms. His gaze slid over her as his hands had done, and when he let his hands caress her again, Emmi closed her eyes and consciously let the soft moan escape from her lips.

Emmi allowed him to peel back the yukata, let him undo the hakama straps and tug it free. She gasped when he pulled open the yukata all the way, letting the cool air hit the burning flesh of her lower half.

"Beautiful," he whispered before kissing her navel. He then licked and kissed his way down each of her thighs and back again.

Emmi squirmed and opened her eyes as a moist heat pooled between her legs. She reached out, touched Kae's broad shoulder, and stroked her hand over as much of his chest as she could reach.

He smiled at her. She smiled back.

He cupped her cheek with his palm and kissed her softly—his lips a whisper against her own.

"So beautiful, like a perfect sakura blossom."

Joy filled her heart, and Emmi slid her hand into his hair, coaxed him down for a deep kiss. He kissed her fiercely, eased himself over her and pressed his hips toward hers. She was nervous at the feel of him pressing against her through the thin fabric of his fundoshi and her panties, but knew as surely as she knew her own name that Kae would do nothing to hurt her.

Though driving her mad seemed to be another thing entirely. When he tugged the bra down, she pulled her arms free of the thin straps and gave herself over to the whirlwind of sensation.

Apprehension washed over Emmi when Kae slid her panties off, but it vanished the instant he kissed her—slowly, almost reverently. When he looked at her, she knew she wanted him completely.

He shifted to lie beside her. With his right arm around her shoulders, he pulled her closer. His free hand stroked, caressed, and turned her into a trembling mass of want and need. She'd masturbated before but it didn't compare to this.

She opened her eyes and smiled up at Kae with sheer joy, more than ready for what would follow.

He pulled her to him, kissed her slowly, and touched himself as they kissed. He did what he needed to do. Without her.

"Kae? Why?"

"It's nothing to trouble yourself over." He sat up and wiped his palm on the blanket bunched behind him. He looked at her and kissed her forehead. "Sleep now. It's very late."

Holding in tears, Emmi turned onto her side. Surprisingly, Kae didn't get dressed and leave. He stayed there, snuggled close, pulled her into the curve of his body and tugged the blanket up over them both. Emmi lay awake trying to make sense of what had happened. What she'd done wrong.

Chapter Twenty

She woke to the feel of Kae's kisses along her jawline. Almost purring, she opened her eyes and smiled as the last vestiges of sleep fell away to reveal Kaemon's handsome face. Last night had been real, not just a pleasant dream.

"Good morning."

"Good afternoon, actually," he teased before flicking his tongue at the base of her throat.

She sat up and realized she was wearing her yukata, though she had nothing underneath. She also noticed that they were in a different room from last night. This room was bigger and much fancier in its few furnishings.

"Where are we?"

"Aneko's room. I had to dress and move you when the workmen arrived to redecorate the other rooms." He grinned. "You're quite the sound sleeper."

Emmi blushed and lowered her gaze. Within seconds, her thoughts began to spin.

Aneko's room meant that the mirror was nearby, and she looked up, calling a triumphant "Yes!" in the back of her mind when she noticed it resting atop a small chest.

But all thoughts of going home faded the instant Kae tilted her face back toward his with a gentle prod of his fingers. Home became the last thing on her mind when his lips touched hers. A steady delicious heat built deep inside her, but then he pulled away and stood.

He walked across the room. She felt stupid for her disappointment. Obviously that Aneko woman was bound to walk in any second. Of course he wouldn't want to pick up where he'd left off last night and really make love to her.

Emmi broke off from her thoughts when Kaemon came back to her with a blue-green kimono, a yellow obi and tabi socks and black wooden geta.

"Put these on. I want to take you out."

"Okay." She looked around. "Where is my underwear, my bra and panties?"

"You'll get them back soon enough." He flashed a wicked grin that made her want him even more than she already did.

Emmi stood. "What are you up to?"

"Nothing at all, Emiko-san. Nothing at all."

"Liar." Emmi kissed him lightly. "Is there someplace I can bathe first?"

Kaemon nuzzled her neck. "Would you like me to wash you?" he teased before nipping at her ear.

Emmi shivered and gave a light laugh. "I would, but then we might never go anywhere."

Kae pulled away. "True, and we have important places to go."

* * * *

"So you have news for me, Yamazaki-kun?" Hijikata Toshizou asked as his chief inspector slipped into the room.

"Some, Hijikata-san." He knelt and presented his superior with a paper copy of his report.

Hijikata scanned the page, his hard gaze intense. "So, it would seem that our troublemaker may very well be telling the truth. A brother of the Maeda lord arrived in Kyoto yesterday to meet with Matsudaira-sama."

"Yes. And I didn't have time to write it in, but I just received word that the girl is expected to appear before Prince Asahiko tomorrow evening."

Hijikata folded the report and tucked it into his sleeve. "There is something about her I don't trust. What of this other relative she mentioned traveling with—Yamauchi? He must be of the mother's family."

"I haven't been able to find any information yet. He could well be a close family friend, and she uses uncle as a term of endearment."

"Perhaps. Still, she's hiding something. I'm sure of it."

* * * *

Nervous, Emmi stepped from Aneko's bedroom, where she'd gotten dressed, into the adjoining reception room where Kaemon waited. She couldn't do much with the obi other than the fairly simple square-shaped back knot that she'd learned as a child. And while she couldn't get her hair into the typical style of a Japanese woman of the time, she got it as close as possible and put it up with the pretty pins Kaemon had given her. She just hoped for the best.

Emmi watched him a moment, staring so intently out the far right window.

"I'm ready," she prompted.

He turned then froze. His soulful dark eyes widened as he scanned her from head to foot.

"I look awful, don't I?" Emmi lowered her head. "I don't know how to tie a fancy obi alone, and I know my hair is all wrong—"

She broke off when Kae tilted her chin with a featherlight touch. He grazed his thumb over her bottom lip and gave her a soft, gentle kiss.

"You look beautiful. Simple and elegant."

Emmi breathed a dreamy sigh and smiled. "I do?"

"You do," he said with a warm smile.

She believed him, but disappointment and doubt flowed through her when he failed to hold or kiss her again as she hoped.

"Let's get going," he said, heading to the door.

"I meant to ask," Emmi said, catching up. "Where is your...friend, Aneko?"

Kae replied without turning as he led the way out of the brothel through the more private rear entrance. "I gave her money to go shopping."

"Oh."

Once outside, Emmi walked slightly behind Kae as her common sense began to lecture her worse than her mother ever had.

That Aneko is his official woman. He obviously supports her like a wife if he sends her out shopping and rents her those fancy rooms at that place. The lecture paused for a moment before closing with a bang. *He rented you the bargain basement with the worn floor mats and crappy food.*

* * * *

Kaemon glanced back a number of times as he led the way to Gion. Emiko was so oddly quiet that he was afraid he'd lost her in the crowd. As they continued on, he wondered what had her so preoccupied. Could she be wondering what punishment her family would hand down now that they had arrived in Kyoto?

Apparently they had forbidden her to come on the journey, so she had set out on her own. But why? From what he had gathered, Maeda Takehito was here for a meeting with the Matsudaira brothers. Saadaki was the new Shoshidai, and Katamori Kyoto Shugoshoku — the official Protector of Kyoto.

Was she simply anxious to see the capital? She certainly was headstrong enough to set her mind to come, but surely she'd seen Edo a few times, so this large city couldn't hold that much of an attraction.

However, what if there was another reason her uncle had come? What if he had come to arrange a marriage for her? A marriage she opposed. Yes, that would certainly make her sneak off to arrive before him then try to dissuade him.

Aren't you forgetting something? A part of Kae asked from deep within. *Aren't you forgetting how she came to you? From within the depths of a smoldering mirror?*

Of course he wasn't forgetting it, because it had never happened. Yes, at first he'd thought it had happened that way, but obviously he had been drugged. He must have imagined the entire thing. Emiko had come to Aneko's room, yes, but she must have been running from someone much as she had been that night when Matsuyama's treachery had come to light. Apparently

Matsuyama had planned an attack upon him at that earlier time, but Emiko's unexpected appearance had prevented it.

But what of her own words about being from another place in time? Kae refused to speculate and silenced his inner questions once his first destination appeared in the distance.

* * * *

"I don't want you to buy me anything," Emmi said flatly when Kaemon indicated the sprawling kimono maker's shop.

"I want to," he said so sweetly that her resolve began to wane. "The garments you arrived in were finely made, but they aren't quite proper to be received at the palace."

"What?" Emmi asked, sidestepping two women who exited the shop.

"My father wants to meet you tomorrow evening after dinner."

His father. The angry, snooty man from the secret passage. He was a scary little noble.

Kae glanced around before stroking the side of her cheek with his fingertip. "He wants to meet the woman who has me so thoroughly distracted these days."

"He does this to all your women?" Emmi muttered.

Kae gave her a long look, and Emmi noticed the earlier warmth in his eyes fading as he spoke.

"Would you rather have your family provide your clothing? It seems that your uncle has arrived in Kyoto at last."

"Here?" Jake was here? Could it be true? Could he have found a way to the past?

Kae pulled her off to the side as more people entered the shop. "Takehito, brother of the Maeda lord."

"Takehito?" Emmi repeated slowly. "I don't want to see him. I can't. Not now." Emmi grabbed Kae's hand. "Please don't force me to see him. Do I have to meet your father? I'm no one important. He doesn't need to meet me."

Kaemon's expression became even colder. "No one refuses my father, Emiko. Not even me."

Chapter Twenty-One

This is not good, not good at all, Emmi thought as she followed Kae inside the fabric shop. She occupied herself by studying the bolts of silk and cotton displayed along the walls and on large tables as a man and woman scurried from the back of the shop to offer Kae assistance.

What was she going to do when she met his father? Why did he want to meet her anyway?

A deep red silk caught her eye and Emmi wandered over to it, reaching out to smooth her index finger along the edge of the bolt. It felt so thick and rich, so different from the filmy designer silk blouses her mother liked to wear.

"Emiko."

Emmi breathed a dispirited sigh and went to Kae's side. She smiled at the older couple and wished they wouldn't lower their gazes or bow so deeply for her. She was no one special. Well, she did have famous ancestors, but still, she was just plain old Emmi from

L.A., and her family was no more important in America than the majority of the population.

Kae placed his hand on the small of her back and gave her a nudge forward. "Emiko, Muroku-san will help you choose the proper fabrics for your kimono while her husband and I discuss the particulars in the back."

Emmi offered the older woman a smile as Kae disappeared through a curtained doorway.

* * * *

Entering the rear room, Kae narrowed his eyes the instant he noticed the lingering odor of tobacco and saw a sake bottle with a half-empty cup beside it. To his knowledge—and he'd been here numerous times—Muroku-san did not smoke.

Muroku quickly swept the half-filled cup away and took two new cups from a small chest. "Forgive the mess, Fujiwara-sama. My wife and I were relaxing when you came in."

"Really?" Kae asked, scanning the room as he removed his katana to sit. He kept it resting across his knees, however, and was quick to note that the action did not escape the older man, who was definitely hiding something today. "And when did your wife take up the pipe?"

The pause before Muroku's nervous laugh was all the confirmation Kae needed. "The pipe is mine, of course," he said as he poured the sake.

"Then where is it?"

Muroku's eyes darted to the left at the same instant Kaemon heard the slow sliding of a shoji door.

"Die, you shogunate pig!" a samurai shouted as he burst into the room, sword drawn and aimed at Kae's head.

The ronin was an equal match to Kae in terms of strength and quickness. He blocked Kae's moves as Kae did his. They locked swords, tried to throw the other off balance, and knocked each other into the walls and furniture.

At last Kae had the advantage and slashed at the other man's waist but, unfortunately, caused little damage as the cut in his clothing revealed chainmail beneath.

When his foot caught a fallen sake bottle Kaemon slipped, giving the ronin the opportunity to land a glancing blow, aggravating his previous injury. Kae gritted his teeth at the pain in his leg but forced himself to stand. He laid into the ronin, slicing the man's arm and breaking his sword.

The ronin dropped the useless weapon and pulled a revolver from inside his yukata.

Kae froze, and the ronin grinned like a fool. What's more, he was a fool, for Kae pulled his iron fan from his belt and threw it at the man's groin. It connected squarely and the ronin's shot went wide, going through the thin wall.

Women's screams echoed throughout the building, and one rose above all the others. *Emiko.*

Charging at the doubled-over ronin, Kae swung his katana with both hands, decapitating the man in one blow. Heedless of his wound, he ran past the cowering Muroku and plowed into the main room of the silk shop.

Emmi was still holding one of the bolts of silk that Muroku's wife had been showing her.

"Kae!" Emmi shrieked, but her eyes remained fixed on the gaping bullet hole in the other woman's head and the growing puddle of blood that was about to reach her own feet.

Blood. So much blood.

Emmi screamed again when Kae grabbed her. "Stop touching me! What are you doing? Trying to kill me, too?"

"Are you injured? Tell me! Are you injured?" he shouted, trying to feel around the blood spatters on her face and clothing.

Muroku stumbled from the back room, fell upon his wife's body and began to wail. The customers and the worker who'd fled now crowded the shop entrance.

Kae threw his arm over Emmi's shoulders and hurried her out of the shop. Three of the Shinsengumi patrolling the area pushed their way through the crowd as well, blocking Kae's way.

"Saitou-san. A ronin in Muroku's shop attacked me." Kae paused and winced. "He had a gun. Muroku may be hiding more or concealing weapons for them."

Saitou ordered a few of his men into the shop and another to secure transportation for Kae and Emmi. He pulled a white cloth from beneath his haori for Kae to use as a bandage.

Saitou said, "Our compound is closer than your home. The doctor is in today. He can tend it."

Kae nodded as he bound the wound. "There's another merchant I have my suspicions about."

"Hijikata-san will be appreciative of the information."

Though her heart pounded like mad and her stomach was twisted upon itself, the shock Emmi felt was easing, but the name Hijikata was the last thing she wanted to hear. She brushed aside thoughts of the obnoxious vice-commander.

Once inside the palanquin, Emmi saw that the makeshift bandage wasn't doing much for Kae's injury.

"The blood has soaked through already," she muttered.

She had to do something but what? She was no nurse. Closing her eyes to focus, she thanked her grade school friend for talking her into joining the Girl Scouts.

"Give me your dagger," Emmi said, reaching out.

"What?"

He looked pale, as though he was about to pass out. How far was the Shinsengumi compound anyway?

Emmi took the tanto and cut through the hem of her kimono. She cut it almost to her knees and folded it upon itself to make a thicker binding.

Emmi loosened his hakama ties to free his injured thigh. Thanks to so many years of seeing her dad and Jake covered in realistic wounds and gore Emmi was no longer squeamish, but she wasn't about to lift the piece of cloth already on the wound. Emmi slid the silk under his leg, wound the ends in opposite directions a couple times, then tied it in a knot. This didn't seem like it would be that much better, but at least it made her feel less helpless.

"Such a fine nurse," Kae said softly.

"If only," Emmi answered, watching as this cloth too began showing spots of blood. "How far is it to the doctor?"

"Not far enough," Kae said, reaching out with surprising strength to pull her against him.

The press of Kae's lips against hers blotted out everything in her mind. Emmi automatically slid her hands up to wind around his neck and gave herself over to the exploration of his tongue against hers. She wasn't even aware of the stopping of the palanquin and the opening of its door until a familiar, sarcastic voice assaulted her ears.

"Why, Yamanami-san, it seems we are to be entertained with an erotic display."

Emmi jerked away from Kae, not missing the glare he gave to the Shinsengumi vice-commander. Nor did Emmi miss the deep, apologetic bow Hijikata gave in return.

"My deepest apologies, it was a most regrettable slip of the tongue."

"See that it doesn't happen again," Kaemon muttered as he tightened his hakama and eased himself out and to the ground.

"Of course," Hijikata responded brusquely, gesturing two men forward to help Kae. "Did you recognize your attacker?"

The kindly Yamanami drew Emmi's attention by stepping into her line of sight. He offered his hand to help her out of the carriage. "Please, Maeda-dono. I'll have one of the kitchen girls find you other clothing and assist you in cleaning up."

While Kae's kiss had calmed her for the moment, Emmi felt her insides tensing and her emotions building into a tight coil when she undressed in the bathhouse. Blood covered her clothing, her tabi socks, her hands... She felt like Carrie when she poured water over her head and saw the red-tinged water pool on the wooden floor before dripping down between the spaces in the floorboards.

Emmi scrubbed herself until her skin tingled. Satisfied that the blood was gone, she stepped into the big tub to soak and try to relax. But no matter what she did, she could not get rid of the blood beneath her fingernails. She got out of the tub, searched her soiled kimono for the long hairpins and used one to scrape beneath her nails. She poked the pin in too deeply in places, but she didn't care.

Emmi dried herself roughly and pulled on the clean clothes the kitchen maid had given her, but tension and fear began to well up inside her once more. This was no movie. This had been real. So real. And she knew from history that it would only get worse from here once the fighting between the shogun's military and the rebels escalated. The stupid anime lines were undoubtedly true—the streets of Kyoto were going to run red with rivers of blood. Next time, she might get swept away.

Emmi was shaking with an inner chill as she approached the door to exit the bathhouse. She opened the door, only to be confronted by the scowling Hijikata.

"Why is it," he began, stepping forward so Emmi had no choice but to back up, "that you are always at the center of violent disturbances lately?"

Emmi trembled as his hard, dark eyes impaled her. This man had killed, and Emmi knew as surely as she knew the sky was blue that he could kill her and feel nothing afterward.

"I don't know," Emmi said, backing up until she bumped against the wooden tub. "These things just happened."

"Well, I certainly have my suspicions," Hijikata said in a tone that set her nerves more on edge. Emmi raised her arms as if to fend off his mean look and words. He grabbed her wrists so tightly they ached.

"Who. Exactly. Are. You. Helping?" he asked, pronouncing each word slowly, inching in closer and closer.

Unable to contain the emotions she'd been trying to keep in check, Emmi shook harder, hating the way this guy made her feel like a frightened girl. "I'm not helping anyone do anything! I don't know why these things happen when I'm around. Do you think I like it? Maybe Kaemon's the cause of it. People are after him, not me!"

"Indeed," Hijikata said. "And you may be the tool they use to get him. It certainly would throw the court into turmoil, perhaps long enough for the rebels to get near the emperor, if his closest advisor and protector were distracted by the death of his only son."

"How dare you!" Emmi cried out, trying to hit the angry vice-commander's chest. He held her wrists in an iron grip, and Emmi tried to pull away.

"Or can it be that you have second thoughts on helping whoever hired you? Perhaps…you've fallen in love with young Kaemon…?"

"I'm not in love. I hardly even know him."

"Is there a problem, Hijikata-san?"

Emmi squirmed free of the vice-commander's grasp and saw Kae standing on the bathhouse steps.

The instant Hijikata let her go, she ran to the door. She reached for Kae, but he turned his back, went down the steps, then spun around to scowl at both her and the Shinsengumi vice-commander.

"How is your leg?" Hijikata asked flatly.

"Fine," he snapped before turning his attention to Emmi. "I need to speak with my father. I will ask Yamanami-san to secure you transportation to the Katsura Villa."

"What?"

"Katsura Villa," he repeated. "Where your uncle is staying." With that, he walked away.

Emmi ran after him and tried to grab his arm, but he shook her off and glared at her.

"I can't go there. I can't."

"You will."

He turned his back and left her standing speechless, more afraid than ever. Emmi couldn't meet her ancestors. They'd think she was some psycho or imposter and have her imprisoned — or worse.

"An unexpected complication, Maeda-dono?" Hijikata asked with a smirk as he strode past like some damn proud peacock.

* * * *

More than once Emmi considered simply jumping out of the palanquin that carried her through the busy streets of Kyoto, but each time common sense — or maybe stark fear — stopped her. Sure she could run away, but where to? She had no place to go, no one to turn to. She doubted she could ever make herself really "fit in" in this century.

The closer the bearers carried her to the Katsura Villa, the sicker Emmi felt. She guessed they'd arrived when the men passed through thatch-roof gates and started down a graveled, tree-lined path. No building was in sight, so Emmi hoped that maybe they were just passing through some fancy park. However, all too soon, the unmistakable outline of a tiled roof appeared in the distance.

Obviously the Maeda in temporary residence here wouldn't be expecting her, since, technically, she didn't exist. Maybe she could pretend to be some distant relative? Some daughter of a cousin five times removed — or something? Emmi wilted. As far as totally dumbass ideas went, that had to be the prizewinner.

Inhaling a deep, calming breath and swallowing the bile that rose in her throat, Emmi stared at the entrance to the villa proper. She almost hoped that the palanquin bearers would drop her and render her unconscious as they walked up the wide steps to the veranda. Maybe she could plead amnesia and forget which possible long-lost relative she was.

Fate could not be so kind as to give her that easy out, and Emmi took yet another deep breath once the palanquin bearers stopped and slid open the door. Emmi nodded and tried to present a pleasant face to the servants who greeted her, despite her fear that she'd throw up and ruin the pristine tatami mats at any moment.

Though her mind was spinning and her stomach was churning, Emmi noticed the covert sideways glances the servant girls gave one another. She didn't look much like a Maeda in the borrowed maid's clothes, did she? More like some stray plucked off the streets.

Emmi's blood ran cold the instant one of the girls said, "Lord Maeda has been expecting you. He is on the moon-viewing platform. Please follow."

Expecting her? Emmi swallowed, though her mouth was close to bone dry, and she followed the girls like a prisoner heading for the lethal injection chamber at You're Toast Now Federal Prison.

Pain gripped her heart when Emmi was shown to the room that led out onto the moon-viewing platform. This was just like the room back home that her parents had added to overlook the backyard and pond. Finally her brain registered the presence standing just outside the door on the rear deck. This was him — Lord Maeda, her great-great-great-grandfather Takehito.

Emmi stood wringing her hands like the heroine from an old romance movie would when about to come face to face with the villain for the first time. Emmi gasped when he spoke — the words that came out were English, very good English.

"Do you find it strange that it pains me to stay in any place bearing the name Katsura?"

"Considering the state of the nation, I suppose not." *Where did that come from?* Emmi wondered as the words poured out of her mouth. Emmi knew that Katsura Kogoro led the rebels, but the political sentiment of her words still felt foreign.

"But it is strange and rather foolish to be troubled by a mere similarity. After all it is my — our — birthright, since Maeda money helped preserve this place."

"I know," Emmi whispered as one of her great-grandfather's old tales came back to her.

'*Then Prince Toshitada married Fu-Hime, the daughter of the lord of the Kaga clan.*'

Slowly her mind finally began to take in Takehito. He still had his back to her. He was rather tall for the time, like Kaemon, but he had a more solid build like her father and Jake had from their martial arts training and stunt work.

Emmi could tell even at a distance that Takehito's clothing was of the quality silk that she had been inspecting today — no, she didn't want to think of that. Instead Emmi concentrated on the details.

His hakama was deep blue, as was his haori jacket, which bore the Maeda crest, visible in the center just below his unbound hair. He wore only a short sword, its golden scabbard tip poking from beneath his jacket.

He turned and Emmi gasped again. He looked so much like her father that she wanted to run and hug him and never let go. Of course, he wasn't her father, and Emmi doubted that he would help her.

"I dreamed of you," he said quietly as he stepped into the room and walked slowly toward her. He stopped in front of her and stroked her cheek. "You are much prettier to my waking eyes."

Emmi blushed and looked down. Takehito tilted her chin up. "You also have dreams of things that come to pass, yes?"

Emmi swallowed. "A few times."

Takehito nodded. He smiled, and Emmi felt that he was relieved to have someone understand at last. Emmi knew the feeling. Jake was the only one she'd ever been able to confide in about her rare "visions" without feeling like an idiot. If only he hadn't been out of the country and could have convinced her father to believe her the day of the accident...

"I believe this belongs to you, Emiko," he said, reaching inside his black kimono. He produced a small square of rice paper and offered it to her.

"You know my name?" Emmi blurted, only to feel silly for thinking no one would have told him her name. Reluctantly, she took the packet. Was he giving her money to go away? Deciding to get it over with, she opened the paper. It was her pendant—the one commissioned and handed down by the very man before her—that she had left with Shinjuku-san.

"It's my necklace. I mean your necklace. I mean your daughter's. I mean... I don't know what I mean."

Takehito laughed and again her heart ached. He was so much like her father.

"Walk with me," he said after fastening the dragonfly pendant around her neck.

Donning sandals, they went out into the expansive gardens that surrounded the palatial estate. For the first time since Emmi had fallen into this nightmare, she began to feel safe and cared for.

It isn't really the first time is it? her heart asked. *You felt very safe and cared for alone in Kae's arms, didn't you?*

Yeah well, that isn't worth thinking about. Not after the look he gave me earlier. What was that about anyway? Emmi wondered as she followed her ancestor along the path of precisely set stepping stones.

It was just best to try to forget about Kaemon for now and concentrate on finding a way home. Maybe this was Fate's way of getting her back on track. If Takehito also had prophetic dreams, then maybe he was no stranger to other weirdness. Maybe he could get her home where she belonged.

Home. *Alone*, her heart chimed in sadly.

* * * *

Prince Asahiko entered his son's rooms as soon as he received word that Kaemon had returned to the palace. He demanded an explanation for his son's latest escapade and received it, though he was clearly not satisfied.

"Why were you at a silk merchant's in Gion, with that Maeda girl, no less?"

"Arranging for her to have something suitable to wear for your meeting tomorrow—which is no longer necessary."

Asahiko stared questioningly at his son. "And why is it no longer necessary?"

"It just isn't. May we drop the subject, Honored Father?"

"For the moment."

* * * *

Emmi grew attached to Maeda Takehito almost immediately. There was just something about him, something so similar to her late father besides appearance, that it almost made her cry every time he looked at her. As they walked along the garden path one evening, Emmi was reminded of the long walks she and her father had taken so many times. When Takehito wandered off the path and to the edge of the wide, decorative pond to skim stones across the water's still surface, the feeling hit her again, and she did cry.

Emmi clung to the sleeves of Takehito's haori when he comforted her.

"Do not cry, child. You are under my protection."

Chapter Twenty-Two

Kyoto
Present day

Jake Hillhouse gave his twin sister a huge hug when he met her at the airport. "You didn't need to come all this way, sis."

"I was worried sick about you and Emmi, and I figure you need backup if the Dragon Lady is coming here."

Jake ran his hand through his long hair. "She's due in an hour, and I am not looking forward to it."

"No word on Emmi at all?"

"Not a one, but I swear I almost heard her when I was meditating this morning."

"What did she say? Did she sound okay?"

Jake's brow furrowed. "Actually, it sounded a lot like 'Oh shit'. But I didn't get any vibes that she was in trouble. It was so faint. I just don't have the connection to her that I had to Laurie. I don't think Em's in the here and now, and I can't reach her across time."

Galen nodded. Her expression was as somber as her twin's. "If anything bad had happened to her with that storm, I'm sure she would have been found by now."

Jake nodded and led the way to a coffee shop near the gate to await the arrival of Emmi's mother, Tara Maeda, and the investigator she'd said she was bringing.

"What the hell kind of P.I. is that?" Galen wondered aloud as Tara and her companion exited the passage leading from the plane.

"He reminds me of a Buddhist monk," Jake said.

"Wearing a kimono top, khaki shorts and Gucci loafers?"

"A gi," Jake said.

"What?"

"The top. It's part of a martial arts training gi."

"Whatever." Galen fell silent and offered a faint smile to Tara Maeda and her odd companion when they approached.

"Have you found my Emmi, Jake?"

"Not yet. She doesn't seem to be in or near Kyoto, but I'm sure she's okay. I have an idea but, well" — he paused and cleared his throat — "it's a bit off the wall."

"Is that so?"

Jake ran his hand through his long hair. "Yeah. I'd prefer to talk to you about it in private."

Tara gave him a cold look. "I'm sure I don't want to hear anything you think you know." She turned to her companion. "Monk Honji will find my Emiko using more than ordinary, mortal resources."

"And that means what exactly? Is he psychic? Some kind of wizard?" Galen asked, shooting Jake a sideways look.

"I have mastered many ancient, esoteric practices and abilities that might appear magical to those on the outside, those who can never truly hope to

181

comprehend," the monk said. He gave Jake and Galen a half bow while holding out his hand, palm up. "Hail the Lotus Sutra," he said before straightening.

Galen glanced over to Jake, who had an expression akin to horror on his face.

"You can't have a Nichiren monk do anything supernatural, Tara. Kenny's people followed the Jodo sect."

"I was married to Kenjiro for twenty-six years, Jake. I think I know that. Besides, Honji-san has transcended the boxed-in teachings of any particular sect."

The monk bowed again. "The Powers of the Cosmos do not avail Themselves of merely one set of sutra. I have progressed beyond such confining strictures to embrace the whole that is incorrupt and entire. I add and extract, compress and expand to create that which is akin to karmic culmination."

Tara and the monk gave the Hillhouse twins identical inscrutable looks then the odd pair walked away, their matching designer luggage rolling along behind them like two inanimate attendants.

The Hillhouses followed. Jake shook his head and muttered, "Man, I have a bad feeling about all this, sis. A bad feeling."

Jake's bad feeling grew progressively worse as the days passed. Tara and Monk Honji canvassed every inch of Kyoto. Although Jake wasn't privy to any information they found, Galen, an investigative reporter, managed to work her particular magic on a few assorted hotel staff. She even got information from people working at the historic sites that Tara and the monk seemed to find particularly interesting.

"If only the Japanese were half as talkative as some of the Irish informants I once knew, we'd have a lot more to go on, but the best I could come up with so far is that they seem to keep lingering on tours to three places — Nijo castle, some estate in Mibu and the Imperial Palace — especially the Imperial Palace. What do you make of it?"

Jake pushed his hair back behind his shoulder. "Not much. Nijo Castle is one of the set pieces for the movie we're doing, since it was a big center of activity when the Tokugawa Shogunate started to hit the skids."

He got up from the chair and paced the room. His steps became quicker and more agitated until he slammed his fist against the wall near the window.

"This is making me fucking crazy. I can't shake the feeling that Tara and that whacked-out monk friend of hers are going to screw something up."

"Do you want me touch base with Jonny to see if he can get through to his mother? He's on work-study in Hong Kong, isn't he? He already told you he could get here pretty quickly if you think it will help."

Jake leaned against the wall. "It won't do any good." He exhaled a deep breath and ran his hands through his hair. "You said they'd been to Mibu a lot?"

"Yeah. Some private estate that's open to tours. Yanagi something. Wait." She grabbed her purse and began leafing through a small notepad.

"Was it Yagi?"

Galen looked up, clearly surprised. "Yeah. Does it mean something?"

"I don't know. That's where the Shinsengumi got their start. Emmi knew a lot about them because of Kenny. They fascinated the hell out him." Jake smiled. "Seeing that place when he did that one action flick here had him acting like a kid at Christmas."

Galen smiled and looked at her notes again. "Oh, I forgot. The concierge said Tara and her mad monk planned to spend most of tomorrow at the Katsura Villa."

Jake frowned. "Kenny loved seeing that, too. The Maeda family has ties to the place through intermarriage with the Imperial Family from way, way back. Maybe they're not picking up on Emmi at all. Maybe it's Kenny. Tara misses him so damn much maybe... Shit, I don't know what to think anymore."

"Try to talk to her, Jake."

"She won't listen." He sighed and pushed away from the wall. "I'm going to hit the bar and have a drink and decide if I need to bail on Cruze and his movie."

Galen set her things aside and went to her brother. "I know you want to stay here and find Emmi, but I think you need to work. I know damn well how you miss the business, and even if you're not doing the stunts, I know you love being the guy in charge of it all."

Jake nodded and gave his sister a fleeting smile. "It's still a rush. I've missed that, being a dull old translator for the past couple years."

"Then you get your ass to Tokyo tomorrow and get to work. You said they'd be coming back here to finish filming once the studio is back up to speed with their repairs. Maybe with you out of town I can get Tara to talk to me. I intend to find out exactly what she and that Honji character are up to."

Jake nodded. "You wanna go downstairs with me?"

Galen grinned. "Why not? That evening bartender is pretty hot. Maybe I can get lucky."

Jake followed his twin to the door and sent his heartfelt thoughts out to Emmi. *I hope luck is on your side, Em-chan.*

Chapter Twenty-Three

Kyoto
1864

An excited maid who looked like she'd seen a ghost woke Emmi up. "A man from the Imperial Palace was here, and Lord Maeda wishes to see you at once."

A man from the palace? Could it be Kaemon?

"Do you know who the man was?" Emmi asked, getting up to dress once again in the simple kimono she'd arrived in. She quickly combed and braided her hair.

"I was told only that he looked important."

That was probably Kaemon. "Does Lord Maeda seem angry?"

"I don't think so."

That was good. Maybe.

Emmi followed the maid to the room where Takehito was waiting. Someone else was there too, a boy about

Emmi's age, who reminded her a bit of her brother. Takehito dismissed the servants before speaking.

"Emiko, this is my son, Sadanori."

Emmi knelt on the floor and bowed forward. "I am honored."

She looked up when Takehito chuckled. He spoke quickly to his son, and she couldn't make out all of what he'd said. "What?"

Takehito motioned her to come join them at the low table. "I told Sadanori that bowing so much must be a wound to your spirit. I have heard Americans are a proud lot who do not bow down to others, and I believe this utterly, from their actions since Perry came."

Emmi blushed and tried unsuccessfully to ignore the nagging voice in her head. *Go on! Ask him who was here!*

"Honored Uncle," she stammered, not quite knowing how to address him since he hadn't told her what he preferred. "I was told there was a man here from the Imperial Palace? It wasn't about me, was it?"

Takehito laughed. "I requested an audience with the emperor. It was a messenger telling me my request was granted for tomorrow. I plan to take Sadanori with me, and I will take you as well."

"Oh, no, no, no. I can't do that. I can't go there. I have no proper clothing. No, I don't belong there."

"I wish you to accompany us, Emiko-chan," he said firmly. "A woman is on her way to see that you have everything you need. You may go now."

Emmi groaned inwardly. Takehito was even better at giving the big brush-off than Kae.

* * * *

Why was it that time zoomed by when she was confronted with things she did not want to face? It seemed one minute Takehito was telling her to get lost, and the next she was being swamped by maids getting her ready to go to the very last place she wanted to go.

Slowly Emmi followed the maid into the main room of the Katsura Villa to await the palanquins that would take her and her ancestors to the Imperial Palace. Of course, following the maid was easier said than done, since the maid was not weighed down in fifty-seven different layers of stuff including towels padding her stomach, above her butt and between her boobs to make her shape into a smooth cylinder.

Emmi couldn't forget the two under kimono, the outer kimono and the *uchikake*, the kimono-ish coat that was embroidered with at least thirty-five pounds of silk thread. To top that all off, there were straps and ties out the wazoo to keep it all in place and to keep her collar at the proper height.

She didn't even want to think about the white makeup covering her face and neck. This stuff could not be healthy. She was positive that the makeup person at the movie studio had rambled about how the 'real deal' once contained lead as a main ingredient.

Emmi hoped Takehito didn't spaz, but there was no way in hell she was going to put that inky black stuff on her teeth. Did these people have no concept of proper dental hygiene? Her parents had spent a fortune having her teeth bleached and straightened in the ninth grade, and she was not going to ruin it now, not even for the Emperor of Japan. She would just keep her mouth shut, which shouldn't be too hard and would probably be a wise thing in the long run.

She took small satisfaction in the way Takehito and Sadanori looked equally uncomfortable in their "Court Costume." Emmi quickly found herself liking her outfit a great deal more. The men looked truly weighted down by the robe-like black tops with the incredibly long full sleeves and backs that resembled a train on a bridal dress. The wide legged pants beneath their robes were longer than their usual hakama, and Emmi knew that if she had to dress in that getup she'd end up entangling her feet and falling on her face. Besides, she didn't have to wear the bizarre, pillbox-type black hat tied on with a thin white cord and sporting a stiff wide fabric tail that rose up then curved down on the hat's back.

Just as Emmi was about to ask if she really had to go along a servant hurried in and said the palanquins had arrived. She winced at the thought of getting into the palanquin, hating the thought that these poor guys had to carry her and who knew how many other people all around Kyoto—rain, shine or snow—for a living, especially when she was weighted down with all this 'stuff' like a gift-wrapped salami.

Emmi let out an enormous sigh—as enormous a sigh as a gift-wrapped salami could exhale—and tried to settle back. Endeavoring to reform the civil liberties of nineteenth century Japan was probably not a good idea, especially if she wanted to get back to her own century just as she'd left it without some freaky Butterfly Effect from her meddling.

A trip to the Imperial Palace mightn't be so bad. She'd at least catch a glimpse of Kae. Not that he cared about her or would want to see her, but still, a glimpse of him, even for a second, would be nice. The memory of him would go with her no matter where she ended up.

Every minute that she'd spent with him ran through her mind as they made their way from the villa. Their time had ended with him giving her that cold, cold look. Just her luck to have a mad crush on a guy who couldn't stand the sight of her.

As they traveled through the big main gate of the Imperial Place, Emmi peeked through the sliding papered window of the palanquin. She caught a glimpse of seriously bored-looking guards, who seemed too lax about who was coming and going. Certainly they would be expecting guests, and the Maeda family was well-known here.

Emmi remembered snatches of the stories about how the Maeda had held court rank since before the days of the first Tokugawa shogun. They'd married into the Tokugawa family on a regular basis ever since and of course had ties to the Imperial family.

Soon the enormity of this evening finally hit her. Certain behavior and etiquette would be expected, and she hadn't a clue as to the intricacies of what that might be. Meticulous details and ceremonies seemed bred in the Japanese blood, and Emmi suddenly felt doomed.

Utterly doomed.

Maybe she should have let them put that black gunk on her teeth after all…

Then again, if blackened teeth were that big a deal, Takehito would have said something before they left. Wouldn't he?

* * * *

They didn't get out as soon as they entered the main gate but were carried farther, through a half-dozen different gates and past a dozen groups of buildings before they finally stopped. She felt guilty at the sight of those palanquin bearers, who looked utterly exhausted, and she hoped they were now trotting off to rest and get some food or something.

The bowing and scraping of the palace guys who soon greeted them bothered Emmi, and she wondered how her ancestors could deal with it as if it was so normal. Of course, to them it was normal. They had been near royalty and would be accustomed to the ado. Emmi would have sighed or groaned if she could breathe better.

Instead she listened and tried to make out what was being said. Thankfully Takehito spoke to her a bit more slowly when he pointed to yet another set of buildings with an entrance gate not far from where she stood.

"While I have the audience with the emperor, you and Sadanori will wait here inside the prince's residence. There will no doubt be food and entertainments offered."

Emmi smiled and nodded, not wanting to open her mouth because something stupid was certain to come out. As Emmi followed the fawning courtiers and her "cousin" into the main building, she was very thankful for the whole "women should be seen and not heard" concept, which would have driven her crazy in her own time.

While she tried not to be a typical gawking tourist, it was difficult. The place was unreal. The painted scenes on the walls and doors and the gold-trimmed lacquer of the cabinets and tables took her breath away. They passed rooms with new tatami mats that smelled of fresh, sun-drenched grass. The scent mingled with the scent of flowers drifting through the doors that opened into the garden areas. As far as palaces went, this was a nice one.

After dinner, courtly women entertained with the same dance that Emmi had watched actresses practicing for the movie. The few times that Emmi was spoken to, she managed to respond with a few quiet yeses, polite nods and close-lipped smiles. She decided that the minute they got out of there, she'd give Sadanori a big, tight hug to thank him for frequently turning the conversation away from her.

Soon, however, her familial savior was snatched away by one of those bowing and scraping crowd who said that Takehito requested his presence immediately. His presence, not hers.

She wasn't sure how long it was after Sadanori left that the courtiers surrounding her decided to move on to the evening's next entertainment, but they bowed and scraped and invited her along.

Emmi wasn't quite sure how she did it, but she managed to give them the slip. She lagged at the back of the group as they wound through the corridors and rooms of the large princely residence, then ducked through a partially opened door. Sliding it shut as softly as possible, Emmi breathed a small sigh of relief.

Relief that was blown away the instant Emmi realized she might just be left behind when her ancestors headed home. They wouldn't do that, would they? No, they'd notice she was gone and look for her. Then she could play dumb or say she'd suddenly felt ill and needed to find a quiet room to rest.

"Hello."

Emmi jumped at the sound of the quiet child's voice behind her. Where the heck did that kid come from? There was only one door here, and she was facing it.

"Hello."

"Are you new here?"

"Yes. I came with my — uncle."

He nodded, and Emmi couldn't get over the feeling that he seemed so sad, almost as if he were as lost in this time and place as she was.

"Do you know Kae-san? Have you seen him? I thought he might play a game with me."

Kae-san? Did he say Kae-san, as in Kaemon?

"I know someone named Kaemon, but I haven't seen him here —" Emmi turned toward the closed door as the sounds of muffled voices and feet quickly padding along the corridor became louder. She turned around to look at the boy, but he'd gone as mysteriously as he'd appeared.

Emmi turned back to the door when it opened, and one of those courtiers on the other side recognized her. Emmi looked down and muttered, "I lost my way. Forgive me."

She was escorted to the room where Takehito and his son were. They didn't look too upset that Emmi had disappeared. In fact, Takehito looked rather happy. No doubt he and the emperor had tossed back a few cups of good sake.

* * * *

The minute they returned to Katsura Villa, Emmi hurried to her room to get out of the silky salami costume and wash the poisonous white gunk off her face. She decided not to bother messing with her hair just then, as it had a bunch of thick, greasy gunk in it to keep it all in place. If the other women of this time could sleep with it in their hair all the time, she might be able to stand one night.

By the time Emmi had finished washing and changing, it was dark. She went to the room that led out to the moon-viewing platform and looked up at the clear night sky. She was wondering if she'd ever see a twenty-first-century sky again when Takehito came in behind her.

"I have a gift for you, Em-chan."

"A gift? For me? But why?" Emmi asked, taking the large, silk-wrapped bundle. She set the bundle on her lap. "You don't have to do this. I didn't do anything to deserve a gift from you."

He sat opposite her and smiled indulgently. Obviously she was being clueless, from the look on his face. She waited for him to feed her the much-needed clue.

"It is a gift from Nakagawa no miya-sama."

"Nakagawa… You mean from Kae?"

"Yes."

"Oh. Oh." Emmi was almost afraid to open it, but she did. It was a length of deep blue silk decorated with gleaming silver embroidery, depicting cranes and chrysanthemums — the prettiest she'd ever seen. "This is beautiful." She looked up, totally confused. "Why did Kae send me this?"

"To formalize the marriage contract Sadanori made for you tonight. I have already sent a gift in return."

The words took a while to sink in, as if the lead makeup and the lack of oxygen from the fancy kimono had stolen her faculties.

"Wait. Your son, who is younger than I am, made a marriage contract tonight? For me? With Kae?"

Takehito stood. "Not with him directly, of course, but with his father's representative. You will be married as soon as the proper arrangements can be made."

He left just as that additional nugget sank into her numbed brain.

But as soon as her brain processed it all, Emmi tore out of the room to confront Takehito and tell him that whatever insane agreements his son made were off.

At least, that was the plan.

When she caught up to him, she began babbling in a mixture of Japanese and English. "I can't do this! Your son had no right! I can't get married! I don't belong here! I have college to go to!"

He gave her a "don't screw with me on this" look in reply, and when he spoke Takehito's voice, though low and calm, carried the same silencing power as his expression.

"You should be honored that a man such as Prince Asahiko has seen fit to agree to this union for his son. I will not allow you to disgrace us by trying to refuse. It has been decided. You have no say in the matter."

Emmi opened her mouth and tried to plead her case but ended up standing there like a dumbfounded idiot for a long time. When Takehito turned his back and walked away, she trudged back out to the moon-viewing platform and plopped down. Looking up at the sky, she noticed that the moon looked a lot like the smirking grin of the Cheshire Cat in *Alice in Wonderland*.

"Go ahead and laugh. You don't have to get married," she muttered to no one in particular.

But you're marrying Kaemon, remember? some traitorous part of her said.

Okay, so maybe it wouldn't be a total disaster.

Of all the things that could happen to her here, if marriage to a hot samurai was the worst she faced, then she'd made out all right, all things considered.

Chapter Twenty-Four

As the days passed, Emmi thought often of her parents, especially her mother, who 'had a thing' for weddings. When she and some of her friends would get together at the house, someone always brought up the latest big celebrity or society wedding. Growing up with so much wedding talk, so much dissection of the high and low points, Emmi realized that she'd developed certain expectations about her own wedding—all of which were shot to hell, considering her current situation.

The biggest thing she'd never have dreamed in a million years was having to go to the Imperial Palace every day, bright and early, to be "Groomed in the Ways of the Court." It might have been fun—or at least interesting—if she actually got to see Kae during some of that time. Even when she did see him, it was only glimpses of him disappearing around corners or walking with his father.

Would it have killed him to seek her out and say hello just once?

With no way to confirm her suspicions, Emmi decided he spent his days off doing who knew what, who knew where, and most likely with that Aneko wench. All the while, she was stuck with a bunch of giggly women with black gunk on their teeth, which caused her to keep her mouth shut as tightly as possible at all times for fear they'd try to indoctrinate her into the Bizarre Dental Hygiene Society.

Emmi didn't try to keep her mouth shut around her "teacher," one Kojima Toshimasa. She was having trouble with some of the language, since what they spoke at court was even further away from the old-version Japanese she'd been hearing since she'd landed here. Still, the fact that she only understood eighty percent of what Kojima-san said really wasn't so bad, because he had the sexiest voice she'd ever heard.

She never would have admitted that to her family or Jake, though, because this guy was almost old enough to be her father, but with that voice and those eyes of his... If he'd been younger, he would have been giving Kaemon a run in the popularity polls. As it was, he seemed to be a hit with the bad-dental-hygiene ladies. They became even gigglier from the time he appeared until he dispatched them to do whatever it was he sent them off to do.

Then he commenced with Emmi's endless lessons. The lessons consisted mainly of where she could go within the compound, what she could do and when she could do it. There were all sorts of schedules for ceremonies, entertainment and meals, and Emmi wondered if that was part of the reason Kae was always off somewhere. That was the happier alternative for her fiancé's absence, much better than thinking he was with that Aneko.

The current reality was that Emmi was still an outsider who couldn't get involved with any of the ceremonial or social activities, at least in this phase of her Almost Princessness. Nevertheless, Kojima-san was a pleasant diversion. He'd take Emmi to walk with him as he lectured, and sometimes he'd cancel class and let her spend time alone in the gardens, which sort reminded her of home. Sort of.

When Emmi wasn't being lectured to or sitting around watching moss grow on pond rocks — or wondering what Kae was up to and with whom — she was being fussed over by seamstresses and used as a living mannequin for bolts of silk. It was beautiful silk, and Emmi had pangs of guilt that they might be billing Takehito for all this.

One day while Kojima-san and Emmi were out walking he said, "The time is right."

"The time is right?"

Kojima-san smiled. He also had a drop-dead gorgeous smile, the best she'd ever seen, even sexier than Kae's.

"The yin-yang diviners have been consulted and have decided that all signs are favorable for the wedding to take place."

He said more that Emmi couldn't quite make out, mostly because her head was spinning with the whole diviners, good signs and omen talk. He sounded like one of those freaky friends her mom knew from Venice Beach. They were old college friends, and Emmi never could figure out how her socially conscious mother hooked up with them at all. Still, she was sure they were the ones who'd brought up that oni nonsense in the first place.

"I am almost sorry the time has come, Emiko."

All Emmi's thoughts skidded to a halt. "What?"

Kojima-san laughed that low, sexy laugh of his and looked at her with those gleaming, dark eyes that made her feel all fluttery inside. "I must confess that I envy Kae-san, and I fear he has no idea of the Perfect...fragile...blossom...he has acquired..."

"Um..."

When he said '*Perfect...Fragile...Blossom*', he closed the fan he'd been holding and slid it down the side of her face. The lacquered wood felt so cool, and her face suddenly felt so hot.

"He is a most fortunate boy," Kojima-san continued in that sexy tone of his.

Was he stepping closer? And when had they walked into this secluded, wooded part of the palace complex? Emmi didn't know and really didn't care just then.

"A Most. Fortunate. Man," Kojima repeated. He touched Emmi with the fan again, this time gliding it down the side of her neck, along her shoulder, then down her upper arm.

She shivered.

He smiled.

He was so close now — close enough to kiss — and Emmi did want to kiss him. Kae, her mind reminded her, she wanted to kiss Kae. She took a deep breath and held it, for a long time.

Kojima-san backed off a pace or two, though his eyes never left hers.

"Kae-san is a fine young man, of course, but it's rather a shame you aren't being married to a more experienced, worldly man."

He gestured for Emmi to follow him back to the palace proper, and she trailed along behind him, not unlike an obedient puppy.

Was he coming on to her? He was! Was he taking her inside to try to seduce her? She wasn't falling for that, but what if he tried anyway? Could she fight him off? Should she make a run for it now? Where would she go? Should she hide? Where could she hide? There were a lot of buildings, but she hadn't been in them.

Emmi's thoughts were still flowing like a raging river when Kojima left her at the entrance to the building where the blackened-teeth ladies hung out. He then went on his way without so much as a word.

Damn, that was close.

Where was that damned alleged fiancé of hers when she needed him?

* * * *

During those weeks, when she had time alone at the palace, Emmi often saw that kid who'd appeared and disappeared the first time she'd been there with Takehito and Sadanori. The little rat refused to tell her his name, though. All he said was, "Everyone here knows."

Emmi decided that this was akin to one of those Hollywood things where if you were *somebody* you'd be on the inside track with such info, and since she was an outsider she didn't matter.

She assumed he was some courtier's son who was also left alone in between lessons as she was. Most of the time he was sort of there one minute, gone the next, but one day after Kojima-san's come-on, the mystery boy popped out of nowhere again. He and Emmi started talking.

She was sitting near the man-made lake, trying to practice her calligraphy and poetry-writing skills — apparently things that were required of a 'court lady' — when the mystery kid appeared behind her. He read over her shoulder, pointing out her messy handwriting and bad poetry.

Emmi very much wanted to tell him that writing with a brush and an ink stone was not the gel pen she was used to, but she couldn't.

"I'm not experienced in writing *waka*. I have to keep stopping to count the syllables to make sure I have thirty-one exactly."

"But it is very easy."

"Not for me."

"It is for me," he said with a typical "pain in the butt" kid grin.

"Then maybe I should get you to write mine for me, so I get praise from Kojima-san, instead of criticism."

"No."

It was so simple, yet said with a tone so high and mighty, so authoritative, that Emmi had to laugh.

"You will marry Kaemon?"

"I'm supposed to."

He nodded. "Do you have many friends? I have only one."

The way he said "only one" was so matter-of-fact, so sad, that it made Emmi think of how alone she felt here sometimes.

"I suppose Kae and I will live here. I can be your friend too."

Emmi tried not to listen to the part of her mind that kept chanting — *Marrying Kae means you have that whole*

Wedding Night thing to look forward to. You have to do like in those old movies and do your 'Wifely Duty'. Every night.

No. She was not going to go there. Well, she wasn't going to think about it right now, anyway.

"I would like you for a friend," the boy said.

Thankfully, his voice silenced the partying slut in the back of Emmi's mind.

"Would you play games with me? Do you play Go?"

Emmi smiled. That ancient checkers-like game was one thing she definitely could do. "Yes, and I will beat you."

"You are not allowed."

"Watch me—"

Emmi was interrupted by the sound of Kojima-san's voice in the distance calling her name. She stood to see where he was coming from. When she turned back to tell her smart-alecky new friend she had to postpone the game, he was already gone. *Maybe the kid really was the son of a super-secret ninja.*

She was straightening her scrolls and writing things when Kojima-san came up beside her. He bent down to help her gather up her calligraphy brushes and put them in their lacquered box. As he helped, his hand brushed across hers, and she jumped. *Oh God, not the flirting again.*

"Forgive me, Emiko."

"No need to apologize," she muttered.

With her brush box and scrolls clutched to her chest, she looked at Kojima and waited for him to lead the way. But he didn't. He just stood there and looked at her.

He looked at her with those dark eyes that had hypnotized her from the get-go. Her hand tingled and burned a bit where he'd bumped her, but it wasn't a bad feeling by any means. He was an older guy, but he was dead-on sexy.

"May I be forward, Emiko, and ask if you'd like to have tea with me before you return to the villa?"

He smiled. It was only a hint of a smile, but it was incredible.

And she was lonely.

"I'd like that."

Kojima could have been giving her the secrets of the universe in with the small talk over tea and pastries, but Emmi wasn't really paying attention. Instead she let herself be hypnotized by that deep, velvety voice and the way he looked at her, the way Kae had looked at her that night at that teahouse.

However Emmi did notice when Kojima sent the serving girl away and poured the next cup of tea for her personally. He handed it to Emmi, and she was positive it was deliberate when his fingers touched hers.

And lingered there, and sort of brushed against hers in a way that sent weird, hot shivers through her.

She was way too lonely these days...and also more than a little horny. Damn.

"I will miss our lessons together, Emiko, and I wish you to know that I will always be available to assist you in the future with any questions you may have on etiquette and what is required of you here."

"Thank you."

"No, Emiko. I. Thank. You. You have brought a breath of fresh air to this musty, ancient palace."

He smiled, and Emmi was certain the room's temperature shot up a good ten degrees.

"I want to fit in here," she said, even though part of her wanted to cry because she mostly just wanted to go home where she belonged. She wanted to be where she knew what was what and how to behave, to be where no dumb mistake might get her killed for being a spy or worse.

Kojima-san's fan was suddenly on her chin, gently lifting her head. He looked at her, those sexy eyes of his full of concern. So much concern Emmi had to force herself not to lunge at him and hug him tight just to feel safe and secure. God but she was a pathetic, needy thing these days. Those women with the blackened teeth were a bad influence.

"Tell me. What is troubling you?"

Emmi shook her head. "Nothing. I'm just nervous about the wedding."

He nodded. "I see." He leaned across the small table. "Emiko. I wish you to consider me a friend. A. Close. Friend. I am here for you."

"I'll remember that."

She would also remember to stay as far away from this seductive older man as she could once she was stuck at the palace all day, every day.

But you'll also be stuck with Kae... As his wife... Maybe in his bed most of the day.

* * * *

Kae was the last person Emmi expected to run into when she returned to Katsura Villa following her semi-flirtatious tea. She was avoiding her room, where the dressmakers were waiting to use her as a mannequin again, when she came upon Kae talking to Takehito.

Takehito made a quick exit, even though she didn't want him to go.

For two people who were getting married, it was a strange meeting. Emmi stared at Kae, he stared at her, and neither of them said anything.

Until he decided to drop a bombshell.

"You know that the wedding takes place the day after tomorrow?"

"I know now. All I was told was, '*The time. Is right.*'"

She thought he muttered Kojima's name and the Japanese equivalent of asshole, but she wasn't sure.

"So, how have you been?" she asked with a bright smile as she folded her arms into her wide kimono sleeves in an effort not to throw herself at him He only stared in return, and she hoped he couldn't read her thoughts as lurid, trashy old movie posters flashed through her mind. *I Married a Nympho…*

"I have been busy," he said simply, leaving far too much unsaid for Emmi's imagination to run with.

Emmi cleared her throat. "I've also been busy learning all about complicated and boring court customs and practicing my calligraphy and poetry that I hate practicing. But I did make a new friend —"

"Stay away from Kojima."

She stared at Kae. "Excuse me?"

"Kojima Toshimasa is no friend to me. He can be no friend to you. I will not allow it."

"You won't allow it?" She laughed. "And who do you think you are to tell me who can and cannot be my friend?"

"Your husband. You will belong to me. You will do what I tell you to do."

Emmi put her hands on her hips, or where her hips should have been under all that padding. "You think I'll do what you tell me, when you tell me, just because you told me to?"

Um, Em, her common sense whispered in her head. *This is 1864 Japan. He will 'own' you, and you will have to do what he says or he could have you imprisoned or killed.*

He wouldn't do that. He liked her. He more than liked her. After all, he'd agreed to this arranged marriage.

Agreed. Right. His father had undoubtedly told him the marriage was a done deal the way Takehito had told her.

She was doomed.

Emmi opened her mouth to say something, to try to make peace with him, but it was too late. Kae had turned and quickly disappeared down the corridor.

With a sigh, she decided that being a mannequin for an hour or two was better than worrying about her pathetic new life, so she trudged back to her room.

* * * *

For Emmi's 'Royal Wedding' there was no golden, horse-drawn carriage, but there was a pretty, painted palanquin. While there was no gown and veil trailing far behind her, she did get to be sausage-stuffed into layers of rich silk that weighed a good twenty pounds.

First there was an under kimono, then a hakama skirt that seemed four feet too long, leaving her feet around where a giant's knees would be. How she was supposed to walk in this thing was anybody's guess. Already she could hardly stand without feeling tangled, but the ancient lady helping her dress added yet another robe then the kimono with multiple half-layers that were sewn together to look like five complete kimono stacked one inside the other next.

Then another one with long, wide sleeves and finally the heaviest, white kimono.

Emmi also had copious amounts of sticky, greasy gunk in her hair so the maids could give her the traditional perfect wedding hairstyle, complete with a lot of tortoiseshell sticks and combs that made her look like some spiky-headed evil goddess.

She looked much nicer than she had for the movie scene, but was it really necessary to put greasy stuff in her hair that was not going to wash out without decent shampoos? They were just going to shove a gigantic white hood on her to cover it all up.

As she made her slow, stuffed-sausage way to the palanquin, the old school hair gel kept the combs and hood from slipping over her eyes, so she decided it wasn't that bad. Walking, however, was still a pain in the ass, and she prayed she wouldn't fall on the skirt that was trailing under her feet.

Takehito and his son were at the waiting palanquin, all smiles and dressed in their equally uncomfortable-looking, court-appropriate attire with the weird little hats.

A wave of sadness hit Emmi as she looked into Takehito's eyes and sort of saw her father there. Part of her girlish wedding fantasies had always revolved around his bright smile as he walked her down a long aisle. She managed not to cry, mainly because it would have left big tear streaks cutting through the Goth-white makeup that the maids had plastered on her face.

They arrived at the palace. Countless bowing and scraping men greeted them before ushering Emmi into a room with a gaggle of chattering court ladies to await the "big moment." It freaked her out to notice that they all had that nasty black crud on their teeth. She was not going to go there, and there was no way Kae was going to make her.

So you think, that slutty part of her brain snickered just before it chose to conjure up a memory of that one night in the teahouse. All right, he probably could talk her into just about anything if he touched her as he had then...

Tonight's the night, baby!

The whole wedding-night-to-be suddenly felt awfully daunting, but she wasn't able to dwell on it. The women became excited when a servant came in with a message. They ushered her toward a small room that seemed to be a half mile away.

Kae was already there. He had his back to her but then slowly turned. While the majority of men present looked rather dorky, he was actually hot in his black and white court outfit. He even made the little hat with the ribbon tail look good. He watched Emmi as she *slowly* made her way in the overly long skirt to kneel beside him. Within seconds, however, he turned his head to stare at the far wall, and a part of her withered away.

While Emmi's family kept close to their Japanese heritage, her cousins' weddings, both in California and Hawaii, had been very Westernized, with the exchange of rings and I do's and the whole nine yards.

But here she and Kae had a girl all of eighteen, who was definitely giving Kae the eye, as if she wanted him for herself. The girl took a small handleless cup, poured sake in it, then gave it to Kae. She refilled it and gave it to Emmi. They did that twice more and the ceremony was over.

No I do. No ring. And certainly no big kiss at the end.

However, they did have something of a reception. After the sake drinking, Kae led the way into a room that was the size of a basketball court. Takehito, his son and Kae's father were there. The bowing and scraping guys who had greeted Emmi when she first arrived were all there as well, along with many unfamiliar faces and one very familiar, friendly one.

It was Kojima-san, and he bowed his head and smiled at Emmi. She smiled back, almost hypnotized by the way he watched her. His stare was even more drop-dead sexy than she remembered.

Up at the front of the room was a low platform with a bamboo curtain pulled almost to the floor. Someone was behind it. A man, it seemed to be, and Emmi realized who it was — the emperor.

Finally it all hit her through the pleasant fog of the fine sake that she'd so quickly consumed. This was really real. She was married, and to a real live prince of all people.

She followed Kae to the empty place at the back of the room, and after lot of breath holding and slow movements, she managed not to tangle her legs in the long hakama. She was able to kneel beside him on one of the large cushions that faced out to the guests who were seated along each side of the room.

All eyes were upon them as they sat together. Takehito smiled. Kae's father smiled. Emmi returned their smiles and was certain that behind the shadowy screen even the emperor smiled. Everyone smiled.

Everyone except Kae. He stared into the big empty space at the center of the room, looking like a guy who'd rather be any place but there and with anyone but her.

Chapter Twenty-Five

Emmi wished this wedding reception was similar to ones back home, where the bride and groom could mingle with their guests. Instead she was stuck, kneeling next to Kae, who struck up conversations with everyone except her.

Her only entertainment was being allowed to change clothes a few times. The ladies-in-waiting ushered her off to change, then she was ushered back to the same reception room and plunked down again and again beside the same cold-as-ice Kae. To make matters worse, she wasn't able to dress in anything more comfortable. Well, she was able to ditch the ridiculously long hakama at the last change.

The long day's one saving grace was that, as the sake flowed, the rules broke down a bit, particularly after the emperor went to wherever emperors spent their time. Takehito and Sadanori came to sit near her, shared a drink or three, and expounded on what a great day this was for the Maeda and how proud and happy they were for her.

That makes two of you, she thought as she watched Kae, laughing with some men who she guessed were his friends, and that babe who'd poured the ceremonial wedding sake. She was right there, pouring for all the men in the group, letting her fingers brush against theirs and batting her eyes like it was an accident.

When Takehito and Sadanori moved off to talk to other people Emmi was left alone, which reminded her of her first few weeks in high school. None of her friends had gone to the private school where her parents had enrolled her. The other freshmen had been together all through junior high. She'd been a class of one. She'd hated it then, and she hated it now that her new life as a princess by marriage was proving much the same.

Who could she strike up a conversation with, and hopefully become friends with, here?

"Such a beautiful bride you are, Emiko."

Emmi pulled herself out of her pity party and looked over to Kojima-san. "Thank you."

"Do not thank me for speaking the truth." He poured her a cup of sake. "I look forward to having many more enjoyable conversations with you as we've had these past weeks." He stared at her with those hypnotizing eyes while that silky-smooth deep voice of his wrapped itself around her lonely heart. "I look forward to it."

"Me, too —" She stopped short when she was tugged from behind.

"Emiko, it is time to leave," Kae said in a commanding, flat tone.

Of course it was time to go. It was time to go because she was finally having fun with her very own friend!

This arranged marriage thing, being the obedient wife, was going to be quite the royal pain the ass, but she was stuck. Literally stuck, she realized, in a tangle of kimono and numbed ankles from being in the kneeling seiza position for so long.

Suddenly Kojima was gone, and Kae was giving her an Evil Glare of Doom and tugging on her sleeve.

"If you help me stand, I will," she grumbled.

With a scowl, he pulled her up and brought home the intoxicating power packed into those many sips of sake. Who'd have thought such tiny cups could contain so much alcohol? The room lurched to a crazy angle. She had to clutch Kae's arm and let him lead her to the corridor.

Her inner slut partied in the far reaches of her brain, shouting giddily, *Woohoo! This is it, girlfriend! The Wedding Night Thing is happening!*

Or not, her inner slut observed when Kae turned her over to a couple of older ladies-in-waiting. They hustled her through this corridor and that corridor, then outside and into another building, through more corridors, and finally into a big room with fancy painted screens and gold–trimmed lacquered cabinets. Inside, the abundance of spicy incense made her sneeze.

She was only vaguely aware of their constant chatter as they pulled her out of the layers of silk and padding. That part she appreciated. She also appreciated the fact that they allowed her to wash the deadly lead-based makeup from her face.

While she was scrubbing away, someone came in with a tray of tea things and a plate of small sugar cakes and rice balls. They set the pot of hot water on the metal warmer off to the side of the table before scurrying away like cartoon mice.

Emmi laughed. They weren't like cartoon mice. This was Japan. They were anime mice with big, big eyes, little noses, short LoliGoth skirts and big boobs.

Laughing harder, she lifted this latest kimono up a bit and plopped down cross-legged on one of the soft floor cushions. She munched a rice ball and enjoyed feeling tipsy. She felt better now that she was out of all that stuff, excluding the greasy hair gunk that she wasn't ready to think about just now. This kimono was very nice. It was light and simple without the overly long sleeves she'd been wearing recently. She felt so much lighter and freer just being naked under this...

Her underwear—whatever happened to her underwear from home? Kae had done something with the bra and panties after that night in the teahouse, but he'd never given them back.

A thoroughly crazy idea hit her. It couldn't be, could it? Was he some nineteenth-century cross-dresser? Did they even have cross-dressers in the nineteenth century? Not counting the Kabuki theater, of course. Emmi continued to munch her rice ball and let her tipsy brain conjure images of Kae in her lingerie. She laughed. A lot.

Maybe she was a bit more than just tipsy from the sake.

Kae dismissed the servants who'd come to tend him. He shed the ridiculous court costume, slipped into a simple yukata and stretched out on his futon, or rather, one of the two new futons that had been placed side by side in his bedroom.

The sound of Emmi's laughter drifted to him through the papered walls separating their rooms. She'd been so beautiful today, so graceful and noble, as if she'd been born a princess. But she hadn't. She hadn't even been born in Japan. She hadn't even been born into the same world that he had.

He knew now that she wasn't an oni, or a potential spy, or even the orphaned niece of the Maeda lord. Takehito had told him the truth, as unbelievable as it was. It had to be truth, the man was no fool. And he wouldn't tell such a tale lightly. It might very well have him branded as insane or a barbarian sorcerer.

Emmi was of Maeda blood, but she would not be born into their family for well over a century. She had come from the mirror. Somehow she had slipped through the barriers of time, and he had saved her from a certain death by fire in the "modern" Kyoto from which she'd come.

His father had no idea of the truth and never would if Kae could help it. He'd arranged this marriage to bring money to his own family and to help strengthen *kobu gattai* — the ties between court and state — much in the way the marriage of the emperor's sister to the shogun had been designed to unite the aristocratic and military powers.

But Takehito had agreed to it solely to protect one lost girl who carried the blood of Maeda samurai in her veins.

How could he not believe the older man who'd prostrated himself on the floor and begged him to marry Emmi, to keep her safe in the ensuing civil war they both knew was lurking just on the horizon of Japan's future?

'I know as surely as I know my own heart that my brother will drag us into the thick of it to support his rebel friends. My retainers and I will commit seppuku before we follow him on that path, but I can't ask Emiko to do the same. I beg you to agree to this union. With you, as a member of the court and your father's house, she will be safe no matter the outcome. And, perhaps you can help her return to where she belongs...'

The soft sound of a sliding wall panel brought Kae from his thoughts, and his hand went at once to the sword tucked under the futon's edge. When he realized who the intruder was, he sat up and bowed deeply before speaking.

"You honor me with such a late visit, my prince. Are you having another sleepless night?"

Crown Prince Mutsuhito, who still liked to be called by his earlier name of Sachi, plopped onto the empty futon as any child might and shrugged.

"Where is your new wife?"

"In the next room, changing and dressing for bed."

Sachi grinned. "Will you still have many mistresses like my father? Will you take turns with them sharing your bed?"

"I don't have mistresses. I am too busy helping my father gather information to better advise yours."

"Will you and Emiko have many children? Will they be my friends?"

"My children would be as honored as I am to be considered your friends."

"Emiko said she would be my friend."

"You've met her? Through Kojima-san?"

Sachi frowned at the mention of the snakelike courtier, and Kae hoped his opinion would remain the same when it was his time to ascend the throne.

"No, I met her in the park. She was writing bad poetry. I told her you were my only friend, and she said she would be my friend too."

Kae smiled at the mention of bad poetry. He would have to see some of this for himself. His smile faded.

"Emiko is not yet well versed in the ways of the court. I respectfully ask that you excuse any small lapses in etiquette that may occur."

Sachi shrugged and got up. "She seems kind. I will let her be my friend."

Kae bowed again, and the prince disappeared once more into the secret passage.

Lying back down, Kae wondered if Emmi had any idea who Sachi was. He should tell her. Then again, perhaps not. If she knew he was the emperor's heir, it might make her nervous, which might cause her to make potentially fatal mistakes of protocol. She needed to fit in here as much as possible. He would simply tell her that it was important to show everyone the proper respect, no matter how young that person might be.

He smiled to himself. So she wrote bad poetry, did she? Did she write bad poetry about him?

Remembering the gift he had for her, Kae got up and went to the four-drawer chest across the room. He removed a cloth-wrapped package and untied it. Inside were the strange undergarments that belonged to Emmi as well as similar silk ones he'd had made. The seamstress hadn't been able to duplicate the strange, delicate metal fastenings on the top piece, so she'd used silk string ties instead. In the absence of the unusual, clingy, stretchy material that the originals used, she'd used more silk ties as well.

He set the package on her futon then went to the shoji separating their rooms. He slid it open, laughing softly when he saw her asleep before the table, bits of sugared cake stuck to her delicate chin.

* * * *

Kojima-san's eyes and voice were hypnotizing. Emmi shivered with delight from the touch of his fan on her shoulder. She murmured when he touched the fan to the skin showing at the vee of her yukata front then giggled when he playfully kissed her chin.

"That tickles. You shouldn't. What will people say?"

"They will say nothing because I am your husband and this is my right."

Hello! Emmi's brain screamed through the alcohol fog cluttering her dozing mind. *That sexy voice was not Kojima's!*

Her eyes shot open and she sat up, bumping Kae's nose hard with her head. "I'm sorry! I was dreaming! Are you okay?"

He nodded, blinked a few times and rubbed his nose, wincing as he did so.

She stared at him and hoped that it wasn't broken, that blood wouldn't start gushing out of his nose. He had a straight nose, and she didn't want to be responsible for screwing it up. And she couldn't forget those cheekbones that led down to a strong chin. And nice eyes too. Not as hypnotizing as Kojima-san's but still fantastic—an intense dark brown with faint flecks of gold in them.

And don't forget how good his mouth feels…

"Emmi," he said softly, his hands resting lightly on her shoulders. He pulled her to him, leaned in for a soft, slow kiss. It made her hot and shivery all at once.

When the kiss ended he stood and pulled her up with him. The sake from earlier hit her all over again and the room went one way while she went another. She practically collapsed, but Kae grabbed her. He wrapped those strong arms of his around her and scooped her up as though she were nothing. He carried her into another room and laid her down on a thick, cushy futon. He slid something out of the way then lay beside her.

Kae looked so gorgeous in the soft glow of the floor lantern, and she kept her gaze focused on his. She placed her hand atop his as he caressed the side of her face.

"I will care for you, Emiko. I will protect you. I will help you go home."

"I don't want to go anywhere," she said, pulling him down for another kiss.

God, but he was an amazing kisser. His kiss was possessive and fierce, yet he was tender in the way he stroked his tongue across hers. As he loosened the thin belt closing her yukata and slid his hands over her flushed skin, she knew he wasn't going to stop. And she certainly didn't want him to.

She was nervous, but it was a good fear, an exciting fright that she was more than willing to experience. And what an experience it was.

The slutty part of Emmi's brain was thoroughly sated and silent when Kae moved off her and cradled her in his arms. Emmi let the pleasant exhaustion, including the effects of the long day and many cups of sake, relax her into a drowsy state. She realized that, for the very first time in her life, everything was perfect, absolutely perfect.

She'd been an idiot to be so afraid. Whatever was responsible for her blast into the past had been a good thing, a great thing, and nothing could spoil it. Not now.

Chapter Twenty-Six

A light but noticeable ache behind her eyes greeted Emmi when she woke, alone. The pain in her head gave her a sharp nudge and she closed her eyes again a moment before a familiar voice teased her.

"The sleeping beauty awakens as in the foreign folk tale," Kae said with a grin as he stepped in from an adjoining room that she hadn't yet entered.

She sat up and gave Kae a smile. "Something like that."

He smiled back as he came closer, his look more intense than it had been the night before. Despite the ache behind her eyes, Emmi was ready to let Kae lead her into anything at all.

Unfortunately he didn't lead anywhere, because he all but ignored her. He finished getting dressed and pulled his damp hair up into a ponytail. Emmi pouted. He should have woken her up, too. She might have enjoyed a nice bath together so she could see if underwater sex really was extra hot.

When he took his swords and slid them into his belt, Emmi felt her pout turn to a frown. "Are you going somewhere?"

"I have work to do," he said.

"But not all day. Just for a while, yes?"

He gave her a questioning look.

She looked around for her yukata and pulled it on. "What am I supposed to do?"

"Not get into any trouble. Call no attention to yourself."

He was gone before Emmi could think of a snarky reply through her growing headache. The next thing she knew, the older ladies-in-waiting came in. One went to the tansu cabinet where clothing was kept, while the other started clearing the rumpled bed things.

"Wait," Emmi said when the woman pulling up the blanket grabbed a small, tied bundle. Emmi took the cloth packet and opened it. It was her underwear and more bras and panties.

Not modern lingerie, of course. These looked a bit like string bikinis. They were made from silk, the primo silk like her wedding clothes. One set was ivory, another pale blue, one purple and the last cotton candy pink. The panties had little Maeda family crests embroidered on the front that matched the ones stitched into the bra cups just below the ties. The older women were staring, and Emmi wrapped the lingerie and shoved it into one of the tansu drawers. She took her Victoria's Secret clearance set and muttered that it was part of a "Kaga marriage custom."

One of the women seemed about to question her, but thankfully another lady came to escort Emmi to the private bathhouse. She felt weird with someone helping her bathe, but was glad for the help when it came time to wash her hair. She didn't even mind that the woman tugged hard with a wooden comb to get out the tangles. After all, she'd been ordered not to get into trouble or draw attention to herself, and this was all she had to look forward to.

Apparently the sense of perfection that she'd felt last night had been nothing but a fleeting dream.

When she returned from her bath, Emmi tried very hard not to behave like some difficult Hollywood diva. She struggled to follow Kae's advice and not draw attention to herself.

But the headache was still nagging at her, and she didn't want to be weighed down in twenty layers of kimono and that ridiculous long skirt. She was certainly not in the mood to get more greasy goop dumped in her hair, or let them totally pluck away her eyebrows and plaster that deadly Goth makeup on her face again.

Even if it was customary for married women to do it, no way would she bring herself to put that stinky black crap on her teeth. The ladies-in-waiting seemed pissed, though they didn't say anything. They simply bowed and left, quietly muttering among themselves, and Emmi hoped this wasn't going to cause some great ruckus with Kae.

Yes, this world was very different from the one she was used to, but she couldn't change who she was. If being stuck here meant having her entire personality crushed, then what was the point? She'd just as well just curl up under a rock and die.

Heaving a defeated sigh, she sank down onto one of the thick floor cushions. Total boredom settled in shortly thereafter with only the painted folding screen and the ikebana flower arrangement there to occupy her attention. She refused to think about the nice, thick futon mattresses and how Kae made love to her. The night before seemed a long time gone, making her more aware of the sudden emptiness surrounding her.

She got up and went to the suite's main room, where a breakfast tray waited on a low table. Emmi took small bites of the smoked fish and rice and drank the tea in half sips to make the meal last as long as possible, which wasn't long at all.

The bell tolled the time. It had rung last right after Kae left that morning, and it was ringing again when she finished that last bit of rice on her tray. That was two hours of non-excitement down and way too many of more deadly boredom yet to come. What she wouldn't give for her cell phone or tablet about now.

Things picked up slightly when a maid came to take the breakfast tray away. She had a letter with her, a letter for Emmi from Takehito.

Emmi opened the letter and groaned inwardly. Takehito and Sadanori were soon heading back to Kaga. They wished her a long, happy life with Kae, and Takehito said he'd try to schedule an audience with her before they left. He had to schedule an audience? Crap. She supposed this meant she couldn't just go over to Katsura Villa to visit them for something to do.

A long, happy life with Kae. Somehow, she had a feeling that might not be the direction her life would be taking. She tucked the letter away then looked around. This room didn't have much more in the way of entertainment or distraction from boredom either, so she decided to check out the room on the other side of the bedroom, the one Kae had come from that morning.

"Excellent," she said when her gaze fell on the floor model Go board in the alcove to the right then found the row of books on the red lacquer cabinet. The thought of playing the chess-like game against herself would normally hold no appeal, but the option felt quite inviting this morning. Fabulous, her life had boiled down to playing games alone, if today was any indicator.

She pushed that depressing thought away and went to check out the books Kae owned. Great. Of course, they were in an old-style writing done by hand, which was much harder to decipher than the modern printed kanji. She leafed through the book anyway.

When she'd first arrived, he had mentioned going through "foreign" books for some governmental agency, so perhaps she'd find one contraband Western book here somewhere... Ancient kanji, ancient kanji, ancient— Oh. This last one was so not ancient kanji or even some boring English or French tome. She'd found a picture book. And what a picture book it was! It was similar to the woodblock porn she'd thrown up on at the Shinsengumi compound.

At least Kae's book wasn't totally like the miserable vice-commander's prints—it didn't contain any yaoi guy-on-guy sex. It was just good old men and women. And women and an octopus? Emmi laughed. So this was where the whole hentai squid and tentacles jokes in anime and manga came from? She winced. Those were some nasty-looking sea creatures in all senses of the word. She closed the book. Even she wasn't bored enough to look at babes with obscene seafood fetishes.

Looking at the closed *shunga* book, Emmi wondered if Kae ever sat and masturbated while looking at it. A tingle formed deep inside at the thought of watching him pleasure himself and an even more delicious tingle at the memory of having him pleasure her. True, she didn't have any experience to compare, but she was sure he would be considered one hell of a skilled lover.

She felt a twinge in her nipples, something like the type she'd get when her hormones were in overdrive before her period. When she scratched herself through her kimono, the action sent one of those electric chills down between her legs. She pressed her thighs together and fought the urge to touch herself and have her own masturbation session. It would be a nice way to pass the time, but it would be better with Kae. Besides, with her luck, one of those ladies-in-waiting would pop in, since she hadn't seen any latches on the doors.

A chill shot down Emmi's spine, and it wasn't one of those exciting sexually charged ones. This one was cold fear. 'Safe sex' was not a concept here. Kae hadn't used a condom or anything like a condom. What if that hooker friend of his had given him some foul, unseen STD? Even if she didn't get herpes or sores, she wasn't on the Pill. Pregnant was not good.

Of course, a baby made with Kae would be a cute little thing…

No. She was not going there. It was one night. It was her first time. Maybe, just maybe, nothing would happen. *But what about tonight and tomorrow and…*

Emmi screwed her eyes shut and balled her hands into fists. Thinking about all this was not doing her any good. She'd always been one to plan things out, but all she could do now was take a wait and see attitude, and pray to high heaven that she hadn't contracted anything disgusting.

She needed air. Yes, a walk should be a safe enough thing to do…if only she could remember exactly where outside was. She wished she hadn't been half drunk last night and concentrating so hard on not tripping over the layers of clothing.

She returned to the suite's main room and went out the door that the maid had used earlier. Another servant, an elderly man, came scurrying out of nowhere like a mouse coming out of his hole after a piece of cheese. He immediately fell to his knees and begged Emmi to allow him the honor of serving her. She wanted to tell him that he had the wrong Maeda here — that he was her mother's kind of butler — but of course she couldn't, so she did her best to tell him she wanted to go out for a walk.

His forehead went to the polished wood floor, he beseeched her respectfully to go back inside so he could fetch the appropriate ladies-in-waiting to assist and accompany her. Emmi touched his shoulder, mostly to get him to just stop rambling and look at her a minute, but from the way he jumped — jumped while still kneeling no less — she'd have thought she'd dumped a stinging scorpion on his back.

"I'm sorry. I want to go outside to take a walk alone. Please, just show me where the door is." *And please wait to keel over until after I leave.*

He was still shocked, but he finally got up and showed her to a long corridor lit only by the light filtered through the shoji panels that led out to the porch surrounding the building.

Freedom. Yes!

Emmi thanked him and bowed, and he scurried away again, backward, bowing the entire time until he disappeared into the shadows. Hearing no thud from him passing out, she picked up the long hem of her kimono and headed for the beauty of the flowering bushes that she could see just through the opened door at the far end of the corridor. Crap. She'd forgotten her shoes and had to go back to where the servant had set them before he took off. She was bending to pick them up when a familiar, sexy voice came from behind her.

"Kuni no miya-sama?"

Emmi stood up and looked around but didn't see anyone else besides herself and the speaker, Kojima-san. He stood just inside one of the open doors on the side of the corridor.

"Did you mean me?" she asked with a smile. And it was a big smile, because it felt great to talk with an actual person she knew. At least for a little while.

He folded his arms inside the wide sleeves of his haori and smiled. "Indeed I did, Emiko-gozen."

"Gozen?" A woman of title? The idea still seemed strange.

She felt frozen to the spot when he came closer. He unfolded his arms with a sleek, smooth motion and took his fan from his hakama belt. He smiled that killer smile and touched the tip of the fan to her cheek.

"You are so new to the world of nobility and its endless conventions that you come across as utterly naive. Charmingly so, of course."

"It isn't every day a girl marries an imperial prince."

"Indeed," he answered simply. He tucked his fan back into his belt and looked at her. "From your simple appearance, I take it that you are not going to any official meetings?"

"No. I wanted to go for a walk and get some fresh air. Getting all done up would make that a bit difficult."

"Indeed, it would." He bowed and smiled again. "If it pleases you, I would be honored to accompany you."

Emmi shivered and told herself it was because she was in a shady part of the corridor and a breeze was blowing around outside.

"I would like that very much. Thank you."

She went to the open door and dropped her shoes out onto the engawa. She held onto the doorframe to balance herself while she stepped into them.

"Please, allow me," Kojima said before kneeling beside her. He wrapped his long, strong fingers around her ankle and lifted her foot, slipped on the right sandal, then the left. He stood and gave her a questioning look.

"Is something the matter, my lady? I didn't quite hear what you said."

Emmi cleared her throat and shrugged. That whimper a second before had not come from her. That was her story, and she was going to stick with it.

"I didn't say anything."

He smiled. "Please, know that I am at your service," he said softly in that velvety voice that slid over her like a thick blanket. "You have but to whisper a command. Any. Command. And I shall do it at once."

Emmi bit her tongue. Hard. There was no way she would let that next whimper come out at all.

Chapter Twenty-Seven

Kae was exiting the building that housed the Bureau of Books and Instruments with a report for his father when he caught sight of Emmi in the distance, walking with Kojima, the courtier he hadn't trusted from the moment he'd set eyes on him.

He'd objected to his father's insistence that Kojima be retained as Emiko's teacher in composition and ways of court protocol, but he had to agree that the best way to keep track of the man's potential treachery was to keep him as close as possible. Still, Kae hated the thought of using Emmi in this way.

He tucked the scroll containing the report into his haori sleeve and proceeded to follow his wife and her escort toward the pine field. The secluded wooded area was thought to be the resort of foxes and demons who dwelt there in human form, waiting to prey on the unsuspecting. Kojima would be drawn there, wouldn't he?

* * * *

"I am surprised, Emiko," Kojima said a short time after they entered the wooded area.

"Surprised?" she asked, looking around, not quite liking how quiet it was here, how cut off from civilization it seemed. Bits of sunlight poked through the thick canopy of tall trees, but it was still creepy. She would never come out here at night alone.

"I am surprised the prince has left you unattended this morning."

He took a step into her path so Emmi had to stop. He smiled that smile that made her feel slightly gooey inside then touched the end of his folded fan to her cheek. Correction—he actually slid the edge of the fan down her cheek and the side of her neck.

"I suppose…he had things to do. He's a busy…man," she said, hoping her voice wasn't as shaky as it sounded in her ears.

With Kojima's piercing dark stare holding hers in place, he slid the fan down until it touched the top of the wide patterned obi, right around the place where the obi mashed her breasts flat.

"We are all busy men," he said before sliding the fan back up the obi, up along her neck, along the edge of her chin. "Yet, were I to have such a lovely young bride, I would see to it that she was my first priority following our wedding day. Only an event of epic and disastrous proportion could cause me to untangle myself from her arms and leave our marriage bed."

Emmi could not contain the half whimper that slid out of her mouth as thoughts of being with Kae filled her mind.

Kojima leaned in close. "The prince. Is. A. Most. Fortunate. Young man."

"We are both fortunate," she managed to say just before an angry growling sound came from behind her.

She jumped back only to see Kae with his sword drawn and his expression furious.

"Emiko. Move."

She approached Kae, despite the drawn sword. "There's no reason to be upset. I wanted to take a walk, and Kojima-san came with me."

She wasn't even sure Kae was listening. He was so focused on Kojima that it looked like he was already mentally dissecting him into a million bloody pieces in advance of doing it for real. Finally Kae's shoulders relaxed a tiny bit and he took a step back to resheathe his katana, though his murderous stare never left Kojima's face. Emmi looked down at the ground, not wanting to see that look directed at her.

Kojima remained silent and left the instant Kae barked at him to do so.

The next thing Emmi knew, Kae gripped her chin and lifted her head up.

"You are mine."

So much for being an independent twenty-first-century woman. She wasn't about to protest the pronouncement, not when he pulled her forward and kissed her long and hard. Her knees grew weak and her hormones raced as Kae backed her up against a tree. He tugged open the top of her kimono and kissed and sucked on her neck where it connected to her shoulder. She was making those whimpering sounds again and feeling so hot for him that she couldn't stand it.

She didn't care if they were out in the woods. All she cared about was having more of this.

The sound of Prince Asahiko's voice bellowing his son's name in the distance was like a bucket of ice water on them both, and Kae backed away so fast that Emmi wondered if she'd imagined the whole 'you are mine' episode.

Asahiko appeared shortly thereafter, and he and Kae had some words. Emmi couldn't make them all out because they spoke so quickly, but she gathered that Kae was on a mission or errand of some sort, and he had to get back to it ASAP. He took a scroll from his sleeve, handed it to his father, then grabbed Emmi by the arm and dragged her back to his suite of rooms. He dropped her off with a warning not to go wandering alone and to always stay far, far away from Kojima.

This time he posted two of those ladies-in-waiting in the main room to babysit her. They sat, doing some kind of embroidery, and looked at her as though she should be thrilled to join in such 'proper pursuits' — pursuits that consisted of more gossiping and snacking than actual sewing.

Emmi passed up the sewing but took part in the snacking and did her best to decipher the court gossip. She heard about all the women who were doing this, that and the other with the emperor in his private room at night. Evidently there were a lot of women in the emperor's bedtime social circle, enough to warrant an entire Bureau of Consorts to keep track of them all. Emmi felt relieved knowing Kae was not in line to become the emperor.

Unable to tolerate much more of the gossip, Emmi retired to the room with Kae's books to have a solo game of Go, since that was about all she could do for now without rousing the wrath of her nannies. She briefly considered asking if one of them wanted to play but decided that she didn't want to spend more time with either of them than necessary.

How dare Kae make her stay here, and how dare he post them to keep watch over her? They were going to discuss this, oh yes, they were. But then, a little part of her brain reminded her as it had before that, like Dorothy and Toto, she wasn't in Kansas anymore, and the rules of conduct in this time and place were very different. To get on Kae's — or especially his father's — bad side could prove downright deadly.

Of course, some things here were very much the same, like Kae's total hotness and the way his touch or even the simplest, probing look from him made her feel. Sinking to the floor, Emmi found herself wishing she'd gotten drunk enough at the wedding to pass out and not have sex with Kae, not just because of the threat of any STD or pregnancy, but because it had only served to turn her attraction to him into something much deeper.

It felt like so much more than simply sex, and she was sure it had been special to him too. The way he'd looked at her, the gentle way he'd touched her and totally possessed her inside and out, hadn't been just sex for the sake of sex. It couldn't have been, which made her entire situation so much more painful and confusing.

She wanted to be with him, but she didn't want to be here with him, not the here of 1864. She didn't fit in, and she knew she never really would. Having the chance to see the real past was exciting, and she'd love to learn more of what life was like in this era, but she missed her own life. She wanted it back — the freedom, the normalcy, the modern conveniences of things as simple as toilet paper and decent shampoo.

As she set the black and white stones on the Go board, Emmi wondered how she could get her mirror back from that Aneko babe. Maybe she could talk Kae into getting it, but that would mean he'd have to go see the hooker. If he went to see her, she'd probably put her hands all over him.

Asking Kojima for any favors would definitely be a bad idea, especially after today, but he might be her only hope. He was the only one she had access to who wasn't a servant. But how could she ask him, and what would she say when he wanted to know why she wanted a hooker's mirror?

"Hello, wife of Kae-san."

The bowl of Go stones slipped out of Emmi's hand and skittered across the tatami floor.

"Where did you come from?"

"My room?" the mystery kid said as he sat across from her.

"I meant, how did you come in? The ladies in the other room didn't tell me I had a guest."

He shrugged and pointed to the game board. "Who will you play with?"

Emmi began picking up the white stones from the floor, dropped them back into their bowl and grinned at him. "Of course, if you're in the mood to lose today…"

The kid went stiff and gave her a pissy look. "I cannot lose."

Emmi smirked. "You have never played against me. I'm very good."

He gave her another pissy look, and she smiled sweetly in return.

Emmi had thought her brother had been a sore loser when he was younger, but he'd had nothing on this kid.

She took it easy on the kid at first, letting him get the advantage.

After he'd gained some territory with his white stones, he started making moves that told her he knew exactly how to play this game. She had no choice but to play full out to keep him from capturing all her black stones. The board was only half covered when he pitched a bitch and knocked all the stones off with a big sweep of his arm.

"I cannot lose!"

"It's only a game. I don't win all the time. I was lucky today."

She turned away at the sound of the door to the next room sliding open with a bang. The sitter babes rushed in to ask what was happening. The mystery boy was gone. *How the hell…?*

"Um, I was trying to teach myself to play and got frustrated. This game is harder than it looks."

"That's why it's best left to the men," one of the women said before walking back out.

"Oh yes, all the interesting things are best left to the men," Emmi muttered before picking up the stones from the floor.

She still couldn't believe how upset that kid had gotten. It was only a game. He'd looked like he was going to cry, and she wondered if there was some way she could make it up to him. Of course, it might help if she knew who he was.

She decided to ask Kae to help her solve the riddle as soon as he came back from his 'secret mission', but she didn't have a chance, because when he came back, he was in a rather pissy mood himself.

The upside to this was that he told the babysitters to get lost and to let the servants know that they didn't need dinner served. Instead he gave her a nicely wrapped bundle and said it was something for her to wear. They were going to be out and about at the Gion Festival as soon as he had a chance to get a bath and put on clean clothes.

So what if the date nights were supposed to have happened before the wedding, she wasn't going to complain. A date with a hot guy was a date with a hot guy, and she wouldn't mind doing a hell of a lot more than just kissing him on the first real date.

"Can I wash your back, or maybe take that bath with you?"

He gave her a look that made her wonder if she'd turned into a gray alien or something.

Her shoulders slumped. *I'll take that scowl as a no, then.*

"Make certain you powder your face and color your lips," he said. "I will send someone to help you with your hair. You'll need to wear the hair ornaments as well." He pointed to the bundle in her hands.

She untied it. There were quite a few fan-shaped silver hair picks with dangly things and tiny bells on them. Emmi stood and lifted the red, flowered kimono out. "This is pretty. Did you pick it out yourself?"

"It is Aneko's," he said before leaving.

Hooker cast-offs? He wanted her to wear hooker cast-offs?

Remember, Em, you're not in Kansas anymore, and you don't want Kae or his dad to call out the flying monkeys.

Flying monkeys be damned. She had pride.

The maid that Kae sent to help her spazzed at Kae the minute he set foot back in the apartment. He, in turn, jumped at Emmi.

"Why are you being difficult? You cannot wear the garments you have nor arrange your hair yourself, and I doubt you will apply the makeup properly."

She stood and stared at him with her arms folded over her chest. "I am not going to go around wearing some whore's hand-me-downs."

Kae grabbed her sleeve, tugged her to the side, then leaned in. She tried not to think how hot he was when his eyes were this intense and his voice was low and forceful.

"I need to gather information for my father. Important information. It will be much easier if I am with a woman from the Pleasure Quarters. I can take you, or I can hire a professional."

Emmi caved. He needed her, and she wasn't about to let him hire some real hooker who might want to give him his money's worth.

Still, she hated wearing that Aneko babe's things, but she figured if she did this and he got whatever info his dad needed, then he'd owe her one. When he returned the dress and hairpins, he could get the mirror back so she could try to go home.

But going home means leaving him here, her heart reminded her.

Stupid heart and its big mouth.

Chapter Twenty-Eight

Kae led Emmi out of the palace through a long underground passage that led to a small alley behind the fenced house of one of the court nobles.

"Stop walking strangely," Kae said over his shoulder once they exited to the main street.

"I'm not walking strangely," Emmi shot back. "It isn't easy in these high shoes, you know."

Kae grabbed her sleeve and tugged her into another alley.

"What did I do wrong now?"

He shut her up with a kiss, a nice, slow kiss. A kiss that made her hot and wet and caused her to forget all about retrieving the mirror. Slowly Kae pulled away, looked at her as though she were the only thing in the world that mattered, then glanced over his shoulder.

"I thought we were being followed," he said quietly before tugging her back to the street.

Great. A fake kiss. The thing that really mattered to him was his undercover operation. Getting that mirror back was a good idea after all.

Even if she would miss him.

Once they began to make the rounds in the Gion section of the city Emmi knew she'd end up missing Kae a lot. Despite the fact that Kae was undercover, that they were following various shady-looking guys and stopping now and again to listen to bits of conversation, Emmi had a pleasant time at the festival.

It reminded her of New Orleans at Mardi Gras. A zillion people crowded the streets. A sea of brightly colored paper lanterns and streamers hung from the shopfronts. There were food stands, puppet shows and little booths with games. One of the games involved trying to catch a goldfish with a paper net. If you caught a fish, you got to take it home in a tiny wooden bucket.

They stopped and watched one young girl who tried and tried but kept losing because her net disintegrated before she could get a fish in it. Emmi felt bad for the child when her mother told her they ran out of money. She considered asking Kae if he would try, but the next thing she knew he'd tossed the man in charge a couple of coins. He shot his bare hand into the trough and captured a pretty silver and blue fish.

He handed Emmi the bucket with the fish and called to the girl and her mother. They came back. When Emmi handed the girl the pail with the fish, the child's smile was brighter than all the hanging lanterns put together. She chattered about how that was the exact fish she wanted and how she knew the gods would reward such kind people.

The little girl's happiness was infectious and swelled up inside Emmi. She turned to Kae, only to have her smile fall away when the look in his eyes went from pleasant to fierce.

She tried to follow his line of vision but couldn't figure out who he was giving the evil eye. Before she could ask, he pulled her to the side in a space between the fish game and the ringtoss game and shoved a few coins into her palm.

"Stay here and amuse yourself until I return. Do not move from this spot. Do not."

She opened her mouth to complain about his domineering attitude but thought better of it. Obviously something was going down that she wasn't aware of. She could let his caveman attitude slide, this time.

Watching the little kids play games wore thin rather quickly. So she tried the ring toss game herself. The prizes were tied to tiny wooden stands all crammed together. The player won if they got their ring to fall over the prize they wanted. It seemed easy enough, with seemed being the operative word.

The item Emmi wanted was a decorative hair comb. A silly wooden hair comb with pink cherry blossoms painted on it. The problem was it was jammed in the center, and she couldn't get the ring to fall on it without being caught on the prizes nearby and bouncing off.

Down to her last coin, Emmi was certain she'd get the comb this time. She was in the perfect position, and the last time she'd needed to add just a tiny bit more of a push to the throw… One… Two… Thr—

"Takeda-kun, is it my imagination or does that 'geisha' look like the woman you arrested for causing so much trouble in Shimabara not long ago?"

Emmi's wooden ring went clattering to the ground just inside the booth after that disgustingly familiar male voice threw her concentration.

She turned around and forced herself to bow to the man that she'd hoped she would never have the misfortune to see again—Hijikata Toshizou and his fifth squad captain, Takeda Kanryuusai.

"You owe me a hair comb, Hijikata-san," she said with a smile, gesturing to the one she'd lost. He and his companion smirked, but she noticed that Hijikata tried to stand straighter to compensate for the fact that in the high sandals she was taller than he was.

"I heard a rumor that your patron married you, apparently the rumor was false, judging from your appearance."

"Apparently, the rumor was true," Kae said, coming up behind the two samurai. They were no longer smirking, but Emmi was. She cozied up to Kae and rested her head against his arm when he moved next to her.

Unfortunately he pulled away almost fast enough to make her lose her balance. He motioned for the Shinsengumi to follow him off to the side between the two game stands and told them to pay an official call on a merchant named Masuya Somethingorother.

They hurried off, which was fine by Emmi, but then Kae said it was time for them to return to the palace.

"But do we have to? We still have things to see. You said there was dancing and—"

"I have work to do, and I can't leave you on your own."

"I'm not a baby. I can look after myself."

"Like the last time you went out on your own?"

She very much wanted to wipe that know-it-all look off his face. "Fine. I'll go home so you can go back to work."

They took the secret passage route back into the palace compound. Emmi was not at all happy when Kae told her to change clothes right away so he could return the things to Aneko.

So that was the work he had to do.

She tried not to feel hurt, not to wonder why she wasn't good enough in that department to satisfy him. Surely he knew the concept that practice made perfect. Of course, she knew the "mistress thing" was commonplace, very commonplace, and probably had some weird deep-rooted ties to an Asian version of the madonna-whore issue, but dammit, they'd just gotten married! Surely the novelty hadn't worn off so this quickly...

Correction. Arranged marriage. How stupid she was to think, since she'd fallen head over heels for him, that he shared the sentiment—or any sentiment for that matter? She needed to go home.

"You'll bring my mirror back, right?"

"What?"

"The mirror. The mirror at Aneko's that brought me here. You'll bring it back with you, so I can go home where I belong, right?"

Kae simply stood and stared a moment. Although he had promised Maeda-san that he would do everything in his power to help Emiko return to her own time and place, he was finding it very hard to let it happen. Obviously she wanted to go. She wanted to leave him.

They'd spent so little time together because of his duties to his father. He'd thought that might change soon, but the information he'd come upon this afternoon was proof that things would be getting even more hectic and dangerous here in Kyoto. It would probably be best if Emmi returned to where she belonged, even if this simple mention of her leaving made him empty inside. He reached out and took her hand.

"I have some time. Time enough for a quiet walk at least."

Emmi nodded. "Give me a minute to change."

She didn't bother closing the sliding door to the bedroom all the way, since only the outer kimono wasn't hers. Her pulse quickened when Kae moved to stand in the doorway and watch while she fought with the simple obi, which she had trouble tying behind her back over the new kimono she put on. This was ridiculous. She'd done it before, why wasn't it working now? Her foot tangled in Aneko's kimono, which she'd dropped on the floor, and she kicked it out of the way.

"You should have folded that first. It's going to wrinkle."

"Yeah, yeah," Emmi mumbled, still trying to tuck in the long end of the wide sash properly.

Kae moved behind her. He brushed her hands away, then slid the obi around and finished tying it behind her back.

"I don't think men are supposed to be so good at doing that."

"I've had a lot of practice removing them. It's only a matter of reversing the process to tie it again."

Emmi grumbled. He laughed, wrapped his arms around her, and pulled her back against him. Her grumble faded into one of those weird little whimpering sounds when Kae kissed her neck.

She reached up and touched his face.

"Maybe…we could just stay inside?"

She slid herself around and kissed him. He kissed her back, erasing her earlier doubts about his feelings and easing her desire to go home. She wound her arms around his neck, pressed in as close as she could and arched forward to feel the firmness of his erection through the layers of their clothing.

Without warning, he pulled away. He crouched down and began folding Aneko's kimono. He placed it and the hairpins into a piece of cloth and tied it closed. Emmi was blinking back the tears from the corners of her eyes when Kae stood and placed his hand lightly on her back.

"Come, walk with me."

Emmi hesitated but then let him escort her to the door, all the while silencing the part of her pride that screamed at her for being such a doormat after the way he'd just blown her off.

"Why are you so silent, Emmi?" he asked after they'd walked in silence for quite some time.

"It's nothing." She looked around. "I thought this forest was haunted by evil spirits after dark. Are you feeling especially brave, or are you hoping one of them will eat me for his dinner, making you the handsome young widower all the pretty girls feel sorry for and want to cheer up?"

Kae laughed.

He had such a nice laugh, so deep, yet light and happy. And he had such nice eyes, so sexy. And his face…

He brushed a fallen piece of hair back behind her ear.

"Do you fancy Kojima-san?"

Where the hell had that question come from?

"Kojima-san is nice enough for an older guy, but no. No, I don't fancy him."

Kae laughed again and stepped closer before leading her to a small stone bench farther along the path. They sat, and he held her hand in both of his and stared at her. His dark eyes sucked her in, making her want to freeze time.

"You are so unlike the other women I know. You are free like a bird that soars just out of reach. We can admire it and enjoy the happiness it brings us, but we can't capture it and place it in a cage."

"I don't know if you'd really like the way the girls are where I come from. We're not the dutiful, proper ones you're used to having walk behind you and do what you say."

Kae let go of her hand and ran his fingers along her cheek. "I would like to see this future world of yours. I would like to see it with you."

Had she really heard what she thought she had? Oh, she wanted him to come home with her, but that couldn't possibly be a good idea. If he turned out to be someone important to Japan's future, someone that she hadn't heard of or simply didn't remember, to take him away could screw up the entire world as she knew it.

"Wouldn't you want to be with me?"

"I would, but—"

Emmi was relieved when Kae's father came out of nowhere and ordered him to get back to business.

Prince Asahiko wasn't a large man, but he was a very scary one. He was a man accustomed to his high position, and Emmi hated the way he gave her that Evil Death Glare of Doom that seemed to say, "If the Maeda family wasn't so stinking rich, you are the last person I would have had my son marry."

The walk back to the apartment was quick, and Kae only accompanied her as far as the main corridor.

"I have many things to do for my father. I may be late in coming home. You don't need to wait up."

"All right. Please be careful. Please."

He smiled. "I will. And I will bring the mirror. I promise."

Emmi gave him a weak wave and watched him disappear into the dark.

She had trouble falling asleep, and when she finally did, she had a strange dream. She dreamed she was small, and her father was giving her and her brother one of his history lessons. He used her dollhouse and stuffed animals to act out the Shinsengumi raid on the Ikedaya Inn in Gion, where the Meiji rebels stayed as they planned to burn Kyoto. In the dream, she looked at the big flowery calendar on her wall. She stared and stared at the calendar and woke up with a start.

It was June 5. June 5, 1864.

Today is June 4, 1864.

What if Kae took part in the raid? What if he was hurt or killed? She knew people had been killed. She thought most of them were the Choshu rebels. But perhaps others had died that she didn't know about, others who, for some reason, hadn't been named in the books she'd read.

What if Kae had been one of the unnamed?

Chapter Twenty-Nine

Kae didn't come home that night, or the following morning, or in the afternoon. By evening, Emmi was worried enough to ask one of the servants to take a note to Kae's father. His reply was a snarky "Your husband will return in good time. Occupy yourself as a wife should".

And mothers-in-law were the ones comedians made fun of?

Consumed with thoughts of Kae's safety, Emmi didn't even jump when that mysterious kid popped in out of nowhere.

"I saw you and Kae-san sneak out last night. Where did you go?"

"He took me to the festival. I guess your parents are taking you? I think there are two days left."

"Is it fun? I hear festivals are fun."

Emmi gave him a long look. That was like hearing a kid back home ask if Christmas was fun. "Of course it's fun. There's lots of food and music and dancing and games and parades. You know — the usual."

"I have never seen a festival. I am not allowed to be outside."

"I've seen you outside before — oh. You mean you're not allowed to go outside the palace grounds?"

The boy nodded.

"That bites," she muttered in English. Emmi gave him a nervous grin when she saw his eyes go wide, and she brushed it off as a Kaga-han saying. "I have no friends to play with. It's boring here! I want to see the festival! I want to see the puppet show!"

Don't even think of going there, Emmi's common sense cautioned. *Not tonight of all nights.*

Yes, it was going to be a dangerous night, but the Shinsengumi raid wasn't going to happen until after dark. Assuming all the movies had gotten facts correct on that point, they had at least two hours of daylight left. And if they happened to run into Kae and got him to come home with them, so much the better.

"Go ask your parents if I can take you. Do you want me to talk to your mother with you?"

The boy shook his head. "My mother does not live here. My father is very busy. I only see him when he gives me calligraphy lessons."

Again, her common sense cautioned. Again, she ignored it. What else could she do? Kae's life was in danger, and besides, she was a good babysitter. She'd babysat all the time back home and for kids way younger than this one.

True, their parents had put her in charge of those kids, but it wasn't as if this kid's parents were that conscientious. His mother lived elsewhere and his father made him stay cooped up here because he was too "busy" to watch him. She'd known many parents like that back home and had seen their kids get into all sorts of trouble, from jail time to long-term therapy.

Besides, what better sitter could this kid have than the wife of a prince? It would do the kid good, probably lift his parents up a notch in the palace social circle. It was a win-win situation, especially since they might be saving Kae's life in the bargain.

"I'll take you to the festival, but you can't go like that." Emmi gestured to his clothing, the same kind of formal court outfit Kae had worn at the wedding. "You need to lose the hat and that robe thing, and the long hakama."

He gaped at her as if she'd sprouted another head.

"You can't go outside the palace dressed that way. It's warm, and you won't be able to walk very far dressed like that."

He continued to stare.

"You have a yukata on under there, right? I can see the collar."

He kept staring.

"Take off everything but that, and I'll give you one of Kae's jackets to wear." He was still staring. "I'll buy you candy, and try to win you a toy."

She could have sworn that kid stripped before she had a chance to blink.

Kae's haori was too long, but Emmi figured it was good enough, despite the look the kid gave her.

"I want to wear a sword."

"What?"

"A sword," he announced, arms crossed defiantly in front of him. "I want to wear a sword like Kae-san. Two swords."

Ugh. This kid was an Uber Pain in the Ass, which reminded Emmi of why she didn't babysit regularly, unless one of her parents' friends asked — twice.

She looked around. Kae had a wooden practice sword hanging on the wall.

"This is all there is, so unless you want to forget the toys and candy, it will have to do."

He replied with a pissy look but nodded and held out his hand. Emmi pulled the sword back a bit.

"I'll give it to you if you tell me your name."

"I am Sachi." He tucked the sword into his obi, tilted his nose in the air a bit in a way that reminded her of Kae's father and said, "Take me to my people, wife of Kae-san."

This kid really needed to get out more. Emmi rolled her eyes and led the way to the secret passage she and Kae had used the night before. Or rather, she tried to lead the way. Sachi pushed past her with some mumbled thing about "inferior women being where they belong."

She grumbled. Oh yeah, this was why she'd never really liked babysitting all that much. Once they made it outside to that alley between the buildings, Sachi stopped and looked back. His eyes were wide with amazement, as though he was surprised to be truly out in the open.

"Come on," Emmi said, jerking her thumb in the direction of Gion. She needed to find Kae soon, and she had a lot of ground to cover.

* * * *

Sachi was awfully quiet as they hurried along the crowded, narrow streets where the various stands and amusements were set up. She let him stop and watch some street performers while she scanned the crowd for signs of Kae. At least Kae was taller than many of the men. Hopefully his topknot of hair would catch her attention. Of course, the fact that ninety-nine point ninety-nine percent of guys had the same hairstyle made things a bit trickier.

Emmi looked down at Sachi when he tugged on her yukata. He pointed. "I want to go there to see the dancing geisha."

"So does half of Kyoto, it seems," she said as she looked at the tangle of people moving that way. "Why don't we go to where the fish game is? Maybe you can catch one."

"I want to see the geisha dance. Why do my people not move out of the way? Why do they look at me? Why do they not lie at my feet and worship me?"

Okay. So maybe there was a reason Sachi didn't get out much.

"Well, the streets are crowded. There isn't room to lay, and you can't help look at someone who is standing right next to you. Oh look, there's a candy vendor. We can get to him." She tugged Sachi's sleeve and led him down the street.

A kid plus candy should have equaled what's-not-to-love, but obviously Sachi wasn't the average kid.

He was horror-stricken as the old vendor scooped up a handful of the sugar candies, put them in a paper pouch, and then gave it to Emmi. He was even more horrified when she took one out and offered it to him.

"Why do you use your hands? Why do you not cover your mouth with paper like the others who serve me?"

Great. Young Mr. Obsessive Compulsive emerges from his cocoon in front of the world. Emmi gave the candy vendor an abashed smile.

"Kids. You can dress them up, but you can't take them out in public."

Good lord, I've turned into my mother…

She grabbed Sachi's hand and pulled him away. He stopped dead and jerked her back.

"I wish to see the dancing geisha."

This boy was strong for such a skinny kid.

"Sachi, you and I need to talk. Let's go over to that nice quiet corner, okay?" *So I can strangle the living daylights out of you, you little brat…*

* * * *

Shinsengumi Headquarters, Mibu

Kae's nose crinkled in distaste as he stepped inside the darkened storehouse where the merchant Furutaka was being interrogated. The air was thick with the rank stench of mingled sweat, urine and vomit.

"He still won't talk?" Kae asked Takeda Kanryuusai, the captain who'd raided the merchant's premises upon receipt of his information yesterday.

Takeda shook his head. "The beatings are breaking his body but not his will. Hijikata-san said he had an idea, though. He went to get something."

Kae turned to face the opened doorway. The merchant had been hiding an incredible amount of rifles and ammunition. The rebel factions were definitely up to something, but what? Where? And when?

"I'm surprised your lovely wife is not here, Fujiwara-san," Takeda teased from behind him. "She seemed quite the adventuress."

His hand on the hilt of his short sword, Kae spun around. The only thing that kept Takeda's head attached to his shoulders was the appearance of Hijikata.

Kae let Takeda pass.

"Fukuchou, what have you decided?" Takeda asked as he approached his commander.

Hijikata handed Takeda the two iron candle spikes he'd brought in. "Turn Furutaka so he's hanging head down and pound these into the soles of his feet. Then light them."

The vice-commander turned to Kae and smirked. "That will loosen his tongue, *ne*?"

Kae ignored the derisive gleam in Hijikata's eyes when he turned to leave the building. As he left, Furutaka's screams echoed through the storehouse.

"Desperate times call for desperate measures, or so Hijikata-san says."

Looking over to the other vice-commander who'd approached him, Kae nodded. "I suppose so, Yamanami-san, but that doesn't make it any more palatable to men of decency and reason."

"But if it saves lives and serves the emperor..."

Kae nodded again, sensing that although Yamanami said "the right thing" he too felt disgusted by it all.

He walked with Yamanami around the outside of the storehouse. The traitor's cries from inside followed them with each step.

The afternoon was drawing to its end when the man finally broke. Kae's blood ran cold when Hijikata relayed the information they had gotten.

"The weapons we found were only part of it. They have banners and lanterns decorated with the crest of the Aizu clan. They plan to raise an army of the ronin in and near Kyoto, execute Matsudaira-sama and march on the Imperial Palace in the guise of Matsudaira's forces." He paused and looked hard at Kae. "They want to burn Kyoto to the ground, abduct the emperor and take him back to the Choshu han. They're meeting to decide it all tonight. Somewhere in Gion."

Rage boiled up inside Kae. "Let me get word to the palace and have someone watch over those nobles we've had suspicions about. They'd need someone on the inside to get away with such insanity."

"Exactly," Hijikata said with a cold look.

Kae dismissed the suspicious look in the vice-commander's narrow eyes. He had far more to worry about than the petty jealousies of a farmer turned self-proclaimed samurai.

Hurrying away from the Shinsengumi headquarters, Kae tried to think of which nobles were the most likely to be involved. Kojima Toshimasa topped the list. It certainly would explain his fawning interest in Emiko. Clearly Kojima was hoping to get her to share whatever information she could regarding those suspicions Kae and his father had.

Luckily, he hadn't had a chance to tell Emmi anything of importance. In fact, he hadn't had much of a chance to speak with her at all.

Oh, but he wanted to. He wanted to walk in the moonlit gardens, sit on the engawa or beside the lake and simply talk. He wanted to know so much more about her and her world. He wanted to know what the future held for not only Japan but also for himself.

He wondered if he would be able to live a tranquil life without her to share it. Kae shook off those thoughts. This was no time to think of himself. He had to think of the safety of the emperor and Japan.

Cursing under his breath, he tried to hurry through the crowded streets. If the rebels were anything, they were clever. They couldn't have picked a better time for their deadly game than during the festival. With this much congestion in the streets, it would be impossible to relay messages quickly or summon help from the local patrol groups without losing precious time. With so many peasants coming in from the outskirts of Kyoto, the rebel ronin could easily blend in with the crowds.

The one saving grace was that the emperor and his family were safely sequestered inside the Gosho. Though the real faction may have their inside sources helping, they were not going to get close enough to —

Kaemon froze in his tracks.

It couldn't be.

He couldn't be seeing what he thought he saw across the way. He was *not* seeing his wife abducting the emperor's only son. Oh, gods. There was only one thing he could do. He had to save Prince Mutsuhito at all cost.

Even if the cost was Emmi's life.

* * * *

"Look, Sachi, you're really starting to piss —" Emmi stopped herself. She was not going to let an eleven year old get to her. "Sachi. I need to find Kae. It's important. He might be in danger."

"Why? Who would dare to threaten him?"

"A bunch of guys who—" She figured she shouldn't spill her guts to the kid and risk doing any kind of time warp damage. She knelt down and tried to put her hands on his shoulders, but he pulled back as though she had the plague. "Trust me. He might be in real danger, and we have to find him before it's too late. So just be quiet and follow me. Please."

"Emiko. Move away. Immediately."

Emmi whipped her head around. She was about to jump up and hug Kae, but his expression stopped her dead and made her stomach twist.

His hand was on his sword.

And he had that look in his eye—the look he'd had when he drew on Kojima-san, the look he'd had when he killed those men at the teahouse, the look he'd had when he'd dispatched those who'd attacked them at Nijo Castle that night.

What was happening? What had she done?

"Emiko," he said again, his tone colder.

Emmi stood up and backed away. She tried not to notice the people stopping to look at what was happening.

Kae went down on his knees and bowed his head at Sachi, and the sick feeling in Emmi's stomach grew. This was bad. It had to be.

"I will welcome whatever punishment you choose to hand down for myself and my unworthy wife," Kae said quietly. "But I beg you, let me take you home at once."

Unworthy wife? Punishment? This was worse than bad... But what exactly was it?

"I do not like it out here. I will go."

Kae barked an order for a man nearby to secure a palanquin at once. After it arrived and Sachi was safely deposited inside, Kae ordered the guys carrying it to head north on the double. They took off at a fast clip with the small boy inside. Kae seized her by the wrist and dragged her as he ran behind the palanquin.

"What happened? What did I do?"

He shot her a look of pure hatred that she would never forget.

"You have issued both of our death warrants."

Chapter Thirty

Icy fear replaced the blood in Emmi's veins, and a sickening shiver ran through her as Kae dragged her along. Tears blurred her vision and she stumbled more than once. Kae didn't care. He jerked her back to her feet and dragged her harder.

They weren't too far from the palace when they came upon Kae's father, Prince Asahiko, who was at the head of a small army of palace guards. Kae ordered the carriage bearers to stop.

Emmi was crying hard by the time the elder prince knelt before the palanquin and also offered to accept whatever punishment Sachi chose to have his own father hand down. He ordered the palanquin bearers to head off again.

They were running again toward the palace. Guards now ran behind as well as in front of them, and Emmi started babbling to herself, mostly in Japanese, partly in English. "Who is that boy?"

Kae jerked her to him, and she tripped again. He pulled her up and hit her with that look again. That look that said he wouldn't have a problem watching the whole "death warrant" thing be handed down upon her.

"That is the emperor's only son," he hissed in her ear.

"Oh, shit!" barely described the dread that settled over her. Emmi was so caught up in fear over what she'd done that she never saw the band of rebel ronin until they were on them.

The clang of swords, angry shouts and screams filled her ears. Blood splattered her face and hands. Shock and fear paralyzed her, until Kae's father slumped to one knee behind the palanquin, now on the ground not far from her.

She didn't know what she was thinking. In fact, she wasn't thinking, she simply reacted. She launched herself at the rebel and kicked his knee. He fell. Asahiko seized the fallen sword and slashed his attacker's throat.

Behind Emmi, Sachi screamed. A ronin tried to reach through the flaps of the carriage. Kae stabbed him from behind. Running toward them, Emmi evaded Kae's attempt to grab her. Before he could reach for her again, another attacker came at him. She made it to the palanquin and looked in.

Sachi may have been the 'son of a living god' but right now, he looked like any other scared little kid. Emmi scrambled into the palanquin and held him, covered him so that if anyone tried to attack him they'd get her instead.

"It'll be all right. It'll be all right. I promise. I won't let anyone hurt you."

Hands seized her shoulders. She fought. Digging her nails into their arm, the other, braced to keep her body covering the young prince. "Stay away from him!" The attacker punched her head.

Sachi screamed and so did Emmi. She was thrown backward and hit the ground hard enough to make the world go gray and fuzzy.

Palace guards took up the palanquin and took off. She was yanked up and pulled forward. It was Kae. He held his sword to her throat for what seemed an eternity, but then lowered it and dragged her into a run once more.

"Your father — ?"

"Alive," he spat as a bunch of soldiers from Aizu charged past to take care of the remaining injured rebels.

The only thing Emmi could think as they hurried the rest of the way back to the palace was that Kae had wanted to kill her.

Of course, they were both as good as dead, since her actions would be seen as a bad reflection on Kae. And — oh God — Kae's father was doomed as well, since the son's behavior would lead back to the father. They were all going to die because she'd been a total idiot.

Oh, no! She was a Maeda! They might even want to take it out on Takehito! Even the entire clan! She might have wiped out the entire Maeda family forever with her own stupidity!

Emmi was nearly hyperventilating by the time they rushed up those few broad steps and through the red-orange main gates of the palace compound. A swarm of guards and furious nobles surrounded them, and Emmi could barely see the palanquin as it stopped and a smaller, similar thing was brought forward to take Sachi the rest of the way to his father's quarters.

Before getting in, the young heir looked back at Emmi, not angry nor scared, but confused.

"I'm sorry," she whispered, knowing he couldn't hear her.

"Shut your lying mouth, girl!" Kae's father shouted. His deep voice rang through the open courtyard. "Get on your knees where you belong!" he ordered.

One of the guards shoved her down so hard she ended up face first in the dirt. Kae ran forward, but other guards with spears stopped him.

"Kill her now," Asahiko ground out.

"No!" Kae shouted. "Emiko is innocent! She has been used. You must investigate first. I beg of you."

Prince Asahiko glared at Emmi then looked to his son. His harsh expression softened just a fraction.

"She stays there until she is sent for," Asahiko hissed. Guards posted themselves around her while others pulled Kae away. Emmi heard him trying to talk to his father, but Asahiko ignored him.

Emmi had no idea how long she was there. The sun shifted and began to go down. She was so thirsty. Her knees hurt so badly, and her ankles and feet were going numb. Finally she gave up kneeling and sat with her legs bent to the side. She tried to rub the circulation back into them, and winced as the pins and needles pain shot through her.

Darkness was falling over the palace grounds when a shadow crossed in front of Emmi, blocking out what little light remained. She looked up to see Kojima-san looking down. His expression was indescribable—his nasty, ugly thoughts were projected outward onto his face.

How could she ever have thought this guy was nice to be around?

"I never would have imagined an ill-bred thing like you could topple the mighty Nakagawa no miya and his insipid son."

"Bastard," Emmi muttered, returning his icy stare.

He said something to one of the guards, and Emmi was jerked to her feet and dragged toward a building that she'd never been in before. But they didn't go in, they went around and into a small, enclosed courtyard. When she saw what waited there, she screamed.

It was Kae and his father. They were dressed in white ceremonial outfits that she'd only ever seen in the movies — the outfits that samurai wore when about to commit seppuku, ritual suicide. Before them were tiny wooden tables upon which lay sheets of rice paper and atop that, dagger blades removed from their hilts.

Emmi tried to break away from the guards and run to the old man who seemed to be overseeing it all. She'd forgotten his name but remembered he and Kae's father didn't get along. Kojima-san went and took his place beside the old noble.

"You can't do this! They didn't do anything wrong! It was a mistake! I didn't know who the prince was! I swear I didn't! I thought he was just a boy who lived here and wanted to go outside!"

"Silence!" Kojima-san shouted.

"No!" Emmi shrieked back. "I wasn't trying to kidnap the prince or hurt him! I was trying to find Kae to make sure he was safe, and that he wasn't caught up in the raid on the Choshu at the—"

Everybody's head turned her way. She'd really done it this time. But what else could she do? She would not let Kae and his father die. She had to spill the history even if it hadn't happened yet. She looked at each of the men assembled in turn and tried to figure out what to say to make them believe her. She noted the usually uber-cool Kojima-san was looking awfully uncomfortable all of a sudden.

Before she could say more, a weird intake of breath from everyone caught her attention, and Emmi looked around to find Sachi and a finely dressed, stately woman standing in the opened door of the building behind the courtyard. Could that be the empress?

Emmi suddenly realized everyone was on their knees and bowing with their foreheads to the ground. Everyone but her. She fell to her knees and did likewise. After what seemed like forever, the noble who'd been presiding over things spoke, and Emmi looked up. Sachi and the lady were gone, and the noble was folding whatever message they'd brought.

"Nakagawa no miya, you and your son are to be confined until further notice, pending an answer to the message his Divine Highness will be sending to Edo."

You and your son...

"But what about me?" Emmi whispered.

She jumped when the old noble turned and stared at her. "You, girl, come with me."

She couldn't move. She was too scared. Two guards roughly pulled her to her feet. Kae tried to jump up, but his father stopped him. Tears were blurring Emmi's vision, but she kept looking at Kae as the guards dragged her inside. She told herself it was her own tears clouding things and making her think that he was crying too.

Her mouth was dry, and fear shook her so thoroughly that if the guards hadn't been pulling her along she wouldn't have been able to stand.

She wasn't sure how many buildings they went through, but when they finally came to a stop, she fully expected to find a samurai assassin waiting on the other side of the sliding door.

There was no assassin inside. There was no one at all. It was only a big, empty room with new tatami mats on the floor. A raised platform was at one end with a bamboo screen in front of it that almost touched the floor.

She heard another door slide open from somewhere behind the bamboo curtain, and when the noble bowed with his head to the floor, Emmi did the same and didn't move until he poked her with the end of his fan.

When she looked up, someone was sitting behind the curtain. Oh no. She knew that silhouette. She'd seen it at her wedding to Kae. It was the emperor himself.

Her empty stomach cramped. He probably wanted to kill her personally for kidnapping his son, or at least watch while the old guy beside her carried out the execution.

"My son has said he ordered you to take him outside the palace walls. Is this true?"

Oh, Sachi, I could kiss you, you princely little dork.

It would have been so easy to go along with the story, but she'd never been good at lying, and there was no point in trying to start now.

"He didn't order me, Your Highness, Sir. I didn't realize he was your son. I thought he was just a little boy who didn't have any friends to go to the festival with. Sir, Your Highness. Please, this was all my mistake. Kae, my husband, and his father had nothing to do with it. I acted foolishly, without their knowledge or consent. Punish me if you need to, but let them go. Please spare them and my family."

Emmi didn't want to cry but found she couldn't help it. She kept thinking of Kae and his dad and Takehito and Sadanori…and seppuku.

She bowed her head to the floor again. "Please let them all live. If someone has to die, take me in their place. Please."

"Go now."

Emmi looked up. The emperor was standing, leaving. Kae would die. His father, her relatives would all die. "Please believe me! I didn't know he was your son! It was my mistake, no one else's! Please spare them. Please!"

He left, and that was that. The old courtier poked her again, and the guards took her back outside.

Kae and his father were gone, but Kojima was there looking like the freaking Cheshire cat from Alice in Wonderland. She wanted to slap that smirk off his face. Someone rushed out and gave the old noble a letter. He read it and looked kind of cheesed off as he showed it to Kojima, who also looked upset.

Kojima walked past her. "You've all been spared for the moment. Enjoy it while it lasts, for it won't last very long."

Chapter Thirty-One

As far as jail cells went, Emmi decided hers wasn't so bad. It wasn't a real jail cell like the ones at the Shinsengumi compound but simply a small, unfurnished, dark room tucked in the back of one of the palace outbuildings that obviously no one ever came to.

Oh no.

Were they just going to leave her here to rot away and die?

Tears stung Emmi's eyes when she realized they very well might, but she sniffed the tears away. Everyone back home probably thought she'd been killed in that weird storm that blew through the movie lot anyway, so it didn't much matter to anyone.

Except to her.

The cramped, dim room was hot and stuffy, but a chill settled in Emmi's bones and she hugged her arms around herself. The most important thing was that Kae, his father and Takehito were alive. At least she wouldn't have to die with the thought that her stupidity had taken innocent men to their deaths as well.

She wanted to go home. She wanted to see Jake and her grandparents. Her brother and even her mother. What she wanted more than anything was someone to hug her and tell she was safe.

And, yes, she wanted Kae to be that person, but that certainly wasn't ever going to happen now.

* * * *

Kae watched silently as the servant women carefully packed up and removed Emiko's things. So this was it. It was over between them before he'd even gotten the chance to really know her, to love her more than he already did.

"Wait. Not that," he said to the girl who was taking the parcel of odd undergarments he'd had made for Emmi in Gion.

"But, sir—"

"Just leave it. Please."

The girl frowned a bit but did as he asked. She set the small wrapped bundle at his feet before withdrawing with the last of Emmi's things. Kae lay back on the tatami and rested his head upon the bundle, certain he could smell Emmi's sweet scent lingering in the fabric.

It had been such a short time since she'd come into his life, and yet it seemed as if she'd been a part of his world forever. He knew he would be lost without her, but what else could he do? Even with everyone sworn to secrecy under the penalty of death for what happened to the young prince, the fact was that Emiko must be divorced and exiled as soon as possible. It was only by the grace of the gods that Emperor Komei and the shogun had decided to spare the entire Maeda clan from the retribution that would normally be handed down.

Kae didn't even bother to worry about where he would be sent. Most likely he'd be exiled to some remote temple and forced into monkhood for the remainder of his days. Not that it mattered. There was nothing for him here, nothing without his Emmi.

"Kae-san?"

Kae's eyes snapped open at the sound of a boy's voice, and he immediately prostrated himself before the emperor's heir. "My Lord, you should not be here."

"Are you no longer my friend?"

"The foolish actions of my wife have brought too much dishonor. Please, my Lord, I beg you to remove yourself from this unworthy one's presence."

"No. I will stay." Sachi sat in front of Kae. "My father is very angry."

"As he should be, my Lord," Kae said with his forehead still pressed to the tatami.

"I was angry, but now I am sad."

"Sad?"

"I have been lonely since they locked you and Emiko-chan away. I miss you telling me stories when I can't sleep. I miss watching your wife write such bad poetry. I miss the happiness she brought me at the festival. I miss your wife, Kae-san."

Kae lifted his head enough to glance up. Sachi was a blurred shape through the tears that formed in his eyes.

"As do I, my Lord, but it cannot be helped. We have offended you. We have brought shame upon our families and ourselves. We must be punished."

"So they say."

The young prince rose and disappeared back into the hidden passage from which he'd come.

Kae sat up and wiped his eyes with the back of his hand. Perhaps death would be the best option for him now. At least it would still the pain in his heart.

* * * *

Kyoto
Present day

Jake Hillhouse shifted nervously and glanced to his sister before turning to Emmi's mother.

"Tara, I have a real bad feeling about this. I don't think you should go through with this ritual or ceremony or whatever it is."

"My daughter is missing. I will do anything to get Emmi back, no matter how crazy it seems. She didn't get blown away in that storm. She's not dead. She's somewhere. I know it, and I'll get her back with Honji's help."

Jake glanced at his sister again, but watched silently as Tara stepped into the waiting elevator with the former Buddhist monk who was certain he could return Emmi to their living world.

Chapter Thirty-Two

Kyoto
1864

It seemed to be a week before they stopped shoving food trays through the door to Emmi's cell-like room. Hana, the girl who brought the food, finally joined Emmi for a meal. Hana also had the dubious honor of bringing her a bucket of cold water to wash with in the mornings and taking away the other disgusting bucket that served as her bathroom.

Emmi almost choked on her rice when Hana said that she would take her to get a real bath and a change of clothes once she had finished her meal.

"I would give anything to soak in a tub of hot water and be able to wash my hair—" Emmi felt the smile drop from her face. Maybe this was not a good thing. Maybe they only wanted her clean and presentable when it came time for the long-delayed execution.

Emmi pushed her food tray away. "I can't eat any more."

Hana looked at her a moment, then nodded and took the tray outside. She came right back with a tray containing clean clothes. A flash of pale yellow caught Emmi's attention, and she reached under to lift the kimono. She bit her lip and tried to blink away the tears that were stinging her eyes. It was the silk underwear Kae had given her.

"I will help you to the bath now."

Emmi wiped the tears away with the back of her hand and stood, clutching the tray with the clothes to her chest.

Emmi felt awkward with the maid hanging around while she undressed and bathed, but she supposed they didn't want her to try to escape or drown herself. At least sitting in the big tub and being able to pour water over her head hid the fact that she was crying like a baby the whole time. The bath should have made her feel better, but it didn't.

Emmi hardly noticed that when they left the bathhouse, Hana wasn't leading her back the way they'd come. Finally she looked up and realized that this corridor was familiar. This was the way to Kae's rooms.

"Emmi."

She spun around so fast she almost lost her balance and had to reach out to grab the wall. There he was. Kae was there—here—standing just a few feet away in the doorway that led outside. She bolted forward and threw herself at him. She hugged him as tightly as she could and buried her face in his shoulder. She didn't even care that the hilts of his swords were jabbing her in the stomach.

"They're going to kill me, aren't they? But I don't care. Not really. Not as long as you and your father are all right. You're going to be okay, right? And Takehito is safe? And Sadanori?"

Kae wrapped his arms tighter around her and kissed the top of her head. He rubbed his hands across her back. "You will not die, Emiko. No one is going to die."

She looked up, sniffled, and wiped her eyes with the back of her hand. "You mean it? You're not lying to me?"

"Have I ever lied to you?"

She cried and hugged him again. It was going to be all right. They were safe and together, and he forgave her for being so stupid with Sachi.

"We will have to leave Kyoto, however," he said softly.

She looked up and rubbed her eyes again. "Leave Kyoto? But will we be together? Will I have to go away alone?"

He smiled and rubbed the last of her tears away with his fingertips. "We will go together. The first thing in the morning."

Emmi nodded and hugged him again. It would be okay. As long as he was with her, it would all work out.

Kae pulled back and smiled at her again. He looked so tired. He looked like she'd been feeling all these days since the Sachi business.

"Are you sure you're all right? You look awful. They didn't hurt you or your father, did they?"

He shook his head. "We were not harmed. My father has disowned me, but I expected as much. He is allowed to stay on here as the emperor's advisor."

Emmi touched Kae's face. "I'm so sorry. It's all my fault. I really didn't know who Sachi was—"

Kae touched his fingers to her lips to silence her.

"None of that matters now. Come with me. I have something for you."

He took her hand and headed down the hall toward his rooms.

Emmi prayed that this wasn't some cruel setup, that he wasn't turning her over to guards for execution. She didn't think he could be so horrible, but if the emperor was testing his loyalty…

She held her breath as he slid open the door. There was no one in the main room. He led the way to the bedroom. Emmi closed her eyes and took another deep breath as he slid that door open.

"Emiko."

The sound of Kae saying her name made her open her eyes, and when she did, she saw it. The mirror. Her mirror. It was sitting on top of a small lacquered chest on the far side of the room, across from the futon. She ran to it, picked it up, hugged it to her chest, then turned to look at Kae.

"It's mine. It's really mine. How did you get it?"

"I had to buy Aneko one with genuine gold trim before she would consider parting with that. I also had to buy her freedom for her and give her enough money to leave Kyoto."

"But that must have cost a fortune. It must have cost everything you had… You did that to get back my mirror? You did all of that for me after everything that happened?"

He removed his swords from his belt and set them in the rack near the bed. He smiled and came across the room.

"I would do anything for you."

Emmi thought she'd cried all the tears she could possibly cry, but she cried again from sheer joy. She was happier than she could ever remember being. She put the mirror down on the cabinet and threw herself back into Kae's arms.

He kissed her long and slow, and she didn't care if she never saw her own time again.

* * * *

Kyoto
Present day

Something was happening, Jake could feel it. The air in the room was unnaturally heavy, and the fine hairs on the back of his neck prickled as if copious amounts of static electricity was spiraling around them, almost the way a tornado swirls and begins sucking things into its vortex.

A chill shot down Jake's spine when Emmi's mother gasped.

"I see her. I see her in the mirror!"

The former monk said nothing—he was deep in whatever trance he'd put himself into with his chanting, which continued in a preternatural drone.

Jake, too, saw something—a distinct blue fog reflected in part of the mirror's edge.

A shadow fell over the room, and Jake looked over his shoulder. Outside the hotel window the waning daylight had totally faded, as if a dark cloud had settled over the setting sun. A boom of thunder rattled the window, and a white-hot bolt of lightning cut directly in front of the glass.

The air raced and howled outside the window, and Jake finally understood the true meaning of the word kamikaze — Divine Wind. This was not natural.

* * * *

Kyoto
1864

Emmi barely heard the clap of thunder through the rush of blood in her ears as Kae kissed her again and again. His hands began to tug at her obi. She felt the fabric give way and fall free, and she sighed. She pressed forward when he slipped his hand inside the front of the kimono to brush his fingers across her silk-covered breast.

"Emiko... Emiko... Can you hear me?"

"Of course I can hear you," she sighed.

"What?" Kae asked pulling back from the kiss.

"Nothing. Forget it," she said, coaxing his head back toward hers.

"EMIKO!"

Pain ricocheted through her head. It was like the accident, when the car slammed through the guardrail. She couldn't see. She couldn't hear.

She couldn't feel Kae's arms around her anymore. "Kae!"

Kae was flung back by an unseen force when Emmi was wrenched from his embrace. He hit the futon flat on his back, and his head bounced off the floor despite the thick cushion. He shook off the impact and pushed himself to his knees in time to see Emmi enveloped in a strange blue mist. He rose and lunged forward, tried to grab what he could see of her outstretched hand.

"Emmi!"

It was too late. The mist was gone. Emmi was gone. The mirror…was broken.

* * * *

Everything was a blur as Emmi flew backward across a million miles of nothingness. She slowed for a minute, but then she was jerked harder until the blackness turned bright.

"Ohmygod!"

Was that Uncle Jake's sister?

"Emmi!"

Mom?

She was in a room. She was flying across the room. She could see a window coming closer, closer…

Someone screamed.

Big hands grabbed her and pulled. Uncle Jake. She fell, hit something—someone—hard.

Her mother grabbed her, hugged her in a crushing embrace.

"Kae. Where's Kae? Mom, where am I? Where's Kae?"

Chapter Thirty-Three

Kaga Domain
1864

Takehito thought he was seeing a specter when Nakagawa Kaemon entered the finely appointed reception room of his home. The young man bowing his head in greeting was not the vibrant young warrior he'd entrusted his Emiko to, and he knew that the incident with the young imperial prince was only a fraction of the cause for Kaemon's current state.

"Emiko is gone," Takehito said flatly as he knelt opposite his guest.

Kae looked at him questioningly with his dark eyes empty, haunted. "You know. But how?"

Unable to explain, Takehito shook his head and shrugged his broad shoulders. "Fleeting thoughts, dreams, nothing more."

Kae exhaled a long, dismal sigh and sat back on his heels, wetness pooling in the corners of his eyes. "I miss her," he said in a dull, soft tone. He managed a faint trace of a smile. "The days are too quiet and predictable without her."

Takehito reached out to touch Kae's shoulder. "She was...unique." His expression hardened when a knock sounded on the shoji. A servant looked in.

"Forgive me, my Lord, but the monk has returned. He insists that you see him. He has had yet another vision. This one clearer. This one featuring a girl riding upon a golden dragonfly."

Kae's eyes grew wide, and Takehito knew he was thinking of the same thing—the charm Emiko wore—the golden dragonfly of Lord Maeda Toshiie.

"I will see him. Nakagawa no miya will see him as well."

Monk Anji entered, and his old eyes grew wide the instant he saw Kae. "You! You are the one! You are the one who torments her spirit. You are the one her soul cries out for!"

Kae leaped to his feet, rushed forward and gripped the old man's shoulders. "You have seen Emiko? Where is she?"

"She is in great pain, my son. Her soul cries out for what it lost. It cries out for...you."

"Then do something!" Takehito shouted. "I have looked into your background. I know what they say near Osore-Zan—you communicate with the dead. You have powers to reach beyond the living world."

Kae faltered, his shoulders slumping. "Emiko is...dead?"

"No, no, no," Anji said. "She is among the living, but it is on a different plane. It is a magical place where great silver birds rule the sky, and where unseen men sing out from small circles of solid rainbows. It is a frightening, wonderful place."

Kae grabbed the monk's shoulder. "Can you take me there? I need to be there. I must see her again."

Monk Anji looked down and wrung his wrinkled hands. "I don't know. I don't know. There may be a way. There are places on Osore-Zan that may be portals to other worlds, but it is all so dangerous." He looked up. "There are no guarantees. You could be killed for daring to use the gods' magic. You could be transported to a place where demons will eat you alive."

Kae met the monk's frightened gaze with a cold stare. "Death is preferable to the empty life I live now."

Takehito removed a small silk pouch from within his kimono sleeve. Pieces of gold clinked when he shoved it into the monk's hands. "You will work your magic, priest."

* * * *

Los Angeles
Present day

Emmi was home, in her own room, in her own house, and she hated it. It had nothing to do with her mother. Her mother was fine. In fact, she was great. She was smiling and happy, much like the way she'd been before the accident. While Emmi realized that her mother had only blamed her for the accident—as Jake had said—to deal with the pain of losing her husband, Emmi felt little comfort in her mother's renewed grace. Emmi's own lonely pain was eating her away inside. She hated everything, absolutely everything. She hated the California sun and the days that dragged by like excruciating months. She had always been proud of the home's tribute to their culture, had loved it, but now she hated it.

There were too many Japanese things here—the low tables, the lacquered chests, the porcelain, the garden—they all reminded her of Kae. There were too many posters and pictures of her father and Jake from their samurai movies, wearing the traditional kimono and hakama. Everything about home constantly reminded her of Kae. She couldn't even bring herself to talk to Jake when he called from Kyoto to check up on her. Simply knowing he was there, where she wanted to be, where she belonged, made her cry.

Of course, that wasn't exactly correct. She didn't belong in the Kyoto of now any more than she belonged here in L.A. She belonged back in old Kyoto. As weird and dangerous and alien to her as it had been, she wanted to be there. She needed to be there because Kae was there. Somewhere.

* * * *

One day, Emmi was sitting in the back yard tossing tiny pebbles into the koi pond when her mother called to her. "Em-chan! It's Grandmother Maeda on the phone. She wants to talk to you."

Grandmother probably wanted to lecture her about returning to college in the fall.

"Emmi!"

"I'll be right there."

Emmi had to cross the patio where her mother and her weird Buddhist friend had been having lunch to go inside to get the phone. Emmi stopped long enough to grab a grape from the fruit bowl in the center of the table and say, "I hate you. Why did you bring me back?"

The former monk put his hands together as if in prayer. "All things have their time and place."

Emmi flipped him the finger and went inside.

Grandmother Maeda told Emmi again that she needed to visit before the summer was over. Her brother always visited every summer, and she would accept no more excuses. Emmi's grandfather had a business meeting in L.A. in two days, and he was going to pick Emmi up and bring her back to Kauai if he had to stuff her into his carry-on bag to do it.

"Fine. I'll come visit." *And, if I'm lucky, maybe a big wave will suck me up and wash me away while I'm there.*

* * * *

Grandfather Maeda's business was with the multinational corporation that he'd worked for before retiring to Hawaii. They flew him in on their corporate jet, and he and Emmi would be flying back the same way. A chilling inexplicable something bordering on a compulsion hit Emmi as she trudged out of the house. A private flight meant none of the usual security hassles and restrictions.

"Wait a minute," Emmi said, grabbing her suitcase out of the back of the car. "I forgot something."

She rushed back to her room and nearly dove into the back of her closet. She pulled out the mirror, which she'd wrapped in the pink silk kimono she'd been wearing when she was pulled back from Kyoto.

Once the plane was in the air, Emmi began to feel like an idiot. The last thing she needed was to have that mirror reminding her of how miserable she felt.

But it also reminds you of Kae, her heart told her. *It almost brings him closer to you.*

Almost.

* * * *

Emmi was reminded constantly of Kae from the moment she set foot in her grandparents' house. Her cousin, Midori, and her fiancé had impulsively set a wedding date, and Grandmother had taken charge of the wedding preparations. Midori's parents were working in Hong Kong and Midori's fiancé was set to begin his medical residency on the East Coast.

"A girl's wedding day is so special! Oh, Em-chan, when you find someone..."

Been there, done that, Grandma, Emmi thought miserably as she trudged back to her room. The sugary sweetness of it all was enough to make her teeth fall out. She'd had the Emperor Komei attend her wedding, had gotten drunk without even trying, and had had the most perfect wedding night anyone ever dreamed of in the arms of the first—and only—man she had ever loved.

Now life just sucked.

She'd been looking into the mirror every chance she'd gotten since she'd come to Kauai but hadn't seen anything. Whatever magic the mirror may have had was gone now, thanks to that meddling bastard friend of her mother's.

She lay on the bed in the dark and stared out of the sliding glass door. There was a full moon, just like that night when she'd gone to the mirror and thought she'd seen her father in it. She knew now she'd seen Kae, and she missed him so badly it hurt.

Hiding from the wedding preparations, as she had so many times since returning to the present, Emmi cried until she couldn't cry any more. Then she went and splashed cold water on her face. She needed air and decided to take a walk on the beach. At way past midnight, the private beach was deserted now.

Impulsively, she grabbed the mirror on the way out.

She walked along the warm sand until she came to the darkest part of the beach. The moon was directly overhead. It was so big and round and bright that it seemed surreal.

She plopped cross-legged onto the sand and put the mirror in front of her. She sat and stared into it for the longest time, but, of course, she saw only her own reflection and part of the moon.

Tears stung her eyes again when she reached out to touch the mirror's frame. She ran her fingers over the metal and around the sakura petals. She touched each dent and scratch, and she even ran her fingers across the glass.

Just one glimpse. One glimpse of Kae was all she wanted. Just one. Just one quick look to see that he was alive.

Faint music drifted on the soft ocean breeze. Great. Her cousin, the bride-to-be, was still up and playing that stupid song she loved. It was "their song", hers and her fiancé's. It was a ballad by a popular Japanese singer.

For the first time in her life, Emmi wished her family wasn't so traditional. She wished they'd left the Japanese customs back in Japan as so many other immigrants had. She had friends whose families had been in California for a lot less time than her family, and they couldn't speak a word of Japanese, except what they knew from the latest anime. But, oh no, the Maeda had to hold onto their culture.

She understood the words to the stupid song and couldn't get them out of her head.

My love for you will remain forever…

The tears came once again—harder than ever—and soon the mirror was nothing but a blur. The glass shimmered through the wetness. Emmi leaned forward until her forehead touched the top of the mirror's frame. She shivered despite the warmth.

"Emmi…"

She missed Kae so much. She missed the way he said her name. She even missed that pissy look he gave her when she ended up doing the dumb things she didn't mean to do.

"Emmi…"

She wanted him back. She needed him back in her life.

"Emiko, I'll be with you."

Yeah, yeah, yeah. Just like the stupid song, he was there in her heart forever.

"Emmi-chan…"

But… But that was real.

She lifted her head enough to look down at the mirror. She blinked. She wiped her eyes. She could see him. Sort of. She saw him inside. No, not inside as he'd been that first time. It was as if he was behind her, as if he was coming closer. It was so much like a real reflection.

"Emiko. My Emiko…"

The Kae in the mirror reached out and touched her shoulder, and she felt it. She felt him kneeling behind her, felt that stupid sword of his poking her in the back.

She'd lost her mind. She was hallucinating. She was seeing and hearing things…and feeling things, like both of Kae's hands on her shoulders, his lips on the back of her neck…

"I have missed you."

Emmi forced herself to turn her head, and she prayed that, if this was a dream, she would never ever wake from it. She couldn't bear for it to be a dream. She couldn't bear to lose him again.

"Emmi-chan."

Hand trembling, she touched Kae's face.

He was real.

He was here.

About the Author

Award-winning novelist Barbara Sheridan grew up a fan of historical novels, TV Westerns and all things paranormal. She also acquired a fondness for J-rock, samurai films and all things royalty related. Coupled with her love of character-driven books, film and TV, all these things have come together to shape her writing interests. Barbara lives in western Pennsylvania and loves hearing from reader and "meeting" them via social media.

Barbara loves to hear from readers. You can find her contact information, website details and author profile page at http://www.totallybound.com.

TOTALLY
BOUND

Home of Erotic Romance